PENGUIN BOOKS

THE DOG

The

DOG

JACK LIVINGS

STORIES

PENGUIN BOOKS

PENGUIN BOOKS

UK | USA | Canada | Ireland | Australia
India | New Zealand | South Africa

Penguin Books is part of the Penguin Random House group of companies
whose addresses can be found at global.penguinrandomhouse.com.

First published in the United States of America by Farrar, Straus and Giroux 2014
Published in Penguin Books 2015
001

Copyright © Jack Livings, 2014

The moral right of the author has been asserted

Portions of this book have previously appeared, in slightly different form, in
The Best American Short Stories 2006, *The Paris Review*, *A Public Space*,
The Pushcart Prize XXXIII and *The Pushcart Prize XXXVIII*.

Printed in Great Britain by Clays Ltd, St Ives plc

A CIP catalogue record for this book is available from the British Library

ISBN: 978-0-241-97012-6

B000 000 015 6210

www.greenpenguin.co.uk

FOR JENNIE

CONTENTS

THE DOG

After Li Yan put the baby down, she joined her husband at the rough table. He was reading *People's Daily* in the brown light of a bare bulb dangling from the ceiling. Li Yan opened her English textbook and began to read a dialogue. It was still early but she was worn out and had trouble focusing on the words.

Pretty soon she looked up and said, "Chen Wei, do you want some tea?"

From behind the paper he said no.

"Okay. It's no trouble. I'll make you some anyway."

"Fine," he said. "Just not too many leaves."

Li Yan filled the electric kettle and turned it on. The light buzzed and the room took on a subterranean murk. Chen Wei rattled his paper at her.

"Hello there," she said. The paper rose again. She unwrapped the tea package and put leaves in a cup for herself, then sprinkled some in another cup for her husband. She thought for a moment about taking a dumpling back to the table for him, then decided against it. She'd sworn never to stuff him the way his mother had. No wonder he didn't like to eat.

It was dusk, warm out, and street noise came in through the open doorway. Occasionally a leaf or a scrap of paper would drift across the threshold. Next door, pensioners slapped their chess pieces on the board outside Old Feng's house. They could get rowdy, sometimes playing until dawn when they had enough to drink, and then Old Feng would sing opera in a warbling voice.

Old Feng's wife was head of the neighborhood committee, but no one had the courage to confront her about the noise. She was paranoid and sharp-tongued, especially when it came to defending Old Feng. No one crossed her. In a way, Li Yan admired the woman's harsh reputation. She'd seen some things in her life.

"Hope they don't wake up the baby tonight," Li Yan said.

"What am I supposed to do about it?" Chen Wei said. He adjusted his reading glasses. He kept them low on his nose and peered over the top of the lenses because his vision was fine. Li Yan made him wear them.

"Just thinking out loud," she said. She turned off the kettle. The lightbulb above Chen Wei's head flickered, burned intensely yellow for a moment, then resigned itself to a dingy glow. She carried the teacups to the table and set one in front of the newspaper.

"If you were more of a chess player, you might have some pull with them," she said.

"You know, not everything you think is worth saying out loud," he said.

"Very wise," she said.

She went back to her dialogue, sounding out the words in a whisper. The book was filled with ink drawings of Alex and Mary, a stylish young American couple. Mary always wore high heels and a tweedy skirt, and Alex a dark blazer, unless they were at the beach or an embassy ball. They bore no resemblance to Li Yan's English teacher, an American college student who sometimes touched his students on the shoulder and wore the same flannel shirt and dirty blue jeans every week. He laughed at his own jokes.

She suspected that he had never been away from home before. During free-talk hour, she and her classmates usually tried to ask him questions about his family to determine whether he was homesick. Everyone agreed that he was terribly lonely so far away from his parents.

I would like to buy a computer. I would like to buy a stereo.

She paused every couple of sentences for a sip of tea, and had fallen into a meditative rhythm when her husband grunted and threw down the paper. His teacup spiraled across the table. Li Yan caught the cup before it tumbled off the edge. A thin pool of water steamed on the table.

"Look at this," he said, stabbing at the paper with his finger.

"What now?"

"Read what it says," he said. "There, on page six."

She peeled the paper off the table and stared at the puddle of water.

"I'll clean it up," he said. "Just read."

"What am I looking at?"

"There, look there."

She read the block of characters he was pointing to. The Beijing municipal government had cracked down on dog racing. The paper quoted a cadre: "'We are committed to stamping out corruption,'" he said. "'As we all know, gambling spoils even the most steadfast heart. Fines will go toward cultural improvement programs.'"

"Politicians. If I had five minutes with one of those guys," Chen Wei said. He shook his fist at the wall. "It's unbelievable. Everything I do goes up in flames."

Li Yan took the cotton rag from his hand and started swabbing at the spilled tea.

"I said, everything I do—"

"I get it," she said. "You're a funny guy." Chen Wei worked for the Public Utilities Bureau. He burned bodies at the Number 7 Crematorium.

"Greedy bastards," he said.

"Would you be quiet? Everyone will hear you."

"I have to go see Zheng tomorrow. Don't expect me home."

"Don't be so dramatic. There's nothing he can do about this."

"I'll take the train after work and be back in the morning." He paused. "If I'm not robbed or killed on the way there." He drew a finger across his throat and bugged his eyes.

"That's very brave of you," she said. "Why don't you just call him from work? Life isn't a movie, you know. Sometimes it's best to stay calm."

"I don't have time to stand around all day yapping on the phone," he said. "Why don't you call him?"

"You're funny," she said. Li Yan was a tailor's apprentice. She had to ask permission just to use the bathroom.

"I'm serious. My work is time-sensitive. The dead are pesky that way," he said.

"Yeah, they're a demanding bunch," she said.

Sometimes Li Yan found Chen Wei's flair for the dramatic endearing. He didn't have much else to recommend him—he wasn't rich and he smelled of greasy smoke and he looked as plain as a flap of burlap, but he had shown up at the gates of her high school every afternoon with a flower clutched in his chemical-stained hand. He'd spotted her walking in the market nearby and he said he'd fallen in love instantly. Right there in the street he'd sung a pop ballad to her. A crowd had gathered, and some peasants watching the proceedings from a fruit stand had screamed, "Young love," over and over, as though a call to arms. At first Li Yan thought Chen Wei was crazy, and she'd told him so, and added that she hadn't appreciated being embarrassed in the middle of the street like that. *It will never happen again*, he'd said, his eyes so stricken she realized the depth of his intentions. Three years later, she still hadn't figured out how to tell his moods apart. He was strange, but there was nothing wrong with that. He worked for a living. That was good. And in the weeks after they'd met, he was always waiting there at the gate, peering through the iron bars like a monkey at the zoo.

Chen Wei told her wild stories about working with his cousin, Zheng, in the western provinces, tales that involved dismemberment, knives, and, too often for her to believe, bare-knuckled combat with wild animals. Later, Cousin Zheng—at the time, just a name Chen Wei waved around like a red scarf—had procured a dress for him to give her. It had a silk rose embroidered on the thigh.

Zheng was Chen Wei's first cousin and, since his parents' deaths, his closest living relative. Zheng had always been a real operator. A stint in the army hadn't reformed him at all, and now he lived near Yulin, where he was in import-export. He made money, but still lived like a peasant.

It had been Zheng's idea to purchase a racing dog, and since he lived in the countryside, he boarded the dog. Every weekend he traveled to Beijing for races. Though Li Yan had only seen the dog once—and then in its cage—she wasn't surprised that it won. It was muscled like a horse. The snout was sleek as a bullet.

The dog had cost six hundred yuan. Then, for a license, another six hundred to the government. And three hundred yearly to maintain the license. After the dog won enough to cover the debts, Zheng declared it a good investment. Li Yan wasn't so sure. Zheng moved in dangerous circles, and though she couldn't forbid Chen Wei from partnering with him, she knew something would go wrong. Zheng had lost a chunk of Chen Wei's money a few years ago in a cigarette-importing scheme—they'd met a shipper from Shenzhen who'd cooked up a plan to import American Marlboros secreted in false-bottomed cargo crates. But he needed investors up front. Chen Wei handed over his share. Two months later, Zheng told him the ship had been hit by a cyclone.

"Lucky only one of us bought in," Zheng said. This was Chen Wei's lot in life. Li Yan hoped the man from Shenzhen had gone down with the ship.

There had been other catastrophes. A pyramid scheme. A plan to export artifacts from Suzhou. She'd argued with Chen Wei about the dog, but he'd told her the animal would pay for itself, and for once he'd been right. It was hard to argue with extra money.

That night she lay awake thinking about the swift dog sleeping three hundred li to the northwest. It had provided them the spoils of a wealthier household—new wool sweaters, silk long underwear, and a grass-stroke scroll depicting the character for good luck, which hung opposite their bed. Chen Wei said the scroll spoke to him. Li Yan thought a microwave would have made better sense.

A few years ago she would have attributed his choice to his romantic streak, but now she wondered if he'd purchased it out of cowardice. They could have just as easily bought a microwave, but Chen Wei worried about attracting the attention of Old Feng's wife, who was reputed to have the ear of a local cadre. They weren't doing anything illegal, but even today you had to watch out for the old guard. There was no point making people jealous.

Perhaps it was better they go back to a modest life. They'd only had the extra income for a few months, not long enough to change their habits drastically. They had enough to eat, a healthy child, a place to live. No one could ask for more than that, Li Yan told herself.

Li Yan nudged Chen Wei with her leg. He sighed deeply and rolled over. She nudged him again.

"What?" he said.

"Don't you think Zheng mistreats you?" she said.

"Not now," he moaned.

"It's keeping me up. Why does Zheng take a bigger cut?"

"It's a business deal."

"Zheng's your partner. You're entitled to an equal share."

"It's a complex arrangement."

"Are you joking with me?" she said. "I can't see your face. Are you joking around?"

Chen Wei propped himself up on one elbow and cleared his throat. Elm leaves rattled in the wind and threw ragged patterns across the wall of their room. Old Feng and his friends were still out there.

"As a husband, I would say that, as a wife, you're really hard to satisfy," Chen Wei said. He tickled her foot with his toe.

"It's not a hard question," she said.

"You're smarter than I am," Chen Wei said. "You tell me why he takes more. What difference does it make now?"

She listened to Old Feng and his friends push their chessmen around the board. They were behaving themselves tonight, voices muted but lively, like a clutch of girls passing around a secret. At one point the baby yodeled and Li Yan tensed, but it was just a cry from a dream, and Li Yan settled back into her pillow.

"You should be more confident in life," Li Yan said.

"Aye, comrade."

"I'm not kidding. You possess the capacity for improvement. Everybody does. But you're too content."

"I do what I can. I have what I need."

"That's not true. Look at Zheng. He is a man of action. Don't you want to act?" It had occurred to Li Yan that those like Zheng— the boors, the idiots, the drooling slobs—in short, those worst-equipped to navigate the slick world of commerce—were somehow the very people who reaped the hugest rewards. People forced to survive on ingenuity and pure will seemed to have luck on their side. She herself could never envy Zheng, but she thought her husband ought to. Zheng was, in a way, a good role model for Chen Wei, who just couldn't seem to figure out how to put his talents to good use. Even at the crematorium he was the number two guy. She wanted him to be a number one guy.

"I do my best, you know," he said.

"I know," she said.

"There's more to me than meets the eye," he said.

"Let's go to sleep," she said.

"Tired of thinking out loud?"

"Let's go to sleep."

After work the next evening, Li Yan rode her bicycle to her parents' house. It was usually Chen Wei's duty to pick up the baby after work, but he'd packed a bag that morning and left the house without saying goodbye. She'd given it some thought, and she was glad he was on the train to see Zheng. But when she arrived at her parents' compound, Chen Wei's bicycle was parked outside. She pushed open the heavy door and walked into the dirt courtyard. Chen Wei was bouncing the baby on his knee, and Li Yan's father was puffing thoughtfully on his pipe. They were sitting on sacks of concrete by the clothesline. Wet clothes were piled in a basket, abandoned by her father when Chen Wei showed up, and Li Yan began draping shirts over the line. Both men looked at her, but didn't break the stride of their conversation. Someone was playing basketball nearby. The hollow sound of the ball clanging off the rim echoed through the maze of alleys surrounding the house.

"This is foolish," her father said. He expelled a bowl of smoke and shook his head. "I know your people are from the North, but this isn't how things are done. It's bad business sense. There must be someone willing to buy the dog."

"Who wants a racing dog you can't race?" Chen Wei said.

"You're thinking too small," the old man said.

Li Yan squatted down beside them and wrung out a pair of socks. The water formed muddy blisters on the courtyard floor.

"Everyone on embassy row has a dog," she said. "Sell it to a foreigner." Her comment didn't seem to register with the two men.

"Look," her father said, "you live in the city now. Your own daughter is going to grow up here. Beijingers don't eat dog."

"Some restaurants in the Yuyuantan are serving it," Chen Wei said. "It's gaining acceptance."

"There is a great difference between acceptable behavior and civilized behavior," the old man said.

"Easy for you to say. Zheng doesn't approach problems the way you or I do."

"I know that," Li Yan's father said. "He thinks like a bandit."

"He's really got me over a barrel this time. That's the trouble with being an investor."

The old man looked to Li Yan for the first time, as if to ask how she could have brought such a weakling into the family.

"Look, man, you still have a say," her father said.

Li Yan tossed the socks back into the basket and took her daughter from Chen Wei. "Zheng's selling the dog to a restaurant?" she said.

"Not exactly," Chen Wei said.

"This should be good."

"We're going to eat it."

She stared at him.

Chen Wei shrugged. "He wants to obliterate every trace of the dog. That's what he said."

"What did you say? You're still his partner," she said. "Even bandits talk things over."

"That's uncalled-for," her father said, but Chen Wei waved it off.

"Zheng's already told the entire family there'll be a feast. You should have heard him. He was furious."

"What's he taking it out on the dog for?" she said.

"He doesn't react well to resistance. I can't tell him what to do."

"He's got a screw loose."

"It's already decided."

Li Yan studied his face for some sign that he might consider opposing Zheng, but she saw only resignation in his hooded eyes.

"He's family," Chen Wei said. "We have a long history."

"Do you want me to call him? I'll give him a piece of my mind," she said.

Her father sucked on his pipe and mumbled, "Behave like a wife," but he didn't put much force behind his words.

"No," Chen Wei said. "I'll deal with it." But she knew he wouldn't.

Early that Saturday morning, Li Yan, Chen Wei, and their daughter crowded into a hard-seat car of the #44 train to Yulin. Four of the hard-seat cars were reserved for soldiers, young men who moved with dazed absence, as though they had been sleeping in the hot sun for a long time. That left only one hard-seat car for civilians—families traveling to see relatives in the country, merchants transporting goods to provincial markets, businessmen too poor to travel in soft-seat. Bundles the size of refrigerators blocked the aisle. There were no seats for Li Yan or her husband, so they fought their way to the back of the car and squatted by the bathroom door. The car was already filling with the low haze of cigarette smoke as the train pulled out of the West Station. Tinny revolutionary songs squawked from speakers in the corners of the car.

Chen Wei laid a leaf of newsprint on the floor between them and took out the playing cards. Li Yan beat him at Catch the Pig and Struggling Upstream before they finally settled on Looking for Friends, which required less strategy. After their third game, the baby woke and cried some, but Li Yan got her back to sleep with a song. As she sang, a farmer wearing rags emerged from behind a bundle of vegetables. He crouched against the bathroom door and hummed along with her, then clapped when the song ended. Chen Wei shooed him, and the farmer drifted back into the car.

At the Xuanhua Station, they got off and found a bus going to Yulin. They had been in transit two hours already, and it was another hour before they reached Yulin, where they boarded a van traveling into the countryside. The driver's crony tried to gouge them once they were on the road, saying the baby counted as a person and needed a ticket, but the other passengers shouted him down.

One old woman called him a wolf and shook her fist at him.

"I've known him a long time," she said. "He'd screw his own mother."

As thanks, Li Yan let her hold the baby until they disembarked at the dirt road leading to the village where Chen Wei had grown up. Hot, their clothes stained with dust and sweat, they arrived at his cousin's house just before noon. Zheng met them at the door and embraced them both. He was a barrel-chested man who looked something like a frog—bulbous eyes and wide lips that seemed barely able to contain his tongue. A cluster of dark hair sprouted from his chin.

"She's really getting fat," he said, pinching the baby's legs. "She'll make a good side dish." He spat out a sharp laugh.

Chen Wei laughed, too, but Li Yan could hear the discomfort in his voice. He would never come right out and say it, but she knew he was ashamed of his family's rough manners, their rugged faces and wide brown feet. She looked at his dust-creased face and saw a refugee. In the country, he drank heavily to disguise his shame, but she never chastised him when he was hungover the next day. She leaned close to her husband while Zheng was rounding up the rest of the family and said, "You are a good cousin. Don't worry, we'll be back in Beijing tomorrow night." He looked puzzled.

Chen Wei spent the afternoon drinking and talking with the men. Aunties floated in and out of the house, an interchangeable cast of thickset women clad in blue cotton who ferried away the baby and left their own children with Li Yan. The children wouldn't stop talking about the dog, acting out great victories they'd heard about from Zheng, scampering in and out of the house on their hands and knees, barking and licking each other on the face. They pestered her to follow them into the backyard to see the dog, but she refused. She wanted to ask the children if they understood the dog would be killed, but couldn't bring herself to ruin their fun. As the afternoon wore on, she felt a dreadful unease set in, misgiving mixed with disdain for her husband's run-down village. Meanwhile, her husband matched Zheng drink for drink, told bawdy jokes he'd heard at work, toasted his uncles, made a spectacle of himself. She could see that he was trying to liquor himself up for the slaughter. Zheng was a hardhearted man whose only goal in life was to become wealthy, but her husband wasn't so naturally equipped for the bloody work that lay ahead.

Late in the afternoon, Zheng rose stiffly and raised his glass in an official toast. "To the Beijing municipal government, which has brought the family together again!" All the men raised their glasses and shouted, "Ganbei." One of the uncles fell out of his chair. Outside, the aunties had dug a fire pit and assembled a tripod for the cauldron. Everyone moved into the walled yard where the dog was caged. Zheng held out a butcher knife to Chen Wei, who grasped it like a sword, with two hands, stiff-armed. Zheng produced a long carving knife from his belt and swung it overhead.

There was no breeze, and it was the hour before birds and bats come out for insects. The golden grass in the hills around them stood still. Everything was quiet.

"Release the beast," Zheng shouted. A little cousin rattled the dog's cage, then unfastened the latch. The door swung open and the dog trotted out. It stood outside its cage and wagged its tail. The little cousin slapped the dog's rump and yelled, "Run!"

Either out of shock or compliance, the dog's claws scrabbled over the hard earth, and it was off. The dog ran directly at Chen Wei but at the last second broke left and charged along the wall.

The children made chase, but the dog was too fast for them, cutting a jagged path through several of the older girls and boys who tried to intercept it at the corner. Zheng waited with Chen Wei, still gripping his butcher knife with two hands. Li Yan watched from the doorway. Beside her an auntie rocked the baby in her ropy arms.

The dog outwitted the children at every turn, doubling back and twisting through their small hands, running with a hint of terror, as though it could smell menace on the air. The children wore down, moving now like a school of fish, unable to block the dog's unpredictable path, parting when it doubled back and ran directly at them, going down in a tangle of legs but quickly forming up again. The dog ran a circuit around the yard, its paws whipping up eddies of dust. Once, it appeared to be readying itself to leap clear of the fence altogether, but Zheng bellowed a command and the dog stopped dead in its tracks. Then he shouted, "Go," and the dog was off again.

Li Yan saw that even though the dog's eyes were wild with terror, it obeyed. It was clear that Zheng took a sporting pride in his control of the animal, but Li Yan watched her husband's face as the dog ran, and knew he was unprepared for this. She knew her husband, and she knew what he was feeling.

Eventually the animal got tired. Its jukes became predictable, its speed was sapped, and it cowered against a corner of the wall, fangs bared, sleek hair spiked the length of its spine. The band of children closed in.

"Don't go any closer," Zheng said. "We'll take over." He punctuated this declaration with a slap to Chen Wei's back, and walked toward the children, who scattered, squealing in mock horror as he swung the knife above their heads. "Come on," he said to Chen Wei. They bore down upon the dog together, their knives raised. The dog snarled. Spittle dripped from its muzzle.

"Sit," Zheng said. The dog sat.

Li Yan couldn't bear to watch any longer. She leapt from the doorway and forced her way through the children.

"Stop," she shouted. "Stop." She was waving her arms over her head.

Zheng turned toward her, his butcher knife still raised, and to someone watching from beyond the fence it might have appeared that he meant to threaten Li Yan's life. But she moved forward, unafraid, until she stood between the two men and the dog. Her husband lowered his knife and hooked his thumbs through his belt loops. He tried to slouch like a gunfighter.

"I should have known," Zheng said.

Li Yan said nothing.

"Move over," Zheng said.

"I'm sorry, Chen Wei," she said, but she did not move.

"Chen Wei, tell your wife to stand aside," Zheng said. The aunties gathered at the edge of the house looked amused. They pinched at each other's sides, and some chuckled under their breath.

Chen Wei shook his head, but he was unable to affect his detached pose while looking his cousin in the eye, so he found a point in the distance and focused.

Zheng scanned the faces ringing the yard. The children were watching him. The aunties were watching him. The uncles were watching him.

He made a fist. "Don't make me use this," Zheng said to Li Yan. She closed her eyes and presented her chin.

Chen Wei dropped his knife. He drew up his shoulders and moved between his wife and Zheng.

Though Chen Wei wasn't steady on his feet, his palm fell on

Zheng's cheek with all the delicacy of a lover's touch. He patted his cousin's rough face. The aunties all got very quiet. There wasn't much they hadn't seen before, and when Chen Wei drew his hand away, they each tensed imperceptibly. Chen Wei turned his slight shoulders to the side, coiling, and brought the back of his hand across Zheng's face with such force that Zheng, twice his size, staggered back a step.

Chen Wei's hand hovered in the dead air between them.

"Ha," Zheng said. "Ha!" A wide smile split his face. "Good one," he said.

If there were terrestrial sounds in the world at that moment, a swallow crying for its mate or a breeze pushing through the grass, they were absorbed into the wake of silence radiating from his voice. For a moment it seemed to Li Yan that the rotation of the earth had locked, that the natural world was pinned like a butterfly to a cardboard frame. She felt the silence enveloping her, the two men, the family, the village, and extending outward like a shadow until it seemed that the entire world was somehow flattened against itself, dark. It was this oppressive airlessness, the locus of suffocation within her own body, that caused Li Yan, desperate to set the world once again in motion, to speak.

"You idiot," she said to her husband. She may as well have clubbed him with a length of pipe. His chin dropped to his chest.

He sighed.

It would take years for him to leave her, but after he had moved out and their daughter had left for America and Li Yan was left alone to pass from the subway to the tailor's shop and home again, where she sat in silence with a cup of tea and tried to rest, to drop the hulking weariness that had sunk itself in her chest, she returned to the yard again and again. Of course she wished that she'd held her tongue. But in her old age, she reasoned it out: standing there in Zheng's barren yard, before his family, the words had risen up out of an unavoidable instinct.

"Give him a break, he's drunk," Zheng said. "We did worse when we were kids, that's for sure."

Chen Wei nodded.

"Well, send her to the market," Zheng said.

"Go to the market," Chen Wei whispered.

"Right!" Zheng said. "You're going to cook for us, right? You saved a dog's life. We'll celebrate life, right? Go to the market, and we'll get the fire going while you're gone. Come on, don't look so ashamed. It's time to make up." He took the couple's hands in his and joined them. Their fingers mashed together. "See? No problem," Zheng said.

Li Yan was lucky to find anyone still selling in the market. Most of the vendors had already gone home, but she found a woman with two buckets of limp carp.

"I want both," she said.

"You're from Tianjin, right?" the woman said.

Li Yan didn't have time to banter. She was sure Zheng would kill the dog while she was gone. "Beijing. How much for both buckets?"

"Beijing! I could tell from your clothes. Why do you want both buckets? Hungry?"

"I'm cooking for my husband's family. How much?"

"Who's your husband? I've never seen you before. Wedding feast?"

"Please tell me how much."

"No need to be rude. What's the rush? If you're cooking, they'll wait for you. They can't eat air."

"I'll give you twenty kuai for them."

"Twenty kuai," the woman said, as though divining a greater truth from the words. "One hundred."

"One hundred," Li Yan said. She looked around the empty market.

"They're worth twice that much right now. Don't try to put one over on me just because I'm a simple country girl." Her teeth made an eerie whistling sound when she spoke.

"Your house isn't worth one hundred kuai," Li Yan said.

"Good thing it's not for sale," the woman said. "One hundred kuai."

Li Yan didn't know what else to do. She held out the money. She'd stuffed her wallet that morning in case of emergency, but this was half a week's salary.

"Who's your husband?" the woman said as Li Yan reached for the buckets.

"Chen Wei," she said.

The woman said, "I remember a Chen Wei who moved to Beijing." But she didn't say any more.

Li Yan started to leave. "Where are you going with my buckets?" the woman said.

"I gave you one hundred kuai."

"But you didn't bring any newspaper. I'll need a deposit for the buckets. Fifty kuai."

Li Yan didn't see the point of arguing. She gave the woman her last note. If Chen Wei didn't have enough for tickets home, they'd borrow from Zheng.

"May your family choke on it," the woman said, but Li Yan was already sloshing down the dirt road to Zheng's house.

The sun had disappeared behind the hills by the time she got there, and her legs were soaked with smelly water. At the gate, she set the buckets down. The fire pit was piled with sticks, dark, just as when she'd left. Through the window she saw the men playing cards at the table. She crept around the side of the house and walked along the wall. The cage was open, and the dog was lying in the far corner of the wall. She patted her leg and said, "Come here." The dog caught the scent of fish on her and trotted halfway across the yard, but stalled, unsure of her motives. She looked at it staring dumbly back at her, its tongue drooping from the side of its mouth. It looked happy. Animals have no memory, Li Yan thought.

She left the dog there. Back around front she lifted the buckets and walked to the door.

"Hey, the chef's back," Zheng said.

The room was packed solid with bodies. Chen Wei didn't look up from his cards when she entered. The children rushed over to see what she'd brought. "Rice fish," one said.

"What'd you expect from a Beijinger?" Zheng said. "They eat like this every day."

Li Yan slopped the buckets over to the iron stove. The aunties had a strong fire burning, and the stove radiated an intense heat. Sweat dripped from her face and sizzled on the cooktop. She hadn't cooked over a wood flame since she was little. In Beijing they had gas. But she'd make do. She plunked the buckets down and the aunties crowded around, doling out judgments about the size and color of the fish. Li Yan wrestled the largest wok onto the fire and the aunties swung into motion, chopping scallions, growling orders at one another, pouring oil and vinegar into the wok. The men's voices were loud and drunk. Each man seemed to be locked in a separate and discursive argument over the rules of English poker, which only Chen Wei knew how to play, but no one was paying attention to him. Wriggling across the floor, under the table, snaking around feet and chair legs, the children did their best to contribute to the chaos.

Li Yan closed her eyes. Her ill-fated cooking stories had gained her a reputation in English class, and the American teacher had nicknamed her "Chef." She knew that women in the neighborhood talked about her behind her back because her husband was skinny.

She would have to be extremely careful with the fish. The aunties would take care of the side dishes, but they wouldn't help with the main dish. She'd brought this on herself, and as she added ingredients to the wok—pepper, sesame oil, coriander, salt—the aunties maintained a loose ring of motion around her without ever coming too close.

Once the oil was popping, she reached into a bucket and pulled out a wriggling carp, wiped it with a cotton rag, and dropped it into the wok. The fish curled tightly, its bony mouth gaping.

"Smells like a five-star restaurant in here," Zheng called from the table. She couldn't tell whether he was trying to make amends or whether it was a joke at her expense. Concentrate, she thought. Concentrate and keep your mouth shut.

Li Yan ladled hot oil over the fish and pressed it flat against the wok. There was room for another one, and she quickly plunged her hand into the bucket. Altogether she had ten fish—with side dishes, more than enough for the family—but by the time she would finish cooking the last one, the first fish would be cold. So she dropped yet another in the wok, three altogether. The auntie who had been looking after Li Yan's daughter peered into the wok and placed her hand on Li Yan's shoulder. Li Yan tucked a strand of hair behind her ear. She knew what she was doing. The men were so drunk they'd barely taste the meal. It was just a matter of presentation.

The aunties had completed a platter of scallion cakes and set them out before the men. There was a great clatter of porcelain and wood, and the cakes were gone. When Li Yan took the first three fish out of the wok, an auntie dropped an armload of spinach in and added soy sauce. "Just one minute," she said, holding Li Yan's wrist. They waited there by the wok until the spinach was transferred to the bare scallion cake platter. Again the platter was laid before the men and scoured clean. Then came tomato soup with egg flower. Then sauced cucumber.

"Enough of the small-fry," Zheng said, and the men all laughed. "Bring the main course!"

Li Yan was nearly done with the fish, but cooking three at a time was depleting the oil at such a rate that she had to add cold oil as she cooked, which killed the boil. She lost track of how many handfuls of scallions she'd added. The fish curled and she smashed them down. They came out of the wok dripping with oil, and more went in. Finally, the last fish looked ready. The aunties had prepared a plate for each fish, a mixed batch of stoneware and porcelain that Li Yan thought hardly worthy of the meal. Each fish was laid on a bed of bok choi, which Li Yan would have said wasn't the proper presentation if she'd had time or space to argue. No matter, she thought, these peasants don't know any better.

The aunties took up plates and stood around the table.

"The fish should honor the head of the family," Li Yan said, laying a plate before Zheng with the glazed eyes facing him.

"No, no," he said, "to our honored guest," and slid the plate to Chen Wei's place. "Now we'll see how they eat in Beijing."

The aunties laid plates before each of the men, fish heads pointing at Chen Wei.

"Go ahead, let us know what kind of cook your wife is," Zheng said. The men leaned in as Chen Wei held his chopsticks aloft. He felt their eyes on him. He felt the presence of his wife behind him.

"Dig in," Zheng said. "Join the Celebrate Life Movement."

Chen Wei lowered his chopsticks to the skin and pressed. Oil seeped out from the scales, but the skin didn't break. He pressed harder and more oil escaped, pooling on the cabbage leaves.

"Maybe you need a fork to eat Beijing cuisine?" Zheng said.

The men laughed and threw back glasses of baijiu. "Do you want your butcher knife back?"

Chen Wei jabbed at the fish, desperately trying to puncture the skin. It wouldn't give. The fish was raw on top. He couldn't turn it over—that was bad luck for the fisherman who'd caught it, even if it had been raised in a rice field. He tried to get at the meat from the side, and succeeded in creating an incision in its belly, but the meat he pulled out dripped with oil and visceral fluid.

"Eat up. Looks tasty," Zheng said, smacking his lips. This time the men didn't laugh. The room was quiet as Chen Wei brought the meat to his mouth. He chewed slowly, his eyes set on a distant point. His mandible rose and fell. He swallowed and laid his chopsticks on the table. Wood crackled in the bowels of the stove.

"You want a drink, I bet," Zheng said, filling a glass. Chen Wei turned to him and forced a smile.

"Hey, don't give me the evil eye. She's the one who cooked it," Zheng said.

Li Yan laid her hand on Chen Wei's shoulder, and as if she had touched the first in a row of dominoes, he lunged forward with such violence that all the men reared back in response. He stood and calmly collected their plates into a pile at the center of the table. The men all looked at their laps. Chen Wei began to stack the plates in two towers, placing his own eviscerated meal at the top of one.

Li Yan backed away.

"No, you're going to help me," Chen Wei said.

He gathered up one tower and thrust it on her. Oil bled over her arms and clothes.

"Come on," he said, his own arms loaded with plates. His voice sounded rough to her, as though his old country accent were again taking hold. He charged out the back door and into the walled yard, the plates balanced on one hand. Li Yan followed him, the family spilling out behind her.

"Hey, waiters," Zheng called. "Get back here with my dinner! Hey, Chen Wei," he said. A laugh caught in his throat.

"Hey." Zheng steadied himself in the doorway.

The dog emerged from the shadow of the wall, its nose high on the breeze.

It was obvious to everyone that Chen Wei meant to exact a measure of revenge on his wife. Sweat rolled over his brow and his jaw was working furiously at something. Everyone waited for him to make a move, and he stood in the yard for an embarrassingly long time, the plates clacking wetly against his chest while the dog arched its back playfully, just out of reach. Finally, Chen Wei turned to his wife and shouted, "You've cooked for a pack of dogs, so let the head of the family have the first bite." And with that, he hurled the plates at the dog. The animal tore at the bounty before it, making a terrible, primal noise. The family watched, enraptured, all except Li Yan. She stood to the side, the plates held tight against her breast, as if to challenge someone to wrest them from her.

THE HEIR

There once had been a time Omar looked forward to fighting the Chinese the way he looked forward to a good meal or sex. But lately he'd been letting his men take care of the dirty work. He could no longer bear the awful smell of the Chinese, their coarse gestures and smacking lips. To make matters worse, everyone was plotting against him—his own people were working with the Chinese to engineer his downfall, he was sure of it. Even Bola, the Mongolian henchman so stupid he hardly knew his own name, had made a play for the old gangster's throne. Not to expect treachery from his men would have been to display a gross misunderstanding of human nature, and Omar wasn't anyone's fool. But he had begun to question his ability to defend himself from their plots. Some of his men would cut their own mothers' throats.

Omar ran the west end of the Ganjiakou market, which was known as Uyghurville. There the crowded market stopped abruptly at an invisible line on the road. Chinese there, Uyghurs here. From the Chinese side, it was possible to look into Uyghurville and see a few shirtless men tending pit ovens outside the mutton and noodle restaurants, old people moving slowly and without intent down the pockmarked road, expats looking to score hash. Bicycle tires and old shoes lay strewn across the roofs of the low buildings. Curtains of acrid steam poured from the paper plant at the neighborhood's edge. Farther west the poorest of the poor had slung tarps at the feet of massive hills of garbage. Uyghurville was unquestionably the worst place in the world, and it remained perched on the edge of oblivion by a mix of swindle and violent refusal to submit to the Chinese city surrounding it.

For years residents of Beijing would not go there for fear of being robbed or killed. There had been uprisings and bombings. The Public Security Bureau, a paramilitary force known for its enterprising use of torture as a public relations tool, regularly conducted sweeping acts of brutality in Uyghurville. Old men disappeared only to reappear months later with weeping stumps for legs. Women were destroyed with lead pipes. In some circles there was discussion of who had struck first, but no one involved in the fight cared one way or another.

The violence advanced and receded like floodwaters.

Then Omar struck a deal with the PSB officer in charge of minority control: in exchange for monthly "advisory fees," the PSB would publicly declare the neighborhood rehabilitated and safe for commerce. Uyghurville hosted a ceremony with ethnic dancing and speeches touting a new era of progress. Chinese cadres, like lions at the kill, hunched over meals of spicy lamb. Later, Uyghur girls were brought in. Though the cadres' eyes lit up at the sight of that primitive flesh, only a few partook, and the rest thought them perverse for doing so.

For a while everything ran smoothly. PSB officers walked the beat and the neighborhood attracted the faddish attentions of Chinese bohemians, the children of high-ranking officials, the first wave of Chinese entrepreneurs. Expats hung around the noodle and mutton places smoking with the kitchen boys. The restaurants kept up their monthly payments and almost overnight the atmosphere of menace began to lift. But it wasn't long before the deal started to unravel. The cadres were swept up in a corruption scandal and replaced with a new band of bureaucrats who as their first order of business doubled the protection fees, reasoning that since they had been clever enough to survive the scandal, they were worth twice as much as the morons who'd been kicked out of office. This sort of Chinese logic made Omar want to shoot himself in the head.

On this point alone Omar and his grandson saw eye to eye. The Chinese were pigs. No amount of money could make up for the defilement they heaped on the Uyghurs. At one point, the government had welded the neighborhood's manhole covers in place and diverted the sewers when the PSB discovered that gangsters were using the tunnels as escape routes. Consequently, shit ran in the streets and Uyghur children died from diseases. Only Omar and a few others had proper homes. The Chinese robbed everyone blind, and no one could save enough to improve his lot. They lived like animals, sleeping in their noodle shops, atop laminate tables. At night, the floors belonged to the rats.

He ordered the restaurants to stop making payments. The Chinese were already bleeding them dry. Soon the PSB patrols thinned and the neighborhood began to decay. There were rumors the Chinese had marked Omar for death. People joked that it was better not to stand too close to Omar in case an inept Chinese sniper had been assigned to the case. With him out of the picture, the Chinese could bulldoze the neighborhood and put up skyscrapers. There was no question about that: the land was worth something, even if the people weren't.

It was with dark pleasure that Uyghurville's residents repeated the gossip about Omar. He wielded absolute power over the neighborhood, and for that they blessed him, feared him, and wished him dead all in the same breath. He was famously vengeful and he had a long memory. Once, a Kazakh had brushed against Omar's wife in the market. The man apologized profusely, prostrating himself, delivering gifts in the following days. It's nothing, Omar had said. He waited ten years to pour hot lead down the Kazakh's throat. In the meantime, he did business with the man, ate at the same table, shared the pipe. The Kazakh had come to feel that he could depend on Omar. This was how Omar operated. He took the long view.

By summertime, the rumors that had simmered for months were being served up as fact: Omar was as good as dead. He didn't pay them any mind. There was always something in the air.

Every night Omar took a walk, as much to assure the neighborhood that he was very much alive as to survey his domain. He wore large square sunglasses, a blindingly white skullcap, patent leather shoes. On this particular night, he was engulfed by a double-breasted suit that hung on him like a hospital gown. A small velvet bag filled with his enemies' gold teeth chattered in his pocket. His capos trailed behind him, and behind them, a few little boys, like gulls in the wake of a garbage scow, worrying the men for betel nuts.

The sun had dropped between the paper plant's stacks, tinting the sky the color of a bloody wound. A hot wind pressing down from above flooded the street with steam.

Despite the PSB pullout, the restaurants were packed on this hot summer night, the streets swarming with Chinese, Uyghurs, expats, shady-looking in-betweens. See, Omar thought, it's worked out fine. When he passed by, the wranglers who pulled in customers kept up their patter—"Come! Come!"—but maintained a respectful distance. Foreigners and Chinese stared openly at this slice of local flavor, the crowd parting to allow him passage.

Near a pile of trash at the edge of the neighborhood Omar passed by some off-duty PSB. They were young and stiff, swallowed by their green woolen uniforms, and absolutely terrified of this place, which lay between their station and the dormitory where they lived. Only through great restraint did they manage to keep from holding hands, as some officers would have done. Two had reached a compromise and walked with their arms locked at the elbows. It was obvious they were only kids, but Omar never let them out of his sight. Children always ran the revolutions, and in the old days these animals would have worked him over with their clubs. He knew they had a nose for his blood. Sure enough, as they passed by, one jumpy recruit thumped his stick against his woolen leg.

Omar was sick of it. He'd been dreaming of open skies and the steppes. The intimacy of emptiness. Endless rivers and the shallow arc of the horizon. It had been thirty years since he'd breathed air so clear a man could detect the hint of a cooking fire an entire valley away. He blamed these fantasies on his grandson, who had been threatening to go home to Ürümqi. The young man was spineless but hot-blooded, and these days they avoided each other except to argue.

After strolling the neighborhood for a while, Omar settled into a table at his usual haunt, where a bad thing happened. A kitchen boy who had no friends among the other boys, seized by a lunatic scheme to prove himself worthy of their respect, stuck his penis into a steaming bowl of noodles meant for Omar. The other boys made such a ruckus that Omar's guards stormed the kitchen. They hoisted the boy onto a table and pinned him there. Instantly the restaurant was empty as a windswept plain.

Slowly, perhaps with a hint of weariness, Omar rose from his chair. Standing over the boy, he opened a delicate knife shaped like a crescent moon and sliced open the boy's pants. He carved the air above the rubbery nub of flesh and stroked the boy's hairless abdomen with his hard fingers, but he felt he was doing it for the benefit of his men, who seemed pleased to have interrupted such an obvious act of disrespect.

"This sort of thing never used to happen," Omar said.

"Please, Uncle," squealed the boy.

Omar was distracted. He needed to eat. "What's to be gained by cutting you up?"

The boy whimpered for mercy.

"Everyone thinks I've gone soft in the head. This is bad for you, understand? It means that I might have to make an example of you."

"Uncle, please."

Omar looked around at his men, their faces those of expectant children. "Have you seen that new movie?" Omar said. "The one about those Yakuza? To punish disloyalty they split it from stem to stern."

Urine spurted from the boy and darkened the table.

Omar was seized by a sudden and deep sadness, and he turned away in shame. His men made a huge fuss about the piss. This is only a boy, he thought. A boy.

"Change this one's diaper and send him back to the kitchen," Omar said. Then, to the boy, he said, "Keep that thing in your pants or you'll lose it." He stroked his cheek with the back of his hand. "Bring me another bowl," he said.

As a younger man he would sooner have castrated the boy than spat on the floor. Maybe he was getting soft in his old age. But what was the point of thinking about it?

The boy, trembling, one hand clutching the waist of his pants, returned with a fresh bowl of noodles. Omar pressed a twenty-yuan note into his palm. He looked carefully at the boy's anguished face, into the black waters the boy didn't even know existed within him, and as if a tumbler had fallen in a lock, with a crisp, unbroken motion Omar cracked him on the side of his head with the knife's ash handle. The boy's lips parted; he wobbled, then dropped to the floor. The other kitchen boys pried the money from his fist and dragged him away, his pants around his ankles, his eyelashes fluttering. It was done and Omar would not think of it again.

After Omar returned home from dinner, he had one of his men fetch his grandson, who was sitting on a crate outside a restaurant down the street, watching the world go by. Anwher was twenty-five, uncomfortable in his own skin. His sharp cheek-bones launched straight out from his deep eye sockets like a pair of cliffs, and, like most young men, he spent the bulk of his time cultivating an air of internal discord, which made him look superficially haunted.

"Boss wants you," Omar's minion said.

"He can wait," said Anwher.

The thick-necked goon stayed where he was, silently exuding thuggish authority.

"Fine," Anwher said. Without a word, they started back toward the house. Anwher studied the man's gait with an almost scientific attention to the roll of his massive shoulders. No one stood in their way, and before long they were at Omar's house.

The man stopped at the door and stepped to the side. Anwher went in and sat on the floor by a low table.

Omar sat drinking his tea for a while, sizing up the boy.

"So?" Omar said.

"So what?" Anwher said.

"Busy out there tonight."

Anwher nodded and took a cup of tea.

Omar sighed. He considered himself an able communicator, but the boy was impossible to talk to. He was lazy as a rug and responded to neither reason nor violence. What once had been a gap between them had become a canyon.

"It's hopping," Anwher offered. "A human farm. Eat, shit, screw. All day, all night."

"Perhaps if you did something besides sit on your ass all day, you'd have a different take on things," Omar said.

Anwher set down his cup and made moves to leave, but Omar held up his hand.

"You have a point," Omar said. "But you might show a little respect for your home."

"Ürümqi is my home."

"This again," Omar said.

"Always. Don't act surprised," Anwher said. "I'll go like a ghost in the night."

"You should write that down," Omar said. "Hand me the smoke." He slowly brought an unlit pipe to his lips and blew through it, moving with the measured patience of a man who routinely found himself talking to people too stupid to come around to his point of view. Anwher dropped a leather pouch into his grandfather's palm.

"And what will happen to the business when you go?" Omar asked.

"Maybe this stomach ulcer will clear up, is what will happen. I can't believe I've lasted this long. If I had any sense I would have bugged out years ago."

Anwher looked out the top of his head when he said this, gauging his grandfather's reaction as best he could without making eye contact. He was ready to run, but Omar said nothing. Then the old man motioned for a knife.

Anwher pulled one from his pocket, snapped it open, and with a flourish presented the handle.

"Where's yours?" Anwher asked.

"Left it at a restaurant," Omar said. He gouged at the pipe with Anwher's knife, the blade rasping against the bowl. "This pipe is a piece of junk."

"It's fine."

"Really? Look at this. It's clogged solid. What am I supposed to do with this?" Omar paused to stab at it some more. "What to do? Cleaning it properly will destroy it. You see what I'm saying?"

"Yeah, I see."

"Ürümqi's not the way you remember it," Omar said.

"It's not the way you remember it, either."

"No Uyghurs left there, you know," Omar said. "It's slope city now. They turned all the Uyghurs into Chinese. You have to cut them open to see the difference."

"You don't say."

Omar stopped working on the pipe and looked at his grandson. "The Chinese have black blood. That's the truth."

"Sure," Anwher said.

"Go to Kashgar if you want to be a man. Go someplace you can behave like a noble human being."

"We'll see. I'm overflowing with noble ideas."

"You're overflowing with something."

"You wouldn't joke if you knew how serious I am about this."

"Really?" Omar roared, his voice thick with rage. "You're serious? Be on your way, then."

"Don't tempt me," Anwher shot back.

"You have my blessing," Omar said. He knew the boy would never go through with it, and that was fine because he wanted him nearby where he could keep an eye on him. He was a caged bird and he'd get eaten alive in Ürümqi.

Omar turned his attention back to the barrel of the pipe. The blade hitched against a lump of carbon fused to the shank. Eventually he gave up on the pipe and located a container of snuff. He scooped one long pinkie nail through the powder.

"Don't think I won't do it," Anwher said.

"It would be the only thing you've ever managed on your own," Omar said.

"I'll do it," Anwher said.

"I'm sure you will," Omar replied. He wrinkled his nose and brought another scoop of snuff to his nostril, inhaled, and waited for the blur to settle into his brain. With his free hand he felt around behind him for a pillow. "Off to see your boyfriends tonight?"

Anwher stood up, shaking his head and smiling crookedly,

amazed as ever at the old man's capacity for provocation. "You truly know how to injure a man," he said. "Good night, Grandfather. Blessings upon you."

"Get a haircut," Omar called after him. "You look like a girl." The boy had always been a torment. He took a beating without a word, afterward never showing any sign of anger. Shot in the head, he'd rise up to commend his assassin. It had occurred to Omar that this trait was the mark of the divine—who else but a truly spiritual man could be so guileless?—but it was dangerous to be known as a forgiving man. Forgiveness had no place in this world. Omar wasn't going to be around forever. What would the boy do then?

He rummaged around for another pipe and smoked some hashish. Before long he was asleep, his hands tucked into his jacket in case a hungry rat picked up the smell of food on his fingers.

The restaurant across the street kept a little monkey. Most of the time it lazed on the warm brick by the pit oven eating Kishu oranges, occasionally rousing itself to harass a customer. It would steal parcels and toss them onto the hot coals where the naan baked.

When Anwher emerged from his grandfather's quarters, he saw the monkey preening the fur on its peach-size face, and he looked around for some trash to fling at it. The hunk of tire he found flew over the monkey's head and thudded against the restaurant's tin roof. The owner came out with fists raised, ready for anything.

"Why? Why?" said the poor man, mortally wounded for the thousandth time.

Anwher shrugged and started up the street.

"Worthless," the restaurant owner shouted. "You're a piece of shit!" As always, Anwher pretended not to hear and disappeared into the crowd.

He wandered deep into the Chinese market, his hands stuffed in his pockets so no one could accuse him of anything, and he tried to walk proudly, meeting the eyes of any Chinese who looked him in the face. The market smelled of garlic and rotten cabbage and was lit by strands of lightbulbs drooping over the street. He caught sight of his barber working behind a cart stacked with chicken cages, and he abruptly turned on his heel and cut through the crowd.

The broad-faced Chinese man was moving gracefully around his customer, a mound of flesh who had established himself, like the cap of a mushroom, on a low wooden stool. From time to time the customer gave his newspaper a shake to clear the hair clippings. Otherwise he was still as a mountain. The barber combed and trimmed in silence, his hands gliding about the man's enormous head. Anwher waited quietly, in a strange communion with the barber, those conjurer's hands, the unmoving customer, until an old auntie pushed him out of the way.

"You're spooking the chickens. Go wait over there," she said to Anwher, pointing at a stool with a folded bib atop it. "I'll get to you in a minute."

He ignored her.

"You deaf?" the auntie said. She held her left hand, palsied and shaking violently, to her ear. Then she recognized Anwher and said, "For a little extra, I'll cut with the right." She laughed like she was choking on a bone.

He knew the type. Like all Chinese, she was working an angle.

"There's only one thing you get paid extra for," Anwher said, "and you're so old I'd probably fall in."

The woman squinted slightly. "Get out of here. We don't serve your kind."

"Sure you don't."

"A haircut's not what you need. Maybe a hatchet between the eyes," she said evenly. Anwher lifted an eyebrow and tried to stay cool. The barber and his patron both looked up slowly, as if they'd been disturbed from the mutual appreciation of a huge, tranquil painting.

"Everything okay, Ma?" the barber said.

"This Uyghur," she said.

The barber limped over, his comb and scissors by his side. He hadn't received enough iron as a child and his legs were crooked. "It's no problem. I know this gentleman." He craned his neck to see the sides of Anwher's head. "Little shaggy on the sides."

"Yeah," said Anwher.

The barber assessed him. "Don't tell me you've started picking fights with old ladies?"

Anwher coiled slightly. "How was I supposed to know she was your mother? Now I know."

"Hey, don't take it so seriously. I'm just messing with you. We're okay, right?"

"It's fine," Anwher answered.

"That's the spirit," the barber said. Then he held up his comb and scissors and said, "We aim to please."

"I don't go looking for fights," Anwher said.

"Of course not. Have a seat over there and I'll be with you in a minute," the barber said. He made a playful jab at Anwher's shoulder, and the young man juked like a prizefighter. The barber smiled and held out his hand for a shake. Anwher rolled his shoulders and tugged on his lapels. Among the Chinese he had no friends, but in this predictable monthly transaction there was a sort of comfort, one that relied on the rules of commerce to ensure that the razor the Chinese man put to his throat would never draw blood. There was, Anwher reasoned, no point in this Chinese doing him any harm. He tipped well and treated the barber like a valued servant. But the old woman had thrown the balance, and Anwher hated her for it.

"Come on," the barber said. He limped over to a stool and snapped out the bib, shaking it playfully for the young bull. Anwher sidled over and the barber tied the bib around his neck. He went back to his other customer.

"It's the heat," the barber said softly. "I saw two old ladies beating each other with their canes yesterday." The fat man chuckled, his paper rattling as he heaved.

"I don't notice it," Anwher said, but as soon as he'd spoken he wished he hadn't.

"Lucky man," said the barber. "Always better to close one's eyes than curse the darkness."

The barber's mother had been studying Anwher all this time. "I never forget a face," she said, shaking a stubby finger at him.

"Take it easy, Ma," the barber said around the comb clamped between his teeth.

Clearly the old woman was deranged, but Anwher couldn't catch the barber's eye to confirm it. The barber cut merrily along while his customer read the paper. The chickens scratched in their cages.

The old woman had spent a fair amount of time in Uyghurville. Those people didn't frighten her. And she knew exactly who this was in front of her. She had given herself to his grandfather in return for a lamb for her son's wedding. The other Chinese girls acted superior to the Uyghurs and complained about every little thing, but not her. She did what was asked, and she got repeat business.

That had been years ago. Sometimes she saw the old gangster in the street. She didn't step aside. A rich Uyghur was still worth less than a Chinese whore.

The boy's grandfather had been rough with her, but she hadn't complained. Afterward they had lain in his murky room, a place composed entirely of desperate corners light could not find, angled shadows where anguish had taken up residence. It made her skin crawl: everywhere the spirit of the dead wife.

After a while, the old man had called out and the boy silently appeared at their feet. He had a shadow of hair on his upper lip. She pulled the sheet over her breasts.

"Take a go at this?" the old man said.

The boy shook his head.

"Come on, I'll show you how. You put your little worm in the slit." He tore away the sheet and grabbed her between the legs.

The boy shook his head, his eyes down.

"Faggot," Omar said.

She set her jaw in case he decided to strike her. People were like that.

Instead he made a sudden lunge at the boy, but Anwher dashed out of the room before Omar's feet touched the floor.

The gangster shook his head. "This is the sort of crime that has been visited on me every day of my life. I should get it over with and buy him a man," Omar said. He went on and on, talking, talking about the boy, the dead wife, business trouble.

As his semen dried to a crust on her thigh, it pulled tightly at the delicate hairs there. He had gone at her with everything he had. She hadn't complained.

From the other room came the sounds of the boy crying, and the old man had stopped talking. He sat up and told her to get dressed.

With only a blanket wrapped around his waist, he'd led her outside. At the restaurant across the street, the lamb carcass had been skinned, gutted, and strung up by its hind legs from the eave. The monkey was making a show of poking at the milky eyeballs, then leaping back to cower behind its owner's legs. In the heat the carcass had begun to sweat and a small crowd gathered as she'd struggled to get the slick body from the rusty hook and into the wooden cart. Without anyone's help she managed to wrestle the viscous thing down. Her clothes clung to her body like a caul. After she'd loaded up and gotten a little ways down the street, the gangster stepped through the crowd and called her name. "Tight Chinese hole," he shouted after her, his fingers forming an O. The crowd laughed. She'd gripped the wooden cart handles and leaned toward the Chinese end of the market.

She knew all about this Uyghur in front of her.

From his stool Anwher catalogued the tools at her disposal. She had scissors. A razor lay on a corroded tray nearby. Rope lay coiled at the foot of the chicken cages, which were stacked in a bank high enough to conceal him from the crowd. Even if he cried out, no one would hear him over the noise. This was his usual means of entertainment. He imagined his own death and cultivated baroque fantasies involving a funeral march through the market. Everyone would be sorry, especially his grandfather, whose heart would break when he gazed upon the beautiful corpse.

After a while, the dim light and heat overpowered him and he dozed off and dreamed about a huge pillowed room filled with bodies twisting like lizards around each other. There were no faces and he lay with women and men alike and never needed to stop.

When he awoke, the barber was close to him, studying his face. Anwher smelled garlic on the man's breath. He glanced down to make sure his erection wasn't showing.

"You have a noble nose," the barber said softly.

Anwher wiped his face with his hands. The barber stepped back and began to move his arm. The razor slapping against the strop sounded desperately final.

"Tilt," the barber said, applying two fingers to Anwher's chin. A metal pot was steaming over a fire, and the barber plucked out a hot towel. He laid it over Anwher's mouth and went back to sharpening the blade.

"This makes some people nervous," the barber said.

"Not me," Anwher said into the towel.

The barber got down to business and neither one said a word until he was done.

Actually, it was the old woman who spoke first. "How fetching," she said. "The boys at the Secret Garden will love it." The barber's scissors snapped around Anwher's head, touching up the tight crop.

"She's bad for business," Anwher said.

"Hm," said the barber. He pressed a small plastic mirror into Anwher's hand. Anwher inspected the cut, then rose from the stool and worked at the bib's knot. He fumbled with it long enough to become aware that everyone was looking at him. "Allow me," the barber said. It was off instantly.

Anwher held out a twenty, a generous sum. He wasn't sure why he'd offered more than usual. The barber bowed.

"If the old woman hadn't shot off her mouth it would have been forty," Anwher said.

She looked up from her bowl of noodles. "Hey, young man, no hard feelings. It's on the house."

"Very funny, Ma," said the barber, flashing the banknote at her. For a moment something other than composed serenity flashed across his face. Then it was gone, replaced by the set line of his mouth.

"What? Speak up," shouted his mother. "We're not so bad off we need dirty money."

The barber winced. Grasping Anwher's hands in his own, he said, "Good night. Be well. See you soon."

"Listen to me," his mother said. "We don't need money from that piece of filth. Give it back. Don't make me embarrass you in front of these people."

The barber tried to laugh, but it was a weak, nervous effort and hardly any sound came out at all. Gingerly he ventured a hand forth to pat Anwher on the shoulder, then thought better of it. "She's not well," he whispered.

"No shit. Who is she, to be talking about filth?" Anwher said.

"Accept my apologies. She's like a naughty child. It happens. It's the heat. The heat does terrible things to an old mind."

"They say the murder rate goes up when it's hot," Anwher said in a tone meant to be menacing. As usual, it hadn't come out right.

"That's true. It's a fact," said the barber. When Anwher didn't respond, the barber added, "It makes us all do things we don't mean."

For reasons Anwher couldn't quite comprehend, the barber's obsequious behavior angered him. He was like a fat bottle fly buzzing over a plate of food, its mere presence ruining the entire meal. "She's no different in the dead of winter," Anwher said. "I can tell these things about people. Bitter old bitch."

The barber stared back at him.

"Look here," Anwher said, crowding the barber, "I don't go looking for fights."

"No one's looking for a fight."

"You should keep her on a leash," Anwher said.

"Beg your pardon," the barber said, backing away. "Beg your pardon."

"That's all you have to say about it? You're a shitty son," Anwher said. "Worthless." Anwher couldn't abide weakness. "Your mother is a whore," he said.

The barber nodded.

"She's a whore," Anwher said.

The barber said nothing.

"You're not telling him anything he doesn't know, boy," the old woman said.

"Shut up," Anwher said. Looking back at the barber, he said, "How much? It's by the hour or what? Doesn't matter. I'll just take my whore right here. That okay with you?"

The barber remained bent at the waist. It was a while before he spoke, and when he did, he addressed himself to the hard earth. "Discuss business matters with her."

"Unbelievable," Anwher said. "Can you believe this?" Anwher looked around for an answer, but the fat man appeared to be engrossed in his newspaper, and the old woman had a crazy grin on her face, so he looked back at the son.

Eventually the barber said, "I know. Hard to believe."

"You need to have your head checked," Anwher said.

"Haircut's on the house," the barber said. He forfeited the bill without looking up. "Please go."

After spitting twice on the ground at the barber's feet, Anwher left. The barber's mother, still grinning ever so slightly, turned to the fat man, that seemingly permanent fixture atop his stool. "That was quite a performance, hm? Did you see that? He walked off without paying. Those people would rob their own kin."

"Ma," the barber said. "Don't."

The fat man shook his head and hauled himself off the stool.

"Ma," the barber said.

"I could give you more than a haircut on the house, you know," she said to the fat man.

He made a show of shuddering.

"You're not much to look at yourself," she shot back.

"I have my charms," he said.

"So does a rattlesnake," she said.

"Aw, you don't mean that," the fat man said. "Come file a report in the morning. We'll take care of the rest."

They came for Anwher while he slept and dragged him from his low bed by a rope twisted around his neck. When they started to beat him the garrote slipped a bit, and in this way he avoided asphyxiation.

They threw him in the backseat of a Volkswagen sedan, a standard unmarked PSB vehicle. Two men sat on either side of him, their large thighs pinioning him. He tried to screw open his swelling eyes, but couldn't see a thing. His ears rang and his face throbbed in time with his heartbeat. They were rolling now, the compartment filling with cigarette smoke that stung the raw tissues of his esophagus. Something cold and hard was in his mouth. One of the men began to punch him in the head.

He awoke in a cell, which in the darkness he first mistook for his room at home. The confusion didn't last long. The scrape of metal buckets on concrete echoed through the cellblock as prisoners passed around the pot to relieve themselves. His body was numb until he moved against the concrete floor and the net of agony tangled around him tightened. He remembered where he was. He drew into a ball and wept.

Omar had stood in the doorway and watched them take his grandson. He could have screamed and waved his arms like a woman, but what good would that have done? Gotten him a broken jaw, probably. He knew how this worked and he kept his distance. Just to be sure, the Chinese had stationed one of their thugs by him, and weapons were made obvious, but he wouldn't have moved even if he'd had an army behind him. It was everyone's fate to be dragged off by the Chinese. Omar, of course, viewed fate as little more than a starting point at which one began his negotiation with the universe. Everyone but Anwher, it seemed, knew how this worked. He'd struggled and made it worse for himself.

Omar went to the slot in the floor and counted out a decent payoff. They'd be sure to liberate him of anything valuable he carried in, so he removed his watch and gold chains and dropped them into the hole.

Then, outside to have a smoke and wait for daylight. He blew out his nostrils and packed the pipe. The monkey across the street was curled on a blanket beneath a window. Omar squatted down and watched the sleeping animal's dim form.

Alone in the cell, Anwher had backed his spine tight against the concrete seam of a corner. His face had become a mask of dried blood and sweat. The unrelenting ammoniac stench of urine was thick on the air. Guards' voices echoed through the corridor. When the prisoners moved, they moved in silence while the guards stamped beside them, shouting, "March, convicts!" Anwher envisioned his own grotesque death, but stripped of the chorus of sympathy usually humming in the background. Allah, mercy, I beg you. Despite the heat, he was freezing, so cold that he felt his hands might snap off like twigs. He knew he was waiting to be retrieved, and that alone kept him awake, his eyes sweeping the dim cell for movement. Finally, the door opened and two guards dragged him to the washroom, where they told him to strip, which he did, as they dumped bucket after bucket of stinging water over his head. He dressed with the deliberation of an eighty-year-old, and they dragged him off to another part of the prison. The barber and his mother were there.

When he came into view, the old woman did a little dance. "That's the one," she said. "Hey, there, Uyghur. How's life?"

"Cut it out," a guard said. "That's inappropriate."

Another guard shook Anwher by the arm. "You stole from these people?" Anwher tried to catch the barber's eye, but the man wouldn't comply. He'd made his decision. Anwher let out a low moan.

"Oh, that's definitely the one," the old woman said. "Coward."

The barber lifted his head to say something, but she cut him off. "You had your chance," she said.

The guard directed himself at Anwher. "You've stolen from a Chinese citizen," he said, "and have damaged the reputation of your minority group."

The old woman laughed.

From behind them a voice boomed, "Behave, all of you." A round man filled the doorway and moved slowly into the room. His face was slick with sweat and the top of his coat was unbuttoned to reveal a roll of flesh at the base of his neck. At first the face was only vaguely familiar to Anwher. This was the commanding officer, that much was clear, and when Anwher placed him, he shrank back against the guard, who pushed him away. It was the fat man with the newspaper. "This is a crime against the People's Republic," the fat man said, "and it will be dealt with according to proper procedure."

"They said it was on the house," Anwher whispered.

"On the house?" the fat man said to the barber. "Is that right? For the record, did you say that?"

"You were sitting right there," said his mother.

"We need to establish the facts."

"Do we look like we're running a charity?" she said, then paused to consider the rules of the game. She had to be sure no traps were being laid for her before proceeding. "Did you hear me say it was on the house?" she asked the fat man.

"I don't recall," he said, his face impassive. It was enough to satisfy the woman that she wasn't going to land in a cell herself. "You understand this kid is connected?" the fat man said.

"Like I care. He walked a tab. And he insulted me."

"Besmirched your good name, did he?"

"You were there," she said. "You heard what he said."

"For the record," he said.

"A whore. He said I was a whore."

"Imagine."

She crossed her arms and gave the fat man the evil eye.

This went on for a while, the fat man extracting his pound of flesh, Anwher attempting invisibility, the old woman needling them both. The barber watched dumbly from the side. Eventually the fat man got bored.

"I'm sure he'll gladly pay a fine plus what he owes you," he said to the barber's mother. "Justice done?"

"He steals from me. He threatens me. He calls me a whore in the open market, and you let him go free?"

"I'm sure you've been called worse," the fat man said. "Don't push your luck." He waved at the door. "Take him back to his cell and get this citizen her money."

The fat man had been promoted hastily in the wake of the corruption sweep. His ascension to the rank of commanding officer was the result of good timing and the luck enjoyed by those who kept their mouths shut and carried out orders. But his men made farting noises when he walked by, and some still called him Fatty Bo to his face. This bothered him.

He had his orders from the new regime and had been waiting for an excuse to move against the old gangster. One could never be too careful. Things had to look right. He'd told the old woman what to do: make your claim, file a report, allow the process to take hold.

Of course, these civilians don't take orders. She'd crashed into the station like it was 1967, invoking revolutionary slogans and a bunch of stuff she'd heard on the radio. "Seek truth from facts," she kept yelling. Before he knew it, the entire station was peering around doors and over the tops of their reports to see what was going to happen next. His men didn't bother to hide their snickering faces. "They're taking over," she screamed. "Threatening old women!"

He had bellowed at the corporal to escort the old woman to a room where they could question the prisoner. The man took his time leading her away, and Fatty Bo had to yell at him again. The corporal's hangdog face hardly registered the abuse, which the other men found hilarious. And the son—there he was, trying to put enough distance between himself and his own mother to signal that their simultaneous arrival had been a coincidence. Fatty Bo motioned him over.

"She's really got a wire up her ass," Fatty Bo said.

"It's the heat," replied the barber. Fatty Bo waited, but that was all the son had to say on the matter. Why she wanted the Uyghur strung up was a mystery, but it sure wasn't because the Uyghur had called her a whore. She wanted this kid out the back door in a body bag. So be it. Embarrassing, yes, to be subject to a crazy old woman's whims, but good luck all the same. Fatty Bo was self-sufficient enough to summon some intellectual appreciation for the situation. It was a blessing, was what it was. Bastards wouldn't call him Fatty Bo after he burned Uyghurville to the ground.

Omar went to the PSB station alone, having left the payoff with one of his toughs stationed down the street.

Every cop in the place jammed into booking to eyeball him. It took two hours to fill out the forms because his Chinese was far from perfect and one of the cops dumped tea on the papers just as he was finishing. This was part of the process and Omar dutifully requested new forms, for which he was charged a yuan and a half. Hunched over like a schoolboy, he began again, pausing occasionally to brush their cigarette ash from the backs of his hands. After the forms, they made him strip and open his orifices in front of everyone before handcuffing him to a radiator in a stifling reeducation classroom. None of this was new to him.

After an hour in that swampy air, his skin had the consistency of boiled chicken and his tongue was so swollen he had to hang his mouth open like an imbecile. A young officer came to fetch him. "Here, now, Uncle, take my arm," the officer said gently, "and we'll go see the prisoner." He led Omar through a series of iron doors, until finally, through a forest of bars, Omar spotted Anwher slumped against the wall, lifeless as a coat left on the ground overnight.

Fatty Bo appeared and offered Omar a thermos of water, which the old man guzzled. Anwher watched the men from his corner of the cell. "This can't be pleasant for you to see," Fatty Bo said.

"It's a shame," Omar said. He had developed a nonchalance when dealing with the authorities that was by this time as automatic as breathing. A man had to wait out the Chinese, figure out their game. Only after carefully considering the options would Omar step forward to engage them.

"Prisoner, hup to," shouted Fatty Bo. He took the young officer's baton and dragged it across the bars. "Up! Up! You have a visitor."

"Go in and get him," Fatty Bo said to the young officer, handing back his baton. A few bold prisoners strained to see from their cells, but the majority hung back, out of sight of the officers. A sidelong glance from a PSB, and you'd be carrying rocks for a month.

The young officer nudged Anwher with the baton and said, "Come on, now. Don't try Fatty Bo's patience."

"Use the proper form of address in front of the prisoner," Fatty Bo shouted.

The young officer shrugged. "Come on, now," he said. "Quit playing." When Anwher refused to budge, the officer, embarrassed to find his kindness rejected, jammed the baton into the prisoner's ribs. "Up," he demanded. Still, the prisoner refused.

Fatty Bo's nostrils flared at this display of ineptitude. Bands stood out in his neck. "Get out," he said, shouldering the young officer aside.

"Boy, don't be an idiot," Omar said under his breath. There was nothing he could do. Fatty Bo pinched Anwher's ears with his thick fingers and wrenched him into a standing position.

"He's got spirit," Fatty Bo said, as if holding up a prize piglet.

"He's an idiot," Omar said.

"If you say so. We should discuss his case." Fatty Bo unsnapped the leather holster on his hip and patted his pistol.

"What's that all about?" Omar said.

"Just watch yourself, okay?"

"Let's discuss the boy's case," Omar said. A gun wasn't necessary for these negotiations and it surprised him that the officer had put it into play. But the Chinese were good at psychology. They had hundreds of clever tricks to knock their detainees off balance.

"His file was called up for a minor charge," said Fatty Bo, "but some research turned up unpaid license fees." He graced the young guard with a wry smile. "What is he? A raisin salesman?"

"A furniture importer," Omar said. "We can take care of this quickly."

"I haven't even told you how much he owes. How much do you think he owes?"

"In range of three thousand," Omar said quickly. He didn't care what the officer was claiming the boy had done. The officer would have the money and Omar wasn't going to stand in his way.

Fatty Bo chewed on it for a moment. "Damn close. It's good that you're on top of his business."

"Four," Omar said.

"Look, it's a symbolic act. A measure of good faith." Fatty Bo focused intently on Omar, his eyes narrowing.

"I wouldn't call it symbolic," Omar said.

"Can I tell you something about myself?" Fatty Bo said. "I'm an unlikely success, you know? The odds were staggering. I was very sick as a child. As scrawny as him." He tipped his chin at Anwher. "Unable to defend myself. Can you believe it, looking at me now? Things change."

"Things change," Omar said.

"And listen to this: My father was taken by the Red Guard, strapped to a log, and pushed over a waterfall," Fatty Bo said. "My mother and I lived like a couple of rats in a hole. If someone had told me I'd be here today . . ."

"You'd never have believed it," Omar said.

"Yes! Exactly." Fatty Bo looked at Omar appreciatively. "You haven't had an easy life, either, but look at you—you've done well for yourself. That's why I feel I can talk to you. So what's money between two men like us? My men tell me you didn't even raise your voice to them. You spoke without speaking, right? It impressed them, I'll tell you that much. Between you and me, you scared them stiff. When was the last time you woke up bloody in a jail cell? Not in my lifetime, am I right? That's a mistake you only make once. But this poor boy. This generation worries me. They're soft. None of this 'eat bitter' bullshit for them. He'll never be able to hold your empire together by himself, that's what you're thinking. Not that there haven't been dangerous homosexuals—remember Queen Li? That guy and his fucking wooden knives!"

Omar kept his eyes level and his hands by his sides.

"You're worried," Fatty Bo said. "Let me put your mind at rest." But that was all he said. He expelled a weary sigh.

"He's been saying he wants to move back to Ürümqi," Omar ventured.

"Is that a fact?" Fatty Bo said.

"It is. He's had it almost as bad as you and I, so it's understandable."

"I very seriously doubt that."

"When he was a child in Ürümqi. Both of his parents. My daughter—" Omar brought his finger across his neck.

"No," Fatty Bo said.

"Yes. Truly. Killed in the street."

"By Chinese?"

"Yes," Omar said.

"That's no surprise. They used to send the top-notch psychos out there. All this bad blood is their fault. Everyone got off to a terrible start."

"And still, the boy wants to go home."

"If only things could have been different early on," Fatty Bo said.

"I've told him to stay here, but he's a grown man. He can do what he wants."

"It's too late to change the course of history. Isn't that what they say?"

"He's a grown man, but I'm responsible for him." Omar brought his hands up, as if to apologize for this insoluble family bond. "I can have the money here very quickly," he said.

"That's a good idea. You should pay the fine and I'll let the boy go." Fatty Bo leaned toward Omar and put his mouth close to his ear. "You understand I'll have to interrogate him. To appease the men. They're animals. No ability to recognize the nuances of the situation. Our history creates expectations."

Only the four of them—Omar, Fatty Bo, the young officer, and Anwher—were there.

"You'll do what's expected," Omar said.

Fatty Bo sighed and held his gun out to the young officer. "Give me your stick. And don't let this old man get the drop on you. He's got a trick or two up his sleeve." The young officer nodded gravely.

Standing over Anwher, Fatty Bo slapped the baton into his meaty hand. "Now, young man. Whenever you're ready to apologize for your crime, let me know." Anwher scrambled into a corner, but Fatty Bo was all over him. With a great sweeping arc he raised the stick above his head, then brought it smashing down on Anwher's back. "This is unnecessary," Fatty Bo said to no one in particular. Beatings no longer interested him the way they once had. But a man did his duty.

He hit Anwher until the Uyghur stopped struggling, and by that time his own back was starting to seize up. It took all of his concentration to ignore the pain. He tried to swing from the hips to minimize the cramps.

He directed some shots to Anwher's head, the baton reverberating sharply in his hand. Then he stopped and looked at Omar. Omar met his gaze but said nothing.

Anwher was making noises. It could have been an apology, but Fatty Bo's back was killing him, the muscles yanking like someone snapping out a wet cloth, and he couldn't think about anything but the cramps. He tore open his jacket to reveal a sweat-stained T-shirt underneath and attacked with a dull furor, the blows momentous, every one a raging earthquake. Anwher's hands crept over the floor, as if he were trying to drag his ravaged body out of the cell, out of the station, away from Beijing entirely. In his homeland, a man could walk in a deep valley for days without encountering another soul.

"Why?" Anwher cried, his voice suddenly clear.

Fatty Bo stopped long enough for Omar to respond to his grandson. When the old man said nothing, Fatty Bo looked up. "This can go on indefinitely," he said.

Omar knew it could.

"So be it," Omar said. "Show us what you're made of."

MOUNTAIN OF
SWORDS, SEA OF FIRE

omeone had hung an enormous red banner across the back of the newsroom that read "Farewell and Long Life, Li Pai!" The man of the hour had positioned himself at a metal folding table directly beneath it. Young reporters came with his memoirs open to the title page, then solemnly presented letters of recommendation they had written for themselves. Li Pai signed them all. Ning had spent the morning watching from his cubicle as they filed by, so worshipful, so eager to drink from the font of the great one's knowledge. The whole damn thing turned his stomach. Had anyone asked, Ning had no quarrel with him: Li Pai was a treasure. But Ning wasn't one for celebrations.

There was to be a party that night at the Green Room. Just thinking about it made Ning cringe. He knew how it would play out. Fang, the economics editor, would kick things off by delivering a speech listing her own accomplishments and thanking Li Pai for his contributions to her stratospheric rise, and old Bang Wen would stutter his way through a selection of Du Fu's poetry. The chief would grunt out whatever he'd written on his Black-Berry on the way over, while everyone, arms crossed, stared at the floor and listened for their cues to laugh. The toasts would go on so long Ning would begin to fantasize, like a man crawling across the Gobi, about a single drop of lukewarm beer. And by the time every editor in the place had said his piece, the drunks from the copydesk and production would feel compelled to chime in. But, much as he wanted to, Ning couldn't escape it. He was the only one old enough to have known Li Pai from the beginning, and the chief's assistant had been hounding him for weeks about his speech.

Like Li Pai, Ning was in his sixties, and for longer than he could remember, he had marked time by the various injustices the thoughtless world visited upon him, the speech being one. Another prime example occurred just after lunch, when one of Li Pai's acolytes called across the newsroom, "Hey, Ning! Great news! You just got scooped by the Baby Reds!"

Ah, perfection, he thought. He'd taken some extra time to do some deep research, and here was his reward. If he'd been younger, he'd have hopped a bus over to the *China Youth Daily*'s dotcom operation and taken it out of the kid's hide—he didn't have to be told who'd stolen this story from him. He already knew. But he had a bigger problem, which was how to explain himself to the chief.

"Hey, no shame, no shame," said the chipper young reporter in the cube next to Ning. He was wearing a necktie and had a pencil tucked behind one ear. He'd been on the job exactly one week, and he'd been a constant annoyance to Ning for the full length of his tenure. "I'm sure this happens to everyone from time to time," the reporter said, his voice expectant.

"What a comfort," Ning said. His phone was ringing but he ignored it. With some effort, like a man feeling his way through a blacked-out room, he located the story on the *Youth Daily*'s site and printed it before turning his attention to his neighbor. "To think. All these years without you. It's a miracle I've been able to find my own dick without your sage counsel." The reporter shrugged and rolled back into his cube, unfazed. It was perhaps the least offensive thing Ning had said to him all week.

Ning didn't much care about good stories anymore, not his own or anyone else's, and he'd given this one about as much thought as he would have the purchase of an umbrella during a downpour. It was about a security guard who'd acted courageously and had been stabbed nearly to death. The doctors had sewn him up, and he was on the mend, but because he'd refused to tell a white lie that would have harmed no one, his case was tangled in red tape and the hospital was refusing to discharge him. Ning had visited the guard, and as he'd listened to his story, he'd felt himself leaning in at one point, eager to hear more, but he'd lost interest again almost as soon as he'd left the hospital. Instead of filing the story, he'd burned the rest of the week doing research on thoracoabdominal penetrating injuries, and now he was going to hear about it.

Sure enough, before Ning had even had time to finish reading the story, the chief's assistant arrived at his desk. Her blue cotton dress had red flowers printed on it, and atop that she wore an apple-green sweater buttoned up to the neck.

"Mercy," he said. "Is it mating season for your species?"

"Don't start with me, old man," she said.

"So you've come down from your lofty perch just to subject me to this thing," Ning said, pointing to her outfit. "I'm nearly blind as it is."

"You don't think I called first?" She had the face of a middle schooler, and though she claimed to be twenty-five and a college graduate, Ning had his suspicions. She was someone's niece, or her father was in real estate.

"I didn't hear it," he said, his chair creaking as he leaned back.

"You didn't hear it," she said.

"Who can hear anything in here?" he said, waving a hand at Li Pai's table.

"If you read your e-mail—" she said.

"I don't read e-mail."

"Of course you don't," she said. "How inconsiderate of the rest of the company to communicate in such a manner. I'll draft a memo immediately and have a copyboy rush it down. Shall I have the little urchin rinse your inkpot and wash your brushes while he's at it? Ning Wang's wish is our command."

"Tell me," he said, "how exactly did you avoid becoming an infanticide statistic?"

She flashed her eyeteeth. "Please, at your convenience, grace us with your presence. I'm sure the chief will be happy to wait," she said, and walked away, her dress cutting around her legs.

"I'm sure he will," Ning yelled after her. He put up his feet to make clear that he didn't take orders from anyone, least of all her, and began to read slowly through the *Youth Daily* story. He paused every so often to laugh derisively, loud enough so that the reporters near him could hear, and when he finished, he made a show of dawdling around his desk before sauntering out to the elevators for the ride up to the eleventh floor.

"Well, I'm here," he announced when he arrived outside the chief's office.

"He'll be overjoyed," the chief's assistant said, picking up the phone to buzz the chief. She waved Ning in. "Always a pleasure!" she called after him.

Inside, the chief motioned for him to sit. "Took you long enough."

"She's as unpleasant as she is ugly," Ning said, gesturing through the glass. "You really ought to kick her down to production. She makes me go soft every time I lay eyes on her."

The chief didn't answer. He was scribbling on a layout for a weekend insert, and Ning waited without saying anything else. When he saw the thick red pencil stop moving, he went on the offensive.

"I know why I'm here, and let me just go on the record as saying that it's a hack job," Ning said. "You know it, and I know it. This kid who filed it—I saw him at the hospital. Probably followed me there."

The chief stared at him.

"Second of all, this is exactly why I don't file to the Web. It's nothing but garbage like this. I've seen better stories in school papers. I bet you haven't had a chance to read the whole thing, have you? I have a printout right here," Ning said, holding up the story. "This thing's got so many holes, you can hear the wind whistling through it. Really, it pains me to read it," he said, before doing just that, aloud and in its entirety. The chief reshuffled the layouts on his desk and went at a new one with his grease pencil. Ning read, pausing every so often to affirm his amazement at the reporter's incompetence. He punctuated the end of the story with a hearty guffaw.

"You done?" the chief said.

"Just give me the afternoon and I'll have a draft for you. For the sake of our readership," Ning said. "For the sake of the historical record!"

"Since when have you cared about either of those things?" the chief said.

"The kid missed the whole point of the story," Ning said, rattling the paper. "Why do you think I've been tied up with it all week? It would take anyone else two weeks to do what I can give you by tonight."

"Is that so?" the chief said. He put down his pencil and pushed his glasses up to his forehead, where they sat atop his white brows like a second set of eyes. The skin on his big bald skull was as rumpled as a plowed field.

"I've been doing some thinking," the chief said. "Li Pai's last day and all. You've been on my mind, I'm sorry to report."

"That can't have been a pleasant experience," Ning said.

The chief snorted. "I don't spend a lot of time pondering the vagaries of the human condition, but I've made an exception in your case," he said. "I'm of limited intelligence, but I've given it my best effort, and I've come up with a theory. You used to be a bull with sharp horns. But, now—" The chief made a puffing sound, his fingers releasing chaff into the wind.

Ning jumped in. "*Youth Daily*'s constantly doing things like this. Those goat fuckers. We'd never go with something this weak," he said, shaking the printout. "You'll see what I'm talking about if you read my file."

"Where is it?"

"I can have it on your desk in a couple of hours. Maybe three."

The chief's expression softened just enough to change the air in the room.

"What?" Ning said.

The chief studied the dark ravines below Ning's eyes. With age, Ning's eyebrows had all but disappeared, his cheeks had sunk, and he wore a permanently severe, gaunt expression, ever squinting into a fire only he could see. At this moment his lips were pursed with impatience, as though he were dealing with a recalcitrant child. Not so long ago, the chief would have told Ning to get out of his office and file the story, but now he had his own job to worry about. The time had come.

On his best days, Ning was petulant, ill-tempered. His presence soured the mood in the newsroom, and he'd gotten worse in the weeks leading up to Li Pai's retirement. The chief had been under assault from the desk editors, who'd banded together in a campaign to get rid of Ning. He told them he'd take it under advisement, but he really had no choice. If he didn't act, they'd go over his head, and for good measure they'd see that he got tossed out on the street with Ning.

The chief was seventy-one, and he harbored few illusions about his own character. He didn't deny his moral failings, but this one, this long-standing weakness when it came to Ning, was unpardonable. When he was covering the American War in Vietnam he had seen the same lazy sentimentalism in officers who got enlisted men killed by allowing them to talk their way into stupid, heroic-sounding missions. The heart had to be kept out of the command chain. Yet he'd utterly failed to obey that dictum, keeping Ning on purely out of loyalty, payment in return for years of service. That he hadn't been able to discard Ning as he would have a broken car part troubled him. He preferred to think that he was coldly pragmatic, if not ruthless, when it came to assessing the utility of his reporters.

"Do you want to hear my theory now? You lost your will after Li Pai's book came out. That's my theory," the chief said.

"You might have something there, Chief," Ning said.

"You thought you deserved more than a footnote."

"That's possible."

"Well, I'm sorry," the chief said.

"What for? You didn't write it."

The chief laid his hands on the desk in front of him. "I'm afraid you're done here," he said.

"That's a mistake, Chief. Story's got legs."

"You're terminated, Ning."

"How's that?"

"Effective today, you're no longer employed at the *Guangzhou Post*," the chief said.

"Because of this?" Ning shrieked, holding up the story. On the other side of the door, the chief's assistant looked up from her screen.

"Because I've got fifty kids down there, each one of whom files ten stories a day. Remember how that works? Report it, bang it out, next story! A guy jumps off a bridge, they're not at their desks pondering the ethical implications of suicide. They're bribing the cops so they can get a look at the corpse! Just like you used to do. For all your deep thinking, you haven't filed anything worth reading in years." The chief didn't mind repaying Ning for all the grief he had caused. Loyalty be damned.

Ning's mouth fell open. He knew he looked like a cliché, his hands lying in his lap like a couple of dead fish, unable to come back with something that would level the chief, or at least wipe that placid, self-satisfied look off his face. In an attempt to get ahold of himself, he fixed his eye on a photograph behind the chief's head, a black-and-white of a PLA artillery crew posing in front of a Type 65 antiaircraft cannon. He'd seen it hundreds of times before, but instead of providing him a lifeline to all those nights he'd waited in that chair while the chief reviewed his copy, he felt as lonely and insignificant as a child who first realizes that, in his absence, his parents laugh and eat and sleep as restfully as ever. The walls of their house do not collapse. The paper without him would go on exactly as it had before. A rasping sound came from Ning's throat.

It wasn't fair. During those nomadic years after Reform and Opening, when the chief had hopped from paper to paper, Ning had followed him like a pack mule, and he'd never said no to an assignment. He'd nearly frozen to death chasing the Panchen Lama on his exodus across the mountains of Nepal. He'd roasted in the sun for weeks at Lop Nur waiting for a subterranean nuclear test. He could have stayed in the newsroom, pulled the Xinhua file off the telex and punched up the copy, but he'd insisted on being there in person to feel the ground tremble. It mattered to him to witness the story. What had all that come to?

It's come to exactly what you always knew it would, he told himself. You've served your purpose and now you're off to the slaughter.

It took an effort of will for the chief to keep from diverting his eyes. He forced himself to suffer this reminder of what happened when he got lazy. Keeping a reporter on past his prime didn't do anyone any good, least of all the reporter. If he'd cut him loose five years earlier, on nothing more than reputation Ning could have landed at another paper. A new start might have energized him. But now he was finished, worn bald as an old tire.

The chief tapped his foot once against the concrete floor to signal that their silent communion had come to an end.

"If you've got anything to say, say it."

Ning had sunk deep into his chair. He shook his head.

"Well, that's a first," the chief said. "Listen to me. I haven't put this through official channels, so we can handle it properly, like gentlemen. Submit an official resignation letter to Personnel and you'll keep your pension. If I have to fire you, no pension. Got it?"

"I'm lucky to have you looking out for me."

The chief didn't respond.

"Why would I resign?" Ning said.

The chief pinched the bridge of his nose. "How about in solidarity with Li Pai?"

"In solidarity with Li Pai," Ning said.

"Yes."

"That's the stupidest thing I've ever heard."

"Your choice," the chief said. "How's the speech coming?"

"You can't be serious," Ning said.

"You should add a bit about yourself. Put in something about how brothers always go down together. Allow yourself to save face. Do you hear me? Don't turn yourself into a flaming monk."

"It's not enough to get rid of me, you're going to put me on parade so everyone can see."

"This isn't a punishment. You've been with him since *People's Daily*. No one knows him better."

"I hardly know him at all."

"Don't give me that. You'll do it, and maybe he'll return the favor. You could benefit from a little character rehabilitation. Maybe he'll write you a recommendation letter, too."

"You're a son of a bitch," Ning said.

"We'll all lift a glass to you at the Green Room," the chief said. "I'm sure Li Pai won't mind sharing the spotlight."

"That'll be the day," Ning said. The chief held out his hand, but Ning didn't take it. He went out to the waiting area, pulling the chief's heavy door closed behind him with a sharp click. His lip curled at the sight of the assistant. Repulsive, the way she sat, her dainty arms poised over her keyboard like an insect worrying over the thorax of its prey. From day one he'd disliked this country girl with the erect posture and sharp tongue, and he was relieved to discover that he hadn't, due to his own misfortune, suddenly been visited by a newfound spirit of tolerance.

"What?" she said, her fingers still clacking at the keys.

Ning put his head down and walked out to the elevator bay.

"That's the smartest thing you've ever said," she called after him.

Back at his desk, he began to work up his resignation letter. Keep it simple, he told himself, but an hour later he had only just begun to air his grievances. He worked on it through the afternoon, and when he was satisfied that he'd communicated his opinions on the matters of the paper's shortsighted appetite for gossip over real news, incestuous hiring practices, inability to recognize and promote talent, and reliance on the fame of its halfwit columnists, he signed it with a flourish and took it to Personnel. From there, he left the building, took a bus across town, and drank at a bar until nightfall, to no benefit other than a slothful heaviness in his legs. When he returned, it was to an almost empty newsroom.

A few stragglers were gathering up Li Pai's gifts and stuffing them into plastic garbage bags, which they threw over their shoulders for the trip to the party at the Green Room. A corner of the red farewell banner had peeled off the wall. One of the young men deftly reached up and with a flick of his wrist yanked the entire thing down. He crumpled the heavy paper into a huge ball before jamming it into a gray trash bin full of beer bottles. Li Pai waved on his coterie and stopped at Ning's desk.

Li Pai was as stooped as an old scholar, his posture the apostrophe's hook and bell. His eyes were pricks of black suspended in rheum, magnified by the thick lenses of his stylish tortoiseshell glasses. Time had worn them both down, but Ning had no sympathy for his colleague's fragility, and he'd lost his appetite for the wandering conversations that inevitably became lectures on Li Pai's singular experience of the world. He couldn't remember when he'd finally stopped admiring Li Pai and had given himself over to jealousy, a soothing contempt for everything Li Pai represented: self-promotion, egotism, shallowness.

"That sums it up, no?" Li Pai said, pointing at the trash bin where the banner was crackling as it unwound itself. When Ning didn't answer, he said, "To the bar?"

Ning made a pained face. "Unavoidably detained," he said. "I'll be there when I can."

Li Pai nodded gravely and gave Ning a pat on the back. "Hang in there," he said, lingering. "You'll find something else."

"Ah," Ning said. "Word's out."

"I hope it's not a show of solidarity," Li Pai said.

Ning looked at him suspiciously. "Nothing like that."

"I could find something for you at Beida. They've asked me to lecture in the School of Communications."

"I think I'd rather not," Ning said.

"Well, it's a sad day for journalism. You and I are the last of a breed."

"Maybe not such a sad day," Ning said. He'd never considered Li Pai much of a reporter, and he didn't appreciate the comparison. In his columns Li Pai had proved himself to be a writer whose self-regard far outweighed his concern for the subjects he addressed. He wrote about poverty and corruption only to make it appear that he was a friend of man, a compassionate soul with a tearstained handkerchief in his breast pocket. Ning had found it impossible to read him any longer after Li Pai held a contest inviting readers to spend a week shadowing him at the paper and three hundred thousand people had written essays explaining why they most deserved the honor.

"You're not resigning because of what happened with your story? There's no point in falling on your sword over a little thing like that," Li Pai said in an avuncular tone that caused Ning to clench his fist underneath the desk.

Ning shook his head. "It's time to move on. Simple as that."

"I see," Li Pai said thoughtfully. He waited for Ning to elaborate, and when he didn't, Li Pai leaned in close, as if to speak in confidence, and said, "I heard the desk editors were after your hide. You know the chief's lost all his leverage. There's nothing he could have done."

"He begged me to stay," Ning shot back. He didn't know anything about this business with the desk editors. He got along fine with them. They respected him.

"Of course he did." Li Pai looked away stoically, with the air of a long-suffering mother whose sons had given her a lifetime of trouble. "A sad day," Li Pai said, patting him on the forearm.

"If you say so."

"You'll come later?" Li Pai said as he walked toward the elevators.

"I'll be along," Ning said, fixing his eye on something beyond his cubicle wall. "As soon as I'm able."

The chief was making his way across the newsroom, and Ning watched as though tracking a slowly accelerating avalanche, calculating the time until his imminent obliteration. When he got to Ning's desk, he banged his fist on the laminate surface hard enough to make the keyboard jump, and loomed over the reporter like he had a load of brick on his back he was dying to drop right on top of him.

"Let's go," the chief grunted.

"I've got to get my affairs in order," Ning said, gesturing at his desk.

"You're not arranging a funeral," the chief said.

"You'd think not," Ning said.

The chief took in the wreckage of Ning's desk—reporter's notebooks piled high against the cubicle's flimsy partitions, boxes of files, printouts of stories stacked like shale deposits on every available surface, newsprint melting over stacks of books, the plunders of a reporter's raids on his fellow man. He drew a deep breath.

"Management defined by its unwavering dedication to mediocrity?" the chief said.

"Too much?" Ning said.

"Every time I let someone go, Personnel gets the same letter. It's a terrible shame I'm never informed of the depths of my moral and ethical insolvency until one of you geniuses gets the boot. Think of the heights we'd reach if only someone would step forward and struggle against my incompetence."

"I'm just a guy in the business forty years," Ning said, "what do I know?"

"Funny how you didn't mention your own contributions to this journalistic morass you accuse me of running."

"I thought that went without saying. As you pointed out, it's been years since I've written anything worth reading."

"And now we know all along you were only saving yourself for a final shot."

Ning shrugged.

"Sort yourself and get over to the Green Room," the chief said.

"Or what?" Ning said. "You going to fire me?"

"You're a real piece of work. You know what? If you don't show up and give Li Pai the finest send-off in history, I'll strip your pension, everything."

"Here it is. My punishment for speaking the truth."

"No one would ever accuse you of that," the chief said as he shuffled off, leaving Ning alone in the bleached fluorescence of the empty newsroom.

Two of the TVs over by Metro were tuned to all-news channels, and the first thing Ning did was change one to a poker tournament from Macau. He put his feet up on his desk and leaned back into the posture of an untroubled man.

To hell with the chief. If he wanted a speech, Ning would give him one. But he wasn't going to get in any hurry. No one rushed Ning Wang.

Ning shifted in his chair and crossed his arms. On the TV, the poker players wore sleek wraparound sunglasses. Some had hats pulled low over their eyes and wore beards like bandits' handkerchiefs. Ning supposed he'd hold his own at the table with these men. They were nothing if you looked past their disguises. He'd once interviewed Johnny Chan, the world champion, and he could read Chan's tells within five minutes of sitting down across from him. That was, in his own estimation, his greatest skill as a reporter, his ability to recognize a man's true intentions.

He watched long enough for a fortune in chips to change hands several times. At the commercial, he reached down, slid open his desk drawer, and pulled out the speech he'd been working on for the last month. It was nothing more than a list of sentimental recollections and professional triumphs cribbed from Li Pai's memoir, written in a style that approximated ground meat shooting into a sausage casing. He'd never been able to work out the introduction. "What can I say about Li Pai that hasn't already been said?" he'd begun the latest draft. The line had been scratched through, rewritten, and scratched through again, the pen scoring deeply into the paper. The more he worked it over, the worse it got. He didn't want it to be good, but he didn't want to make a fool of himself.

He dropped the speech and slammed the desk drawer closed. He wasn't going to fire sugarcoated bullets. Tell it straight or don't tell it at all. Over the years, this stance had cost him friends, but he tallied those losses not as indicators of some failure on his part, but as the inevitable consequence of maintaining his ideals.

The poker game ended in what Ning could tell was a staged win, the victor thrusting his hands aloft as his vanquished opponent lowered his face to the felt. They'd probably meet in a hotel room later to split the winnings.

An F1 race came on next, and he watched, vaguely hoping for a crash.

A cleaning crew of blue-bibbed women wheeled their carts through the newsroom, dumping trash cans and chatting to each other across the cubicles, oblivious to Ning's presence. He checked his watch. He supposed it was late enough, and he gathered a few mementos—a press pass from the '08 Olympics, a sliver of *Shenzhou 1*'s heat shield encased in resin, a photo of him at the U.S. Embassy protests in '99—and stuffed them into the pockets of his coat. He opened the desk drawer again and pulled out the speech.

When Ning got to the Green Room, he nearly turned around and went home when he saw who was posted at the door.

"You've got some balls," the man said. He was called Baby Zhou. So painful an example was he of the shopworn convention by which hulking men are given petite names that Ning cringed every time he set eyes on the guy. Baby Zhou was, indeed, a man of infantile proportions—a perfectly round head, high, perpetually rosy cheeks that gave the impression he was always smiling, stubby arms that seemed to project from the sides of his neck. Because of that, Ning had always caught a whiff of cruelty in the name, the possibility that it had been bestowed as an act of retaliation. If that was the case, Zhou seemed blissfully unaware. Whatever the name's origin, Ning considered it a sad commentary on human nature.

"Nope. Nope. Not a chance," Baby Zhou was saying.

"I'm not going to tell you how to do your job, and you'd probably be right not to let me in," Ning said.

"Not a chance."

"But you might show some respect to a man twice your age," Ning said.

"If I killed you and threw you in a ditch out back, do you think anyone would care?" Baby Zhou said, stepping closer.

Ning noticed that Baby Zhou's eyes were incredibly puffy. "No, probably not," he said.

"I'd get a cash reward," Baby Zhou said. "Do you think anyone's forgotten about what happened last time you were here?"

"That kid should have known better than to go shooting his mouth off," Ning said. Just then the metal door screeched open, and he found himself face-to-face with Li Pai.

"You made it!" Li Pai said, throwing his arms around Ning. He was drenched in the sour musk of beer, and he slumped soddenly against Ning's shoulder.

"Good grief," Ning said, trying to back away.

A couple of young reporters Ning recognized from the newsroom came out after Li Pai. When they saw Ning, all joy drained from their faces.

"Ning," Li Pai said, suddenly very serious. "I saw you through the window. Like a shimmering in the mist." Li Pai looped his arm through Ning's and announced, "My dear friend has arrived! Let the celebrations begin anew!"

"Yes," Ning said. He'd meant to arrive late enough to miss the celebrations entirely, to give his speech to a nearly empty bar, but peering inside, he could see the place was packed.

Baby Zhou blocked the door. "Mr. Li, all due respect, I don't know about letting him in."

Li Pai tilted his head to the side.

"What am I supposed to do?" Baby Zhou said. This was a

quandary. He sank a finger into his ear and rotated it a quarter turn, then back. Ning could practically hear the rocks banging around inside.

Li Pai said nothing.

"You'll vouch for him?" Baby Zhou said.

"Who?" Li Pai said. "This man? I've never seen him before in my life." He doubled over laughing.

"That's helpful," said Ning.

"Let's say he is my best friend in the world," Li Pai said. "Is that not enough? Here." He pulled out a wad of cash and stuffed it into the breast pocket of Baby Zhou's suit jacket. Baby Zhou gave the money back.

"Your word is enough, Mr. Li," he said. Then he took Ning by the lapels and pulled him close enough that Ning could smell his mealy emanations.

"If you so much as raise your voice to order," Baby Zhou said, "I'll snap off your fingers. You blink wrong, I break fingers. You have a bad thought, fingers. I've been authorized. Got it? Won't type so good then, will you?"

"You smell like a barnyard," Ning said. He smiled grandly.

Li Pai pulled him through the door before Baby Zhou could remove his head from his body.

The Green Room was a long corridor about as wide as a boxcar. It had an arched ceiling that in the wet season condensed and dripped onto the patrons below. A hundred years earlier, it had been part of a club for English traders, and the walls above the chair rails had been upholstered in a rich green velour, but now only mold and cracked plaster remained. The wood floors were beer-soaked, and beneath that familiar sour smell was something else, earthy and dank, as though the entire place had slipped subterranean. Reporters loved it because it was the embodiment of condemnation, and hookers loved it because of the reporters. You could smell the disrepute for blocks.

Li Pai steered Ning to a table in a corner where a couple of kids from the newsroom and the chief's assistant were seated. Ning had worked a story with one of the reporters, and he didn't hate him. Ning allowed that someday he might be a decent journalist. He was an empty bucket, thick in the way the best reporters must be, incapable of developing a full understanding of anything he was being told without a complete and detailed explanation.

Ning nodded at him. "Here's a man always ready with another question," he said.

The kid ducked his head.

"One's greatest asset as a reporter," Ning said, addressing the table, "is stupidity. A reporter with a brain never knows when to shut up. He can't stop answering his own questions. Not a problem for this one," he said, gesturing at the young man.

"It's late," the chief's assistant said. "I'd better be going." She reached across the table to shake Li Pai's hand. "Mr. Li, it's been an honor."

"The honor has been all mine," Li Pai said.

"We'll go with you," the reporter said to the assistant. "Mr. Li, we'll drop your presents off tomorrow."

"That's very courteous of you," Li Pai said.

"It's the least we can do." Ning saw that the empty bucket was visibly moved. He had enfolded Li Pai's hand in both of his own, and appeared unwilling to release him. "I became a reporter because of you, Mr. Li."

"Be well," Li Pai said with great import. "Be well."

"Where's the film crew?" Ning said to no one in particular.

"I don't suppose we can trust you to see that Mr. Li gets home safely," the chief's assistant said to Ning.

Ning didn't respond. He signaled the waitress for a beer.

"From the day I met you, it's been a trial," the assistant said, drawing her shoulders up. "In fact, it's been a nightmare. I've never met anyone so awful. When I heard you were leaving, I wept with joy." She was gaining courage from the power of her own words, and she stood and steadied herself on the table for another salvo. "You're a rotten piece of shit, Ning Wang, and I hope you spend your remaining years alone, suffering for all you've done. After you're dead I'll find your grave and piss on it."

One of the kids tugged at her arm.

"I'd piss on you now but I wouldn't want to waste the beer," she shouted as they pulled her toward the door. Some of the reporters nearby gave a rousing cheer.

"Well, wasn't that something?" Li Pai said.

"She's charming. Chief find her in a Vietnamese massage joint?"

"She's a survivor, that's for sure," Li Pai said.

"Had a thing for me from day one."

"You don't say."

"She's young. She can't handle how I make her feel. You've seen how I make her loins quiver."

Li Pai, realizing that Ning might be serious, let it drop.

Ning felt around in his pocket for the speech. "I didn't get you anything," he said.

"I wasn't expecting anything," Li Pai said. "Your friendship has been gift enough."

Ning frowned.

"Of course, you remain, as ever, a waste of humanity," Li Pai said.

"That's more like it."

"What've you got there?" Li Pai said, nodding at the speech in Ning's hand.

"Just some thoughts. I don't think they're appropriate."

"I'd be disappointed if they were. Let's hear them." He rose to call everyone over, but Ning stopped him.

"How about a drink first?" Ning said.

Li Pai agreed, and they drank—or, Ning drank while Li Pai reminisced about old colleagues, friends lost to retirement and the grave. There came a point, after his third glass, when Ning felt something like comradeship rise up in his heart, even if it was only because he recognized all the names and beer made him sentimental. The bar was filled to capacity, the noise forcing them to sit closer than Ning otherwise would have chosen to. Every so often reporters would stop by to shake Li Pai's hand. Then they'd drift back into the crowd, which, Ning found hard to ignore, was a forest of youth. The few old-timers looked like men adrift, mossy and damp, flapping jowls and eye bags thick as melted icing. It was during one of these scans of the crowd that he spotted the back of the chief's mottled head. He was on a stool at the bar, hunched over his drink like an inmate protecting his bowl of soup.

Ning spat on the floor, and when he looked back up, he saw the kid from *Youth Daily* sauntering toward their table. It was just one thing after another. The kid was hard to miss in his pink Izod golf shirt and knockoff Italian loafers. He was wearing a nice watch, an Omega, but it all looked wrong on him, as if he'd borrowed the ensemble from his older brother. He had given up a banking job in Hong Kong to become a reporter, and he had a hurt, angry look about him, as if he'd recently come to the realization that he'd made a terrible mistake, for the first time in his life double-crossed by his own desires.

"Here comes the great scribe," Ning said.

"Who's this?" Li Pai said.

"This is the retard who wrote my last story out from under me," Ning said.

"Ah, one of the Red Guard," Li Pai said.

The kid was at the table now, and he held his hand out to Li Pai, and then to Ning.

"You really put my balls in a vise," Ning said.

"Sorry, sir?" the kid said.

"The security guard. That was my story."

The kid turned red and rubbed the back of his neck.

"My editor was all over me to file it. I didn't have any choice."

"These things happen," Li Pai said. "Editors are beasts."

"Bullshit," Ning said. "This kid saw me at the hospital and knew I was onto something."

"That's not true," the kid said. "That's not true at all."

Ning grunted. He was enjoying himself. "It's one thing to beat an old man to the punch, but you got it dead wrong," he said to the kid. "When you're a little older, you'll have more respect for the undertones of a story like this one. You'll see. There's more to this business than facts."

The kid bowed his head. Then he directed himself to Li Pai. "Mr. Li, you've had a great influence on me. I'm here today because of you."

"You honor me," Li Pai said.

"It's a great loss to the profession," the kid said.

"You're too polite," Li Pai said. "Mr. Ning is retiring today, as well."

Without making eye contact, the kid bowed slightly in Ning's direction. "Mr. Li, I wish you all the best." He reached across the table, his armpit in Ning's face, and shook Li Pai's hand vigorously. Ning watched him go, and when the kid got back to his friends, he saw the heads turning to look at him, and he heard them laughing.

Li Pai saw it, too. "You remember Xiang Xue?" he said.

"Which one was he?" Ning was still looking at the back of the kid's head.

"Rental tuxedo at the Reagan dinner."

"Sure," Ning said. "'New Beijing style,'" he said. That had been Xiang Xue's response to the American president when he'd pointed to the rental tag dangling from the sleeve of the reporter's dinner jacket.

"You know he died last year," Li Pai said.

"I hadn't heard that," Ning said.

"That young man reminds me of him. Same wardrobe problems. Perhaps a certain lack of self-awareness, but sometimes that can be a good thing. It can put people at ease."

"He'll never be half the reporter Xiang Xue was," Ning said.

"Is that a fact?"

"No question."

"What was it that our young friend missed?" Li Pai said.

"He missed the story. He got the facts and he missed the story."

"What's this deeply complex story about?"

"It's just another story," Ning said, pushing on the rim of an overflowing ashtray. "To the uninitiated."

"It's a shame. Your last one, and you never got to write it."

Ning drew a deep breath. "There's this peasant from Yunnan, probably grew up in a cave and went to school in a tree. When he gets old enough, he sets out for the golden shore. He has a trustworthy face and he gets on as a night guard at a building down near the International Finance Centre. Mostly he sits behind the lobby desk and reads comics. One night, he hears screaming. He looks up from his copy of *Sui Tang Heroes* and sees, just on the other side of the glass, a woman struggling with two men. One's got the collar of her coat, and the other one has her arm. They're dragging her away. At first he's frozen with fear. But then honor asserts itself and he attempts to rescue her. No regard for protocol, which dictates that he phone the security team that patrols the outside perimeter. No, our hero goes it alone, and for his trouble he's stabbed eight times and left for dead."

"And the girl?" Li Pai said.

"No sign of her. Disappeared."

"Probably a setup," Li Pai said, rubbing his eyes.

"All for two kuai and a subway token."

"People have done worse for less," Li Pai said. "So that's the story?"

"That's just the first inch of it," Ning said. "This noble boy winds up in the hospital. No money, no insurance, but his boss at the security company is a clever fellow. He walks up to the nurses' station and signs the guard in under the name of another employee who's covered under the company policy."

"Clever," Li Pai says.

"And it works like a charm. They wheel him into surgery, sew him up, prognosis excellent. All this kid has to do is lie in bed, flirt with the nurses, and answer to someone else's name. But after a couple of weeks, he decides he's tired of pretending to be someone else. He makes a stink about it. At first, the hospital refuses to recognize him by his given name. If he's readmitted under his real name, they have to give back all the insurance money. But he insists. Then he calls the insurance company and fesses up. And now he's liable for a hundred and fifty thousand in bills, and they won't discharge him until he pays up."

"This is the problem with heroes. Far too honest," Li Pai said.

"The question you have to ask is, why? Why would he do such a thing? You see? That half-wit from *Youth Daily* didn't even bother to ask. What does this peasant think he's going to gain? Now he's trapped like an animal. Why would anyone behave that way?"

"You asked him?" Li Pai said.

"Of course I did," Ning said, smacking the table with his open palm.

"And?"

"He says, 'I woke up, and I'd forgotten who I was.' That was his explanation. He forgot who he was." Ning shook his head.

"How peculiar. A real-life existential crisis."

"Hardly. Nothing more than pride, I'd say. He's twenty-five

hundred li from home, he's broke, he doesn't even have a change of clothes. He's got nothing but his name. The only problem is, now he doesn't even have that. How can he send home an article about his heroism when his name's nowhere in the story? What's a hero without his own name?"

"Or perhaps he's just too virtuous for his own good."

"I just wanted the damn story to ask the right questions," Ning said.

"They don't make them like us anymore," said Li Pai, raising his glass. "To age and wisdom!"

"To age and wisdom," Ning said. "These kids. They have no curiosity. They're just happy little story factories shitting out copy all day long."

Li Pai nodded slowly, as if digesting a sage truth.

"Even when I was their age," Ning said, "I pondered the larger context. Even at *People's Daily*, even when I knew there was no chance the truth might make it into print, I thought of the greater good. I wrestled with my conscience. I tried to behave honorably. We both did, didn't we?"

"We did," Li Pai said. "We reported for the greater good, not for selfish reasons."

Ning narrowed his eyes, but Li Pai's face gave away no irony, no sense that he was calling out Ning's bloated self-adulation, or something worse.

"Maybe so," Ning said. When they'd first met at *People's Daily*, he'd never before encountered anyone more deeply resistant to the lures of ambition than Li Pai. He'd forgotten that. He'd forgotten his earnest face, his dedication to serving the People's Republic. Li Pai had always been a model worker.

"We were all different then," Li Pai said, as if reading Ning's mind. "I remember you, brave boy. You scaled the mountain of swords, swam the sea of fire."

"We all ate bitter," Ning said, deflecting, but inwardly he was pleased at this recollection of his exploits.

"You even assisted with the *People's Daily Extra*," Li Pai said.

Ning stared at Li Pai. "How's that?" he said.

"You collected the student flyers at Tiananmen for the *Extra* edition. Don't be coy. You risked your life for the protests. You did your part to protect the students. You're a hero."

"I don't know what you're talking about," Ning said. He looked around to see if anyone had heard.

"Ning Wang. We've been friends for longer than either of us wants to admit. Surely you can grant an old man a final wish."

"What do you mean?" Ning said.

"Tell me how you avoided the purge," Li Pai said.

"I want to know who's been spreading these lies about me," Ning said. "I had nothing to do with the *Extra*. That was a band of revolutionaries who got what they deserved. They defied the Central Committee and were punished." His breath was coming fast and he drained his beer in a swallow. "I had nothing to do with that."

"No, I know you did," Li Pai said, laughing. "Qian Liren told me so."

"Why would you bring this up now?" Ning said. He leaned close to Li Pai. "What have I ever done to harm you?" he said. "Why would you bring this up? Someone will hear."

Li Pai reached out and placed his hand firmly on Ning's shoulder. From across the room it might have appeared to be a comradely embrace, but Ning understood Li Pai's true intent. "You were a man of such bravery," Li Pai said. "And yet when everyone else went to prison, you were spared. Such luck! So brave and so lucky." His fingers were squeezing Ning's shoulder.

"Yes, very lucky," Ning said.

"Lucky boy," Li Pai said. Suddenly he drew back and picked

up his beer. "Let's toast to luck, then," Li Pai said. He held up his glass, unsmiling. Ning picked up his own empty glass and touched it to Li Pai's. He made the motion of drinking from the empty stein.

"What are you toasting to luck for?" a voice said from behind Ning. It was the chief. "Toast to something appropriate, like senility or amnesia."

"Indeed," Li Pai cried, tossing back the last of his beer.

The chief collapsed into the chair next to Ning.

"You look terrible," the chief said, nudging Ning's arm. "Cheer up. Your days of taking shit from me are over." The old man was drunk. "Everyone's waiting on your speech," the chief shouted.

"Yes," Li Pai joined in. "Let's hear it."

Of course it hadn't been luck. Two men who said they were from the Ministry of Water Resources had been waiting inside Ning's apartment one sweltering night a couple of weeks after the protests. Since the crackdown he'd been living like a man in a diving bell, waiting for his air hose to be severed at the surface. Colleagues had been taken away in broad daylight. He'd known they would come for him, too, and he'd decided. Once he'd seen all the empty desks in the newsroom, he knew he'd tell his inquisitors whatever they wanted to know. It's pragmatic, he told himself. Either way, they'll get what they want. Just give it to them and preserve your career.

That night at his apartment, they'd asked him to take a seat, and before turning on the lights, one of the agents had pulled the cord anchored on a nail at each window frame. The blinds had come whipping down, one by one.

The chief struggled back to his feet and, wobbly, turned to face the crowd. "Quiet," he shouted. The noise died down quickly. "We're here to see off a cherished colleague—a beloved colleague—our brother Li Pai. His contributions to the *Guangzhou Post* are unchartable. He has set a new standard for journalists in China.

In all my years, I've never seen such an outpouring of sadness from the readership." The chief looked back at Li Pai, and Ning understood that the old man had paused because he was genuinely choked up, flooded with longing to embrace Li Pai, to gather him up in his arms as one might a child. No one would have thought less of him—it was the right time for an outpouring of emotion—but he turned back to the crowd. "Li Pai has been like a son to me, but no one has known him as long as Ning Wang. He's volunteered to say a few words about his dear friend."

The chief sat to a round of applause that abated as soon as Ning stood up. As he maneuvered himself into position, his chair scraped loudly against the floor. Uneasy, eyes down, he felt in his pocket for the speech. There was a great silence all around him, and when he looked up at the crowd, he saw that they all hated him, and only the chief's authority kept them from shouting him down. He unfolded the speech and held the paper out before him. He took a deep breath and began to read without understanding the words of praise, and without hearing his own voice, but hoping that he might, by some magic of language, acquit himself.

THE POCKETBOOK

Claire was standing outside the cafeteria door and she could hear them laughing. Go, she told herself. Go. She pulled open the door and went directly to the service line, from which she could safely survey the seating arrangement. Her ex-roommate, Alicia, was at a table with her friends, doing her Teacher Wu impression, and it was brutal. Teacher Wu was sitting at the next table over, oblivious as ever and, Claire thought, pretty much begging for it. He was shoveling noodles into his mouth and sauce was dripping off his chin. He had that misty, philosophical look about him, the one that said, This world does not my reward hold. She wanted to take him by the shoulders and shake him until he turned blue.

When he spoke English, his facial contortions brought to mind the painful passage of objects from the body, and Alicia's imitation was consummate. She made her face flush. She did the stutter and the gape. A strand of saliva swayed from her lip, then snapped and dropped to the tabletop. This went over big with everyone except Claire, who, given the choice of sitting with Teacher Wu or with Alicia, wasn't so principled as to make herself part of the joke, at least no more than she already was.

When Claire put her tray down, Alicia turned to her and said, "Oh, sorry."

"What?" Claire said. "I don't care." Everyone was sure Claire and Wu were sleeping together. Alicia wiped her mouth and went back to her meal.

It was Friday night and after dinner a pack of Claire's classmates were headed to the Kunlun. The Thai guys were rounding up people to hit the Globe Club out on the Third Ring Road. The stoners were going to the Red Dragon, and Claire heard Alicia say something about stopping by a dorm party at Beida before going to Maxim's. No one asked Claire to go anywhere.

The students departed in flights of three or four. Anticipating the moment of complete abandonment, Claire had pulled out her paperback copy of *The Fountainhead*, but she couldn't focus, and once she had the book out, she couldn't put it back, so she wound up moving her eyes over the page in a way that simulated reading, killing time until she was left at the table all alone. Not even Alicia had bothered to say goodbye. Stay cool, Claire thought, sit in and stay cool. None of it had registered with Teacher Wu. Claire was shooting daggers at him, but he didn't notice. He was useless. Empty, the cafeteria had all the ambience of a surgery theater, its zombie fluorescence glowing on the pots of plastic bamboo and assorted Chinese yard sale art catching dust in the corners.

Claire had had a talk with herself in which she'd acknowledged that, like a drop of detergent in a pan of greasy water, she'd succeeded in repelling every student at Capital Normal University School of Foreign Languages. She couldn't make herself any friendlier than she was, and, as usual, when it became apparent that she had opinions of her own, whoever she was talking to went in search of more compliant company. Claire didn't suffer fools gladly, and fools, for their part, tended to avoid her. As did the wise. And those of middling intelligence. She knew she could be brusque, but she wasn't combative, a word Alicia had swung at her like a mallet. Alicia was the combative one. A person who couldn't hold up her end of an argument wasn't worth talking to. Neither were backstabbers, and Alicia was a backstabber.

Claire had spotted Alicia as soon as they'd deplaned at PEK. She'd been impossible to miss. She was Chinese American and gorgeous and Claire could hear her voice clear across the gate, as though she were addressing the entire group from onstage, which annoyed Claire, and then everyone in the group had broken into laughter and Claire had felt like she wanted to commit a homicide. At the time, she was standing by herself because on the flight from Tokyo she had gotten into an argument with a grad student from Duke about Chinese policy in Tibet, and he'd accused her of being a contrarian and she'd called him a fat prick, and that, it appeared, had pretty much put her on social death watch. On the bus from the airport, Claire had watched Alicia, who was sitting at the back, surrounded by a bevy of suitcases, smacking her gum, staring into the middle distance like the air had done her wrong. Everyone else was looking out the windows. Claire could tell Alicia was one of those people who hardly bothered to breathe unless someone else was paying attention to her. This is a girl, Claire thought, with a trust fund and a shoplifting problem.

When they arrived at the dormitory and she checked the roommate postings, she nearly threw up. Of course the administration had stuck her with Alicia. Why wouldn't they? Claire thought. Just perfect. But she talked herself down and decided on the spot to make the best of it. That first night, they had stayed up late smoking cigarettes, Claire nodding along to Alicia's crystalline recollections of club shenanigans in the Meatpacking District, a crashed BMW on the Vineyard.

Wow, Claire said, wow, expelling jets of smoke through her nose. She hoped she didn't sound as bored as she was.

It's not like we're rich, Alicia said. You don't know rich if you think I'm rich. But Daddy does fine, she said, laughing so loud that Claire winced. Alicia declared her enemies to be numerous, which was why she'd come to live in exile in China. Even her best friends were assholes of the lowest order. Cretins, she'd said. I know that makes me an asshole, she said. But it's true. They're all assholes. Isn't everybody an asshole? she said, flopping back on her bed.

No way was Claire going to utter the polite answer, which was, No, you're not an asshole, I hardly know you but I can tell you're a good person, primarily because Claire thought Alicia was a spoiled bitch, an asshole if ever there was one. Instead, she decided to retaliate with some biographical information of her own, and Alicia propped her head up on her hand and looked irritatingly engaged, her eyes a little too fixed, her interest too measured, like the practiced sympathy of a grief counselor. She'd listened and nodded so intently that it had thrown Claire off a little. Claire wasn't sure why, but she'd even made up a story about having an affair with a professor back home. And that's why *I'm* in exile, she said.

Two weeks later, Alicia moved to a single room. It came out that she'd petitioned for a single the day after they'd arrived.

"It'll be good for both of us," Alicia said to Claire. "Haven't you had enough of me? I know you can't stand it that I come in so late and bang around. And now you won't have to deal with my stupid-ass whining anymore. Win-win—you'll have a single!" She smiled like a Dallas Cowboys cheerleader, and Claire had stood there thinking she'd believe in god if only he'd drop a Volkswagen on this horrible person.

"How? They won't let anyone switch. You have to cough up a kidney just to get a spare door key," Claire said.

"I don't know. I asked. I thought it would be better for both of us."

"No, you didn't," Claire said. "What did you tell them about me?"

"Paranoid much?" Alicia said. "Christ. Don't get all weepy," she said. "I'm just moving upstairs."

"Why? What did I do?" Claire said.

Alicia gave her the grief counselor look. "It's not personal," she said.

Bitch. That had been a month ago.

And now, here was Claire, finishing her meal alone, telling herself she was fine. Single. When she walked out the cafeteria doors, the pack of students milling around by the bike racks went silent.

"Oh, come on, people," she said. She unlocked her bike, mounted up, and pumped across campus, cutting through courtyards and taking blind corners at suicidal speed, spouting a slew of bad Chinese at terrorized pedestrians.

Outside the front gates she swung into an alleyway bordered on one side by the college wall, a ten-foot concrete slab topped with broken bottles, on the other by a public bathroom, a long row of pit toilets attended by an ancient man on a folding stool. The alleyway jogged left at the corner of the wall and passageways branched off into the hutongs behind the college. The students had been warned not to use the alleyway as a shortcut to the market. Claire used the alley every chance she got.

Near the mouth of the alley she rattled past a cluster of brick hovels attached like barnacles to the college wall. Families squatted outside tending cooking fires and talking over chessboards. Children yelled at her. It occurred to Claire that Alicia would never take the alleyway. She would never experience this side of China.

It was here, Claire told herself, with the college behind her and the market ahead, that she felt most at home. She told herself she savored the taste of the unsettled air between the two arenas of existence.

At the edge of the market she dismounted. There was an hour of light left, and she could go east into the Chinese market or west into Uyghurville. Occasionally, as a test of her mettle, she ate in one of the restaurants there, and in her bag she was carrying a souvenir of her last visit, a kernel of hard brown hashish. She'd been saving it, hoping she wouldn't have to smoke it alone, entertaining the vague notion of casually mentioning to Alicia that she had it and just seeing what happened.

In the market, strings of lightbulbs hung between vendors' stands, snaking around skeletal trees and up electric poles. The street was choked with smoke, and she couldn't hear herself think for the cacophony of transistor radios, searing meat, motor scooters, the frenzy of vendors screaming into the crowd. Teenage lovers took advantage of the tight crowd to press against each other as they moved slowly up and down the road. Claire wondered what it said about the Chinese that at the end of the day they repaired to this clanging cowbell of a settlement to unwind. Scattered along the roadside like weeds, men seated on low stools sipped tea and played chess. A few stared off at nothing, puffed on pipes, and fiddled with their crotches. Beneath a loudspeaker blaring a tinny pop song, a sculptor worked dung into detailed miniature animals.

Claire felt like a snorkeler on the open sea. She couldn't read a billboard or a street sign and she knew just enough Mandarin to get by. But what she saw felt authentic, not like the pantomime that surrounded her back home. Here, there were dusky men perched atop motor trikes, buildings that fell apart before construction was complete, panes of glass peeling off skyscrapers and spinning down onto pedestrians. Swarms of bicyclists so thick she couldn't cross the street. Bread-box taxis held together with duct tape and spit. In a letter to a professor back home, she'd called it a human drama played out on a life-size stage. She'd been proud of that line. She'd seen couples in the park humping under blankets, crowds cheering bloody street fights, legless beggars trundling along on wooden pallets. Alicia had told her she had colonial fever.

She never saw the purse snatcher, though she was as obvious to him as a cinder block dropped into a pond. He was a pro, a shadow of a boy who existed between pauses in conversation, clinging to the underside of memory like a fly. She would have felt a dead weight in her chest if she had seen him. His hair fell in heavy ropes over his face, which was brown as old leaves and crossed with amber scars. Ten years old, he was wastewater wrung from the sponge of the world.

At the age of six he'd been grabbed off the street in Turpan and sold with a band of other children for seventy yuan a head to a dealer who transported them to Shenzhen and doubled his investment selling them to a gang. The men who ran the gang taught fast hands by placing the children in front of a pot of boiling water with a coin at the bottom. Failure to grab the coin got them a beating with a hose. After three years of picking at markets in Shenzhen, he'd managed to escape on a train to Beijing, and he'd avoided being absorbed into Beijing gangs mostly by good luck and a studied eye for kidnappers. He was a good thief. Confident, direct. It couldn't have been easier if Claire's pocketbook had jumped out of the bike basket into his hands, and with it hidden under his cotton shirt he slipped into a narrow gap between the foundations of two buildings.

He gouged the purse with a scrap of aluminum, forgoing the zipper for the pleasure of opening a hole of his own in the soft leather. With a satisfying pop it gave way: her wallet, two photos, a tampon, which he quickly unwrapped, tasted, and discarded, her student ID card, for which he had no use, a set of keys, a red pocket dictionary, a small tube of hand lotion that tasted like flowers and fish and which he drained in one gulp, followed by the ball of hash, which he swallowed whole.

In the wallet he found five 100-yuan banknotes, the most money he'd ever pulled at once. He rolled the banknotes into a tight stem and packed them into the channel between his gum and cheek. It was the safest place he knew. He could give a blow-job with the treasure secreted in his mouth, but if forced to present his backside and he'd hidden the money there, it would be lost for sure.

The thief slipped back into the market, passing within feet of Claire, drifting through the crowd like a leaf until fetching up on Sanlihe Street, a wide boulevard he had in the past avoided because the shopkeepers there cracked him on the legs with their brooms. But now it seemed to welcome him. This was as close to happiness as he'd ever been, this feeling of inner radiance spreading from his chest, warming his bones, and he began to imagine a future in which he would wear fine clothes and stride with intent through the crowded market. People would step aside.

Late that night, on a deserted street near the zoo, a pack of boys attacked him. He'd vomited out the hash by then, but its lingering effects made him an easy target. The other boys, too, had been in the market, hovering near the American, but this was a much safer play. One pried his jaws apart while another crammed a hand into his mouth. After they had the money, they beat him until he stopped struggling, and there he remained, on the cracked pavement, his lips moving wordlessly.

For a while, Claire stood at the edge of the market scanning the faces of passersby. A loudspeaker over her head was blasting Chinese opera, the wailing voice crackling and fuzzing against her eardrums.

Fuckers, she said. She didn't care about the money, but not having an ID was going to cause real problems. Traveling was out until she got a new one, and she had wanted to take a trip to Beidaihe to enjoy the last of the good weather, even allowing herself to imagine she might meet someone there. Behind her anger she slowly became aware of an expanding seam of loneliness, a black mood settling around her like fog.

She told herself to cut it out, that she was being stupid, that it was only a bag, but she took the long route back to the college, pushing her bike out to Sanlihe Street first, riding a mile out of her way, not even daring to look down the alleyway as she passed through the college gates.

The following Monday after classes, she paid a visit to Teacher Wu in his spartan office beneath the dormitory stairs. He was charged with tending the American students, an assignment a rising star in the English Department might have considered a temporary setback, at worst a character-building exercise, but that, in Wu's case, had precipitated the full collapse of his ambition.

He was young and opinionated, and had a habit of speaking out of turn in departmental meetings. His petitions to be allowed to return to teaching at the beginning of the next semester had been ignored, and though he tried to bear those rejections with the grim fortitude of a condemned man, he'd begun to believe that his reassignment had placed him permanently beyond redemption's reach. He had no real work to do. For the last two weeks he'd only been able to stare vacantly at the Scenery and Natural Wonders calendar hanging on the wall opposite his metal desk. With his head tipped slightly forward to accommodate the slope of the eave behind him, he chain-smoked and rearranged papers. There was a chair for students, though in the two months he'd been at his post, only Claire had visited.

When she arrived, he lit a new cigarette. He was thin, had a large mole on his cheek and heavy, reptilian eyelids. She'd been to see him three times the previous week, twice the week before that, and though he'd at first thought she was a bellyacher, he'd come to recognize a familiar loneliness in the way she stacked questions atop one another, fending off the moment when she'd have to leave. It was not unusual for students to develop feelings for their teachers, and he could see from the frequency of her visits that she was experiencing emotions for him. He could not offer the kind of help she seemed to be after. He took his responsibility to the American students seriously, and he adhered to proper interaction boundaries. When Claire brought him oranges from the market, he permitted himself to offer her special-issue postage stamps in return, nothing more. Very recently he'd had a dream about her and upon waking he'd soaked in the memory of her big white thighs before coming to his senses. He fought mightily not to think about that dream.

There was, in fact, a single reason Claire had made a habit of visiting Teacher Wu's office: to pump him for information. It had been killing her that she didn't know why Alicia had moved out. Telling the administrators that they were incompatible wouldn't have been enough. Surely Alicia had fabricated untruths about Claire—that she stole or didn't bathe or had emotional issues— and if the administrators believed the untruths, then her teachers knew about them, too, which meant that every day Claire sat in class her teachers knew something about her that she didn't know about herself. Wu must have heard something.

No, nothing, he'd say.

She'd narrow her eyes. Nothing?

I am sorry, nothing. I am always asking.

But on this afternoon, she'd come with a different story. When she told him what had happened in the market, he was outraged. Yet, as she went on about needing her ID card to travel to Beidaihe, he realized that he'd been presented with an opportunity to redeem himself in the eyes of his colleagues. An immense gift, this robbery. He closed his eyes and reminded himself to breathe. His long, aqueous fingers moved loosely on his legs. Though Teacher Wu did not consider himself a brave man, he was sure he could ignite the tight blue flame of anger flickering within him.

"So you'll get me a new ID," Claire said.

He rose into a stoop, his head canted in such a way that he looked to be bowing solemnly, and motioned Claire out the door, as there was not room for him to move from his post behind the desk unless she first left the office. Once they'd emerged, he said, "Please follow me."

Claire had to jog to keep up with him. At Central Administration, a dilapidated building that smelled of wet plaster and ashtrays, Teacher Wu dashed from one pea-green office to the next, gesticulating wildly to the accounting staff, ideology monitors, anyone who would listen. Claire hung back in the hall, and a couple of times she thought to leave entirely, but she wanted to get her ID sorted out. Without Wu, it could take months to get a new one.

There was always some story making the rounds about Uyghurs kidnapping Chinese virgins. They were never above suspicion, hailing as they did from a place so far away from Beijing that it was said the clocks hung upside down. They were diseased and they bred like livestock. Their acts of terrorism had been well documented. Now, finally, Wu told his colleagues, these murderers, these pale-skinned dope peddlers, could be made to suffer. Rapists. Cowards, pickpockets. Robbers of defenseless American female students.

"We must extract the rotten tooth," Teacher Wu exclaimed. He fell easily into the cadences of zealotry, a strange nostalgia fueling his anger. As a child, he'd marched with his schoolmates, emptied his inkpot over his teacher's head, watched as older middle school students had stuffed their teachers' mouths with dirt. He still had long passages from the Little Red Book rattling around his brain. His colleagues, patriots all, agreed that the Uyghur problem had to be dealt with once and for all. The foreign students had too long been at risk, and it was only a matter of time before one was kidnapped, raped, hacked into pieces.

By the time Wu was done, he'd cleared the building and a crowd of over a hundred administrators had gathered outside. Claire tried to slip away, but Wu grabbed her arm and ferried her to the front. The crowd swept like a mudslide through the college gates, diverting a stream of cyclists into the street, snarling traffic. As they turned onto the wide sidewalk, a traffic cop, whistle bleating, stepped off his pylon, waving his white-gloved hands, then stepped back up, perplexed. The mob was nothing more than middle-aged academics from the language college. They weren't shouting or holding signs. He watched the crowd march up Fucheng Road.

But by the time they breached the front door of the Public Security Bureau, they had worked themselves into a frenzy, and the noise went up like a cannon. They poured into a long room resembling a drained swimming pool, the sound of their voices echoing off the bare walls. A squadron of junior officers who had spent the day slogging through paperwork shot to their feet all at once, their metal chairs clattering across the floor. Most of them would have fled if they'd been able to, but there was nowhere to run. Some of the officers had been students at the School of Foreign Languages and recognized the administrators in the front ranks.

A voice commanded them forward, and the officers complied, running headlong into the crowd, arms extended against the wall of humanity bearing down upon them. Teacher Wu stabbed his finger at the nose of a young officer whose peaked hat had gone sideways on his head, its leather chin strap jogging across his eye. The officer, though attempting to adhere to training protocols by displaying the dispassion of an agent of the state, was churning inside, and his cheeks were flushed a deep crimson. To a man, the officers were scared out of their wits. The administrators had waded into a wave of fresh technical school graduates, a skinny bunch whose collective specialties ran to electronic eavesdropping and code-breaking, all awaiting reassignment, in the meantime cleaning up six months of back paperwork at the Ganjiakou station in Beijing.

Lacking any slogans to chant, the academics targeted individual officers and shouted into their faces, creating an unintelligible wash of noise that only served to further frighten the officers. After a while, the protesters began to feel bad for the young officers, and the mass action lost some of its passion. In the middle of the crowd, administrators looked at one another abashedly, as though they'd been caught in a collective act of masturbation. Their voices waned, and those in the front rank stopped pushing against the officers. Teacher Wu tried to rouse them, but no one seemed interested in taking up the charge.

At the same time, in the rear, some younger administrators, who'd only just arrived after hearing about the protest from colleagues on campus, were trying to make up for lost time, shouting and shoving at those in front of them. Claire, on the front line right next to Teacher Wu, felt the crush of bodies at her back grow more insistent. She braced herself, locked her knees, and tried to set her feet hard against the concrete floor, but she, along with several other administrators, was sliding forward, borne ever closer to the line of officers by the bodies packed tightly around her. Her heart throbbed in her ears, and she tried to lift her arms but they were pinned at her sides. Then her legs became tangled with those of the administrators on either side of her, and she lost her balance, tipping forward into a ruddy-cheeked officer, who backpedaled as if he'd opened a closet door and a rotting corpse had fallen out. Claire hit the floor in a puff of dust.

The fallen administrators quickly picked themselves up, and the crowd backed away, forming a ring around Claire, the human loupe that never failed to materialize at Beijing's car accidents and public heart attacks. The floor was gritty, and she tasted coal dust on her lips. Teacher Wu crouched next to her.

"Now is a good time for you to speak," he whispered.

"Now?" she said. "Some help?"

He tentatively reached for her arm, and was relieved when two other administrators stepped in and scooped her up by her armpits.

"Where's the officer in charge?" said Teacher Wu to one of the recruits.

"Here," said the precinct captain, standing off to the side, a smoldering cigarette wedged into the corner of his mouth.

Teacher Wu pushed Claire forward, forcing her onstage. "Now is a good time for you to tell your story," he said.

"Careful with the merchandise," Claire said.

"Speak now," Teacher Wu said, nodding in the direction of the precinct captain.

She looked around, then started to speak in elementary Chinese, but Teacher Wu stopped her.

"English. Speak English. You are tired. I translate," he said. "Tell about the Uyghur who robbed you."

"I didn't see anyone. My bag just disappeared," Claire said. "I told you that."

Teacher Wu smiled and looked around at the room magnanimously. "Okay, okay," he said. "You talk, I translate."

"All I wanted was a new ID card," Claire said. "What is all this?"

That blue flame again. Wu turned a grim smile on Claire and then began to relate his version of events to the captain.

The room reeked of sweat and tobacco smoke undercut by the tang of pickled cabbage wafting out of someone's desk drawer. The precinct captain sucked on his cigarette. His face had the heavy quality of wet cloth, and he surveyed the room from behind a monkish brow, his eyes never alighting on any one person for very long, as if committing a pointillist version of the crowd to memory. He had a gift for faces.

Teacher Wu, intent on proving himself worthy to everyone gathered, spoke with his clearest voice.

"Our motherland has failed to protect its children. This neighborhood has become unsafe! University students and foreign guests have been endangered, and now one of the students entrusted to us by the government of the United States has been robbed! We demand action. Illegal influences from the western provinces have taken over! We can no longer walk the streets without fear. How many of us will be attacked before you will act to protect us?"

Wu paused to gauge the administrators' reaction, but especially Claire's.

What beauty, he thought. Even with dirt all over her face and her hair askew, she was a heavenly spirit. She stared back at him impassively, and he understood immediately that of course she couldn't understand a word he was saying, and that even if she could, she wouldn't allow her emotions to surface unless she wanted everyone to know that she harbored romantic feelings for him. Her cold eyes excited him. He knew that beneath her mask of disregard, she was urging him to continue. She never took her eyes off him.

All the administrators were watching him, and he felt alive, electrified, as though delivering a lecture to a packed hall. The PSB officer in charge was watching, too, waiting for him to speak. At last, thought Wu, at last.

He brought his voice to its full register, turning this way and that to address both the administrators and the captain. As he spoke, he allowed his emotions to course freely, until he had broken through the wall dividing self-preservation and martyrdom. Perhaps the government, he said, had planted the Uyghurs to facilitate the neighborhood's downfall so cadres could sweep up land on the cheap. Perhaps local government was profiting from the drug deals. Perhaps PSB officers were on the take—no one in the room, but an investigation surely would expose graft.

"This is the worst form of oppression," he shouted, "ignoring the dangers to the Chinese people so that a few cadres can become rich! Look what's happened. A defenseless American student has been attacked. She could have been killed!"

The administrators stood with their fingers locked, eyes on the floor. If only someone would step forward to restrain Teacher Wu, they were thinking. But no one wanted to risk his own skin. Finally, a bold administrator placed her hand on Wu's arm and said, ever so softly, "That's enough."

The precinct captain had nodded thoughtfully throughout Wu's speech, and now that it appeared to be over, he called to a pair of plainclothes officers posted across the room. They rushed at Teacher Wu, grabbed him, and without ceremony hustled him to a stairway in the back. He twisted and fought, shouting the whole time, "Justice! Justice!" Claire thought he looked like a bug, his legs skittering this way and that. As they reached the staircase, Wu cast a wide-eyed gaze back at her and moaned when he saw that she was content to let them take him away. He went limp and closed the book on another chapter of his mournful life.

"He doesn't speak for the group," the head of administration said to the captain.

"No one authorized him to say those things," someone else said. "There was no need for him to go so far in his criticisms."

The rest stood as silent as children before an unpredictably violent parent, praying to be dismissed without a beating.

"You have all done your patriotic duty," the captain said, waving his cigarette at the administrators. "We will investigate the allegations. Rest assured, citizens, that your welfare is in the hands of the People's Republic, and your concerns will be met with action!" A few of the protesters nodded in approval. Most were already backing toward the exit. Suddenly a young teacher in a white shirt thrust himself through the crowd and, fist raised, shouted, "Your words are shit! We demand immediate action!"

Two more plainclothesmen grabbed him by the yoke of his shirt, wrestled him to the floor, and dragged him across the room, his flailing legs banging against desks and toppling chairs. By the time they got him up the stairway, he was screaming hysterically, struggling like an animal off to the slaughter. Pens spilled from his shirt pocket and tapped down the concrete steps.

The head of the college Maintenance Department, who'd joined the protest only because he'd been in a meeting at the administration building when Wu had burst in, was muscling his way through the crowd, fighting his way toward the door. "Not involved," he was saying in a low voice, "not involved." He threw himself against the heavy door. The exodus was under way.

No one looked back to see that the captain held Claire in place. When the room had emptied, she said in Chinese, "What? What did I do?"

The officer rolled the cigarette around in his mouth. He had been posted to the embassy in Ottawa for several years, and spoke careful, slightly accented English.

"Scholars are China's great pride," he said. "They are the heart of modernization. So much excitement today. I think perhaps too much for you?"

"Yes," Claire said.

"Yes, this is old-fashioned behavior. We must modernize our attitudes." The captain thrummed his chest and nodded.

Claire nodded, too.

"Do not worry about your teachers," he said, waving his finger at the stairs. "We will speak with them for a little while. Perhaps they will spend the night. Please accept my apology for any problems," the captain said. "We are here to protect you and to promote friendship."

He offered his hand with such gusto and camaraderie that without thinking Claire took it and pumped right back. The captain then swept his arm toward the stairs, a master of ceremonies directing her to affix her gaze upon the opening curtain.

"For your safety, you should remain here for a while," the captain said.

"Up there?" Claire said.

"Yes," he said, then pointed at the stairs until she began moving in that direction. Halfway up, she glanced back at him, and he smiled and urged her on with both of his hands, as if shooing children out of a kitchen.

On the second floor she was met by an officer who first saluted her, then shook her hand. There was something adolescent about him, his face a bevy of angles, his twiggish wrists and hands so small they disappeared up the cuffs of his coat like moles darting into their burrows. He motioned stiffly that she should follow him, and he marched off down the hall.

The reeducation classroom's white walls were cracked, but scoured clean. They were the cleanest walls Claire had seen in China. She squeezed into a desk. There were bars on the windows. The officer straightened his uniform.

These were, for him, highly unusual circumstances. He'd been told only to escort the white woman to the classroom. No further instructions. Perhaps it was a test of his allegiance to the Party, if, as they said, a Western woman could corrupt a pure heart with a flutter of her eyelashes. He looked sternly at the woman and she smiled at him. His stomach jumped. She was, indeed, powerful. Suddenly he wagged his finger in the air, a gesture he'd seen in a movie—sit tight, I'll be right back—and hop-skipped out the door.

He returned carrying a vacuum bottle of hot water and a teacup, which he placed on the desk before her with the decorum of a waiter at a four-star restaurant. As he poured the water, Claire noticed he had a small bandage on his right index finger. It was grimy, and she felt like that was all she needed to know about this poor boy. He probably wasn't much older than she. Her fingers brushed the back of his hand. He tensed, and when the cup was full, he left the room, ran down the stairs, and out the building via a side door, where he vomited against a low wall.

Claire understood that he wasn't coming back and that she was to remain in the hard wooden chair and self-criticize or something. The whole day had been a waste, and she was about to get up and leave when she thought of Alicia. She picked up the teacup and took a sip, and as she did, her mind glazed over, wandering from one torture scenario to the next. What would Alicia think if she were to return to the dorm black and blue, her stomach dotted with cigarette burns? By the time she'd emptied the bottle, it was dark outside. She'd been there long enough. She stepped into the hallway. It was as if the place had been evacuated.

There were no signs of life in the corridor, no creaking desk chairs, no scraping pigeons on a windowsill. The station's windowless interior was lit by bulbs in wire cages screwed to the wall. She walked to the stairwell and at the bottom stopped and imagined what it would be like to be subdued for attempting to escape. The front room was dark and quiet as a deserted theater. A streetlamp's orange light cut through the window, and in its glow she made out the desks, returned once again to orderly rows, the papers stacked neatly. Slowly she made her way toward the door, her hands trailing from the cool surface of one desk to the next. At the last one, she let her hand drift to the stack of reports. She ran her thumb along the edge of the pages, and, looking the other way, flicked her fingers outward. The reports fluttered down in the dark. She walked to the door, grasped the smooth brass bar, and pushed.

It was dark outside, and beyond the courtyard endless waves

of commuters rattled by on their bikes. Blurs, insubstantial as ghosts, they flashed through the cone of light cast by a streetlamp and were gone. The paving stones clucked beneath their tires, shifting like a rickety wooden bridge. The door clattered closed behind her. She passed unnoticed out the gates of the PSB compound.

At the college gates, the old watchman didn't even glance up from his movie magazine when she walked by the guardhouse. She made her way toward the dorm through pools of light separated by spaces of abyssal black. The adrenaline from the police station had long worn off, leaving in its place the cold exhaustion of a long swim. After all that tea she needed a bathroom, and began to worry she wouldn't make it from one yellow disc of light to another without wetting herself, and she kept moving, dashing ahead to the box of light proscribed by a window, then to the murky glow of a series of bulbs dangling over the glass cases where the newspaper was pinned up, eventually, gritting her teeth, reaching the chain-link fence around the athletic field. The dormitory lay just on the other side of the field. Claire laced her fingers through the cold metal diamonds and pressed her lips against the back of her hand. She clenched her legs together, pausing to imagine again that she'd been tortured at the PSB station and was just going to make it back to the dorm before passing out. Weak, disoriented, her back covered with bruises, she'd stagger into the lobby and collapse in a twitching heap on the dirty floor.

But then she realized she could have stayed out all night—handcuffed to a radiator at the PSB station, for all anyone knew—and no one would have even noticed she was gone. Not one of her classmates would have said, Hey, where's Claire? It stunned her a little, the unbidden cruelty of this thought, and, lacking anyone other than herself to blame for its formation, she felt for an instant that there must be something wrong with her.

So no one missed her. So no one cared. That was freedom, wasn't it? She reached for the button of her jeans, unzipped, pulled them down, squatted, and released a stream of urine onto the packed dirt. She groaned with relief. Mud splattered against the insteps of her shoes. The puddle grew beneath her, and she tipped forward to grab the fence. She didn't care who saw her. She knew no one would see her.

DONATE!

Yang had come home from the factory for lunch. The courtyard was covered in brown peach blossoms, exactly as it had been when he'd left that morning. He was standing beneath the old peach tree, debating how best to punish his daughter, who hadn't even touched the broom he'd left leaning against the trunk for her, when the earthquake hit. The branches above him shivered and dropped petals and twigs on his head. Must be something big up there tearing around after a pigeon, he thought. He was looking up, hoping to spot a yellow weasel, which would have been good luck, when suddenly the tree shook off its remaining petals and he found himself staring directly into the sun. He felt unsteady on his feet, as if, in the middle of choppy seas, he'd decided to stand up in his rowboat for a better view. He threw his arm around the tree's rough trunk just in time to catch himself from toppling over backward. His stomach churned. Across the courtyard, a terra-cotta roof tile landed with a thunk on the packed earth. The mahjong players who congregated outside his neighbor's gate, an excitable bunch to begin with, were yelling like madmen; the public toilet attendant, a Korean War vet in his seventies, reliving a nightmare of American shelling, cried out for the mahjong players to take cover. Horns wailed on Fuchengmen Street as traffic locked up. Dogs yelped. A windowpane popped. A single clay flowerpot tipped over and fell from its perch by the front gate, landing with a thud-crack against the pavers. Wind chimes clattered in the still air. Yang crouched down and felt around on the ground in front of him, trying to steady himself with his free hand. The broom fell over and whacked him on the shoulder, and he saw his wife coming toward him from their bedroom, waving her arms and shouting. At first he couldn't make out what she was saying over the storm of noise in his ears.

"Bing Yang! It's an earthquake!" she was saying.

He looked down at the fresh blanket of pink petals on the ground. "Are you hurt?" he said.

"I'm fine," she said. "It's only tremors. Nothing serious."

"You know my inner ear is unhealthy," Yang said.

"Watch the horizon," she said.

"I'm doing what I can," he shouted.

"Be calm."

He looked up at her with the eyes of a wounded animal turning to its predator.

"What?" she said.

"Help me up?" Yang said.

Gong crossed her arms. "Get up yourself. You're fine. Given any thought to Little Li?"

"Do I look like I've had time to make a phone call?" His knees cracked as he stood, and a wave of light-headedness washed over him. "Where's my phone?" he said.

Gong waggled her cell phone at him. "She already sent me a text. They're evacuating to the soccer field. The epicenter was hundreds of miles from here. This isn't such a big deal. It's over."

Yang moved away from the tree and swept flowers off his shoulders, bits of bark from his shirt and trousers. Gong reached out and brushed some blossoms from his hair. Yang fished around for his phone and dialed his daughter.

"You've evacuated?" he said when she picked up.

"What?" she said. "We're on the soccer field."

"Did the school collapse?" he said.

"Yang!" Gong shouted. "Leave her alone."

"I'm asking serious questions here," he said. His daughter was laughing, but not at anything he'd said. She was fourteen, a cipher to him.

"Bing Li," he said, "come home right now." He made a face at his wife. "And when you get here, sweep up these peach blossoms like I told you."

Gong grabbed the phone away from him.

"Hey!" Yang said.

Gong put the phone to her ear. "Little Li, stay put. Don't move a muscle until your teachers tell you to. Goodbye." She sighed and crossed her arms.

"Well, let's go see what this is all about," Yang said. "And you can rub this knot out of my shoulder." The broom's blow, glancing enough, had hit the site of an old injury.

"Who in heaven did I offend to get stuck with you?" she said, laying her hand on his back.

"Clearly you're cursed from a former life," he said, giving her a weak smile.

When Little Li arrived home from school, the first thing she did was ask Yang for a donation.

"My class is sending money to the victims," she said.

"How do you know about victims?" Yang said. "What victims?"

"Daddy. I'm not five."

"Yes. Sure," he said. He turned the television back on.

"It'll be a miracle if anyone survived. And this isn't the end of it," she said. "After Tangshan in 1976, the aftershocks were five-point-zero on the Richter scale, and they kept coming back for months and killing more and more people." She shook her head.

"You weren't even alive in 1976."

"And you were still a peasant in 1976," she said. He didn't respond.

"Daddy, there's not a building left standing in some villages. Everything's collapsed."

"Such unshakable optimism," he said. "Who told you this? Your teachers?"

"What would they know? They've been teaching all day. I got texts. Ming Weilin's cousin lives in Sichuan. He told her everyone's dead."

"Everyone's not dead," he said. "The administration organized the donations?"

"No. We did it ourselves while we were waiting."

"That's very industrious of you," Yang said, pulling a ten-yuan note from the roll in his pocket. "Let this be a seed that grows tall."

"Okay," Little Li said. "Embarrassing."

"You're welcome."

"Mama," she called. "Mama, I need money for the earthquake victims."

"Hey," Yang said. "That's a family donation. Ten-kuai family donation," he shouted after her as she crossed the courtyard, bound for her parents' bedroom, dragging her feet through the peach blossoms.

"Zhou Hao's dad gave him fifty kuai when he came to pick him up," she shouted back. "Mama! I need money! Daddy's being a tight-ass!"

"Watch your mouth," he muttered. On the TV, rescue workers in red jumpsuits and hard hats stood precariously atop slabs of gray rubble. A scene of unimaginable destruction, the newscaster said, and Yang thought, It's not unimaginable. The camera zoomed in on a woman covered in gray dust, clawing at chunks of concrete, desperately plunging her bare hands into the tangle of rebar, glass, jagged planks of wood, stone. She was digging for her child. The camera remained on her until Yang had to cough down the ache in his throat and look away.

"Come here," he called hoarsely.

After a while, Little Li slouched back in.

"Here." He pulled a hundred-yuan note from his pocket and closed her hands around the crumpled paper.

"That's more like it," she said. She looked at the TV, which was replaying images of the mother digging in the rubble. "Nobody's alive in there. That woman must be suffering from post-traumatic stress disorder. She's going to end up in an asylum."

"Her child is buried."

"She looks ridiculous."

Without understanding what he meant to do, Yang jumped up from his chair, violence coursing through him. He had never before raised his hand to her, and Little Li flinched. When Yang lowered his hand and looked away, Little Li reassembled herself and set her face to register disregard. There was a tear in the corner of her eye, and her cheeks were flushed. Yang was vibrating with anger, unable to look at his daughter, unable to defuse. Breathe, he told himself.

"Keep your comments to yourself," he said. A spasm bit into his shoulder when he reached for his jacket. "And help me get this on." The spasm widened into a bright, electric grip gathering up the muscle in his shoulder. He made a face.

He chased the sleeve around with the tips of his fingers, unable to gain purchase on the nylon lining, flapping his arm weakly.

"Do you need some medicine?" Little Li said.

"No," he responded, too sharply, he realized, but there was nothing to do about that.

Little Li dipped her head. She reached for the jacket, taking it by the collar as she exhaled in exasperation, her hip cocked at an angle of supreme impatience. Yang wondered when she had become this person.

She gave the jacket a weak shake.

"Do I need to take my donation back?" he said, wincing as he guided his other arm in.

"No," she said, holding the jacket still. "You look weird when you make that face."

"I wouldn't wish this on my worst enemy," he said. "I'm going to the hospital."

"Really?" she said, dropping her guard and turning toward him.

"To give blood," he said.

"For your back?"

"Are you serious?" he said.

"No."

"To donate," he said.

She pondered this, then said, "I don't have to, do I?"

"No," he said. "You're too young."

"Oh, good." She picked up the remote and skipped through the channels. "When is this going to be over? It's just the same old rubble." She was testing the waters and waited for her father to laugh, but he didn't. "It's been two hours already. Mama!" she called out into the courtyard. "What if the earthquake is still on tonight? What am I supposed to do about *Lovely Cinderella*?"

She cocked her ear and, hearing nothing, shouted, "Dad's going to the hospital to give away his blood!"

"You don't have to make it sound like a crime," Yang said.

"Then why were you trying to sneak out of here without telling Mom?"

Gong came shuffling across the courtyard, moving as though underwater, every step weighted, a diluted, slow-motion replay of the actual event.

"Did you take pills?" Little Li asked her mother.

"I'm fine," she answered, holding Little Li's eyes for a moment.

"Okay, so he's giving his blood away for free," Little Li said, opening her mouth wide in an imitation of shock.

"Your father and the rest of the Revolutionary Guard," Gong answered, turning to Yang. "Take off your jacket and sit down. Wait for them to issue a formal request and then you can get a little credit. You, of all people, running to the rescue. They'll drain you and then a doctor will say they need a kidney and you'll say, Where do I sign? Just wait for Old Gao to come around asking for volunteers. If you do it through her, maybe she'll mind her own business for a week."

They lived near the Forbidden City in an ancient hutong neighborhood. Most of their neighbors were Chinese yuppies whose boredom with the practical elements of communism, like work groups and neighborhood committees, was a source of wonder to Yang. He'd grown up in the countryside in the late sixties and early seventies, and as a child he'd pulled yams next to intellectuals sent down for reeducation. He respected the Party's ability to whip citizens into a storm that could flatten everything in its path. These days, when a yuppie butted heads with the neighborhood committee over a plan to install a bathroom in his three-hundred-year-old home, he bribed a cadre in the municipal government who directed the committee to issue a variance.

The rest of Yang's neighbors were foreign executives, Swiss and Germans who levitated above the quaint diktats of local governance. The neighborhood committee's power, such as it was, had concentrated in seventy-five-year-old Gao Lin, a woman who had fought off real estate moguls and the municipal government when they'd tried to evict her from her house, a gold mine to whoever could sell it out from under her. None had succeeded, and her gate now bore a white plaque marking the house a cultural and historical treasure. Her family dead and gone, she was the last soldier encamped behind crumbling fortress walls. When she went out, she shuffled around the hutong like a shrimp on its tail, stopping to take note of infractions and issue tickets, which she pinned to her neighbors' heavy wooden gates. She fined them for improper bicycle parking and for failing to sweep their entrance stones. She fined them for neglecting to report their neighbors' infractions. No one bothered to pay the tickets or remove them, and when a breeze blew through the hutong, the papers rustled like leaves. The rain pulled them down, and she replaced them with tickets for littering.

She was hard as nails, and none of the Chinese left in the neighborhood would have tried to have her removed from her post. Even the municipal-level cadres were slightly afraid of her.

"When she comes around I'll tell her I've already donated blood. They'll give out certificates," Yang said.

"She'll talk you into giving another pint," Gong said.

"Are you watching this?" he said, pointing at the television. "I'll gladly give another pint."

"Don't have a heart attack," she said. "We lost a clay pot and some flowers from the tree. This could have been a lot worse."

By the time Yang got to the bus stop, the news had hit the evening papers, but most people were lost in their own thoughts and looked to Yang not unlike a bunch of unplugged televisions. At the hospital, he had to pay a scalper one hundred yuan for a ticket to cut the admit line and, once inside, he searched four floors before he found someone who could direct him to the proper department for donations.

When he announced his desire for his donation to go to Sichuan, the volunteer behind the desk, a young woman wearing heavy black glasses and a white paper nurse's hat, told him that per regulation, all donations would be apportioned according to need. "Local injuries are our immediate concern," she said. "People were hurt inside city limits and the suburbs. Fifteen people were injured on the Fifth Ring Road."

What a robot, Yang thought.

"There's real carnage down in Sichuan," he said.

"There have been no reports of casualties."

"Give me a break," Yang said. "The province is a graveyard. It's a disaster zone."

"The central office for disaster response has issued no such statement," she said.

"I'd prefer this donation should go to Sichuan," Yang said.

"For the earthquake?" the woman replied.

"For the snowstorm," Yang said.

"There's no need for that," she said sternly.

Yang sighed. He could keep arguing, which inevitably would cause the volunteer to leave her post for a break that lasted until he gave up and left, or he could acknowledge that the woman on the other side of the desk maintained unassailable power. "I understand," he said. "The blood goes where it's needed most. I just want to help." He palmed a twenty and offered his hand. She looked up, and without pretense plucked the bill from it.

"It's rare to meet someone as civic-minded as you," she said. "I'll ensure your donation goes to Sichuan." She wasn't much older than Little Li, and he took a hollow satisfaction in having bent her to his will.

He filled out some paperwork and she directed him to an exam table covered with green paper. An orderly wearing large silver headphones came and swabbed his arm, then slipped in a needle. "Relax and be cool," the orderly said. "I'll check on you in thirty."

"Where's everyone else?" Yang said.

The orderly pulled one of the cups away from his ear and said, "Whassat?"

"The other donors?" Yang nodded at the empty exam tables around him.

The orderly crinkled his brow and released the earphone, which snapped back with a muffled pop. He disappeared into the hall.

Yang lay back on the table. He'd grown up in a farming village, his only possessions two blue Mao jackets, one stuffed with cotton for the winter, the other without cotton for warmer months, and a family of wooden frogs that fit into the palm of his hand. In 1980, a migrant work program brought him to Beijing, where he bored holes in door hinges and small-gauge gears at a state-run metal-stamp factory. Twenty years later, he had become co-owner of the factory. He was worth twenty million yuan, but most of his neighbors assumed he was a schoolteacher with a patrilinear claim to his hutong house. This aggravated his wife to no end. They'd paid cash for the house. It put Gong in a murderous state of mind when a neighbor asked her husband about his employment and he ducked his head and chuckled like a mountain hermit. "Metals," he'd say, if pressed. She had given up trying to explain to him that to be rich was glorious and there was no shame in having means. Even total strangers felt a sense of relief and pride in the presence of success.

Yang looked down at the tube, dark, almost black with his blood.

His parents were still alive, and though they accepted his money, they wouldn't move in with him. They were perfectly happy living like two turtles under a rock out in Xianghe. There was no way he and Gong could ever be so content in each other's company. Someone would have to surrender first.

A while later, the orderly returned and with surprising care slipped out the needle, affixed a bandage, bent Yang's arm up at the elbow, and placed a rice cake and a cup of juice on the exam table next to him. He picked up the blood bag and left without a word.

Yang was nearly home when he realized he hadn't asked for a certificate to prove he'd donated. He gave it a moment's thought and kept walking.

It was the first thing Gong asked about. She made a strained face before he'd had a chance to answer.

"There must be a name for it," she said.

"For what?" he said.

"This psychological disorder of yours."

"They were very busy. You should have seen the line. There was no time to fill out certificates."

"Sometimes I think you go out of your way to oppose me."

He peeled back the gauze to show her the petal-shaped bruise in the crook of his arm.

"Show that to Old Gao when she comes around."

"What's the big deal?" he said.

She opened her mouth to speak, then stopped herself.

"There's no way to know how many were hurt," he said. "How many children are dead?"

"Be quiet," she said very softly, almost as if addressing a voice in her head.

"In the larger view, a pint of blood isn't much, but it's something," Yang said. "It's part of a philosophy of, well, compassion."

"Don't you dare say I'm not compassionate," she said.

"I didn't," Yang said.

"Why don't you show some compassion for your family before you help total strangers?"

"You have no sense of logic," Yang said.

"And you do? You'd rather remain anonymous than do a simple thing I asked of you? How's that logical? Could you have done one simple thing to make my life easier?"

"A certificate makes your life easier? Your life is hard?" Yang said. "Do you go hungry? Does Little Li cry because the stones cut her shoeless feet?"

"Stop making fun of me," she said.

Yang shrugged, and he felt, high on the left trapezius, a seizure of the muscle exactly where the broom had struck it.

"I have to lie down right now," he said.

"Did you even bother to ask for a certificate?" Gong said.

Oh, why did she have to ask? Yang thought. There was no

point in trying to answer. Unanswerable questions led to evasions. He didn't reply.

"Go lie down," she said.

This was the standard procedure to preserve his back, which would cripple him for days if not accorded the proper respect. The method, part traditional medicine, part common sense, required him to lie perfectly still for hours, staring at the ceiling. Normally Gong would bring him the radio or read him a book, but two hours passed before she entered the room.

"I'm sorry," he said.

"You better be," she said. She set a steaming cup of water on the table and emptied a packet of Yin Qiao San into it. Yang's nostrils flared at the scent, but otherwise he was still as a corpse. Gong lowered herself to the edge of the bed and leaned in, her lips on his ear. "Behave like a child and I'll treat you like one."

"Hm," he said, closed his eyes, and reached up to touch her cheek. The thorny fist in his back clenched tighter. He could beat the pain if he drank the herbs and remained as still as possible. He gently laced his fingers together to form a bridge across his chest. In through the nose, out through the mouth. He tried to visualize old paintings of sleeping philosophers soaring out over vast canyons, borne up in their dreams by mystical forces, but the image of the mother digging in the rubble kept coming back to him. He stayed there until he fell asleep.

The next morning he awoke at dawn and slid out of bed. There was still a finger of pressure against his shoulder blade, but the silver wire of pain had left his body. Gong didn't stir. Her lips were parted and her braids lay splayed out at right angles on the pillow.

The sky was pinking over the roof on the other side of the courtyard, and he stopped to look in on Little Li. Her sheets were in a pile on the floor, and she was strewn across the bed as though she'd crashed through the roof. Yang feared for what her life would bring.

He set out for the post office, stopping to pick up an egg-and-scallion crepe from a street vendor he knew, and still arrived before the doors were opened. Bicycle postmen streamed out of the alley adjoining the building. By the time the doors opened at eight, he was surrounded by a crowd of early birds balancing parcels in their arms. They all went inside together and assembled in a rough line, each one ready to dash for the window should this tenuous civility break down. In February the year before, the government had declared the eleventh of every month Queuing Day, an attempt to reduce the scrums that formed wherever people congregated to wait their turn at a window. It was May, and as the summer Olympics got closer, rhetoric had increased, and people did their best to satisfy the rules, but no one expected the newfound order to survive once the foreigners had gone home.

Only one window was open, and Yang kept eyeing a wooden table set up in the corner of the lobby. When it was Yang's turn, he told the clerk what he was there for and she called into the back, then directed Yang to the table. Another postal worker struggled through a door with a steel voting box held to his chest. He crashed it onto the wooden table, the steel biting into the wood, the metal table legs scraping across the stone floor. The worker settled into the chair behind the table, sighed, and motioned for Yang to step up.

"Donations for the Red Cross?" Yang said.

The employee behind the table nodded mournfully. Yang wondered if he had lost relatives in the earthquake. Or maybe he'd merely gotten into character when his boss told him to man the donation box. Some people were like that. Given a chore, there was no limit to what they'd do to succeed. Yang had planned to give three hundred, but he stuffed one thousand yuan into the slot and left without a word.

While he'd been waiting inside, the PLA had erected three green canvas canopies on the sidewalk, each one bearing a poster-board sign with blood types. A young man in fatigues and a Red Cross armband ran up to him.

"Sir, what blood type?"

"I've just made a donation," Yang said.

The young man narrowed his eyes. "Blood?"

"Money. To the Red Cross," Yang said, pointing at the soldier's armband. "I gave blood yesterday."

"You gave blood yesterday?"

"At Beida. Beida Hospital."

The soldier leaned in to Yang like a prosecutor trying to catch a witness in a lie. "At Beida Hospital?"

"That's what I said."

"Whole blood or plasma?"

"What do you mean?" Yang asked.

"Which did you donate?" the recruit said, his voice rising. "Blood or plasma?"

Yang wasn't entirely sure, but he said, "Whole blood."

"Good. You can donate plasma."

Yang pulled up his sleeve to show the bruise.

Glancing down at Yang's arm only long enough to confirm that it was, in fact, an arm, the recruit said, "You're the picture of health. Why are you trying to wriggle out of this? Don't you care about your comrades in Sichuan?" People were staring. Comrades? Who used that word anymore?

"Where do I go?" Yang said. The recruit grabbed his arm and pulled him over to an officer in a lab coat, then double-timed it back to the sidewalk.

"Quite a trapper you have there," Yang said.

"Blood type," the lab coat said.

All business, Yang thought.

The lab coat had to stick his arm four times to get a vein, and by the time the needle was in, Yang was ready to strangle the stone-faced bastard. An hour later, he was unceremoniously dismissed, his right hand pressing a hunk of gauze to his arm, the left clutching a bean cake. He couldn't stop yawning and his stomach was an empty pit, and he got in line at the nearest noodle shop. The TV was going in the corner: scenes of rubble, children's backpacks, more footage of distraught mothers throwing themselves against blank-faced fathers. Yang tried not to watch.

A construction crew was hunched shoulder to shoulder around the shop's flimsy linoleum tables. They parted to allow Yang a place without breaking the shoveling motion of their chopsticks. Yang nosed into his bowl.

The heat from the smooth porcelain warmed his fingers, and after he'd eaten most of the noodles, he began to feel more like himself. He wished someone would turn off the television, and he tried to tune it out as he ate, but it was hard to ignore. Then his phone began to ring.

"Better get it," his neighbor said, smiling. "Might be the office." Some other guys laughed. It was an offhand remark, but Yang understood its meaning, and it set his teeth on edge. The men sharing the table with him wore dusty canvas jackets with heavy gloves jammed into the chest pockets, and here he was in a button-down shirt and pressed trousers. But his arms were as sinewed as any man's at the table. He made a fist. He could teach anyone there to operate a thirty-ton H-frame press. He hadn't forgotten.

The phone stopped, then started up again.

"Sounds urgent," the construction worker said.

Yang backed away from the table to take the call.

It was Gong. "Back's better?" she said.

"Ah, it's better, thanks."

"Where are you?"

"On my way to work." On a normal day he'd have been at the factory since just after dawn, plowing through production logs and calling customers.

"Where are you?"

"Noodle shop," Yang said.

"You sound funny," Gong said.

Yang knew the construction workers were listening. "On my way," he said, and hung up. Then, as a precaution, he turned the phone off.

The TV droned on over the slurping of noodles. Back in the kitchen, the cook was whipping a rope of dough through the air, strands multiplying as he strung the noodles like yarn on his fingers, then a twist and smack against the counter and into the boil. The cook's arms were loose, extensions of the noodles themselves, and he proceeded through the operation with so little attention to what he was doing that Yang felt no shame in staring. There was an automatic quality to his movements, the thoughtless perfection of repetitive motion, the perfect state, Yang thought, of doing without thinking. All his life, thinking had gotten him in trouble. When he'd acted on impulse, he'd always been rewarded.

He hadn't noticed that one of the construction workers was standing next to him.

"This is sick stuff, eh?" the man said, pointing at the television.

"Yeah," Yang said, still watching the cook.

"I'd have expected better from Yao Ming. But he probably eats white bread and speaks English at home," the man said.

Yang nodded absently. "Now," he ventured slowly, "what is it that Yao's done?" he said, only just then turning to see that the basketball star was on-screen.

"Cheap bastard's only pledged five hundred thousand yuan to the relief effort."

"I see," Yang said.

"He's going to miss five hundred thou like I'd miss a fen."

"True," Yang said. "He's in a hard position."

The man cocked his head and took in Yang's clothes and shoes. "I don't see what's so hard about it," he said. "But I guess you guys have got to stick together."

"I haven't played ball in years," Yang said, but the construction worker didn't laugh. He hadn't meant to defend Yao, but Yang suddenly felt that he'd rather be misunderstood. "What a man does with his money is his own business," Yang said.

"How much have you given?" the man said.

Yang looked back at him blankly. He presented both arms and pulled up his sleeves.

"Blood?" His mates turned around and Yang was aware of their eyes on him.

"You look like you might be good for five hundred thousand," one of them said.

"I've already made my donation," Yang said, moving toward the door. "I've done my part."

"Keep walking, asshole," someone shouted as he hustled out the door. "Say hi to Yao Ming for us."

Yang walked back to the post office and donated another two thousand yuan.

Then he caught the 451 bus to the industrial park in Fengtai District, where his factory was located.

His partner, Rabbit, a middle-aged number cruncher whose round black glasses would have been more at home on a French painter, met him at the industrial park gate. Rabbit seemed always to be bathed in light sweat, no matter the temperature, which made customers nervous, but he was good under pressure and had an elephant's memory. His hair was neatly combed in the front but in back looked slept-on. Every day he wore the same brown tie that, with the perennial bags beneath his eyes, gave him the harried air of a salaryman who'd barely survived his latest bender. Yang and Rabbit had known each other since childhood and Yang recognized that it was all a ruse, Rabbit's mannered fumbling, the rumpled bedsheets he called clothes. Rabbit was a hard, calculating man. He'd worked the same fields as Yang in the days when school had consisted of memorizing passages of

revolutionary poetry. In another life, he'd have become a professor of mathematics, but history had conspired against him. Yang
understood the machines and tended to customers and Rabbit
kept the books and dealt with the men on the floor. He had the
common touch.

"What's the good word?" Yang said.

"Come on, come on," Rabbit said, holding Yang's arm as they
walked toward the factory. "You picked the wrong day to leave for
lunch, pal. You should have seen this place. The lights were swaying like a fat lady's tits. I can't believe you weren't here. Sounded
like a tank battalion rolling through the place. The boys were
scared to death. Zone Chief Zhou's been calling for you."

"What's he want?"

"Donations. The zone committee's hitting up the workers when
they leave at the end of shift, and the workers' union has a separate
donation drive. These guys' danweis are pushing for donations,
and their kids all came home from school yesterday asking for
money. It's chaos in there. There was a fistfight in the locker room
this morning—one of the Huis said that he'd donate five kuai but
no more because none of his people lived in Sichuan, and Brother
Chu—you know Chu Pi, from Baiduizi—he slams this Hui against
a locker and next thing you know, Brother Chu has a broken nose
and half the room's standing on top of the Hui. This isn't good.
We're going to end up all over the papers."

"Idiots," Yang said, quickening his pace. "I thought Chu Pi had
some sense."

"He claims it was his patriotic duty," Rabbit said. "Meanwhile,
we're losing ten thousand an hour while they're standing around
waving their dicks at each other." Rabbit pushed through a pair of
heavy fire doors and looked over at Yang. "You hear about Yao
Ming?" he said, a wry grin on his face.

"I heard," Yang said.

"Cheap bastard," Rabbit muttered as he pushed through another pair of doors and they hustled past the men's toilets and the men's locker room, through another pair of fire doors that opened to the factory floor. The space was heavy with silence. Lit like a subway car and as long as a soccer field, the factory floor usually vibrated slightly. Searing noise forced everyone to wear ear protection, but without the mechanical thrum that marked time twenty-four hours a day at full production, the workers' voices rose and fell like winking stars in the black sky.

Yang and Rabbit climbed the metal stairs to the platform outside their office. Yang rapped his knuckles against the metal railing until the workers milling around below turned their faces upward, most squinting as if looking into the sun. A couple of the guys took off their hard hats.

"Where's Brother Chu Pi?" Yang shouted, surveying the crowd.

"At the hospital," someone shouted back.

Yang nodded. "Gentlemen," he began. He had no idea what he was going to say to still the men's spirits. This made about as much sense as trying to talk away the rain. Yang heard the purring of an air compressor and, somewhere in the thermoforming area, the tinging of cooling metal. He cleared his throat and began again. "Gentlemen, our country is suffering. We are lucky to have been spared—" He stopped, aware that among his men there would be those with relatives in the South. "Those of you who are concerned for your families—I am concerned for your families, too. Don't ignore the fact that our factory is still standing and we have our lives. We can help best by keeping production high."

Some of the men clapped weakly.

"That is the best thing for China. Maintain production," Yang said, drawing out the words.

"Why?" came a voice from the back.

"Isn't it obvious?" Yang said. But it wasn't obvious even to him, and at that moment he caught a whiff of his own woolly sweat wafting up, and found himself considering a wild notion:

he should bus the entire workforce to Sichuan to aid in the recovery effort. But by the time they got there, the men would have been drunk for two days. They'd have beaten each other to a pulp and would get off the bus in worse shape than the quake survivors. "If we fight about small things," he shouted, "we miss opportunities to help. This is not about fighting. This is about helping."

Rabbit pushed his glasses up onto his nose, leaned over the railing, and shouted, "And you're all going to help run this factory out of business if you don't get your lazy asses back to work, and then where will you be?"

A wave of laughter went up from the men. Rabbit had a way with them. A balled-up rag flew out of the crowd. Rabbit snatched it from the air and dramatically shook his fist at the men. "Get back to work before we call in the riot police on you assholes," he said.

"What are you going to do to aid the victims?" someone shouted.

"We're doing plenty," Rabbit shouted back.

"This isn't funny! We're making personal donations," the worker shouted, "so where's yours?"

Another man said, "My wife's factory is covering her personal donations!"

Rabbit looked at Yang, who smirked at the man's obvious lie.

"We should be compensated for our donations!" another man shouted.

Yang held up his hand. The men quieted down. The year before, the factory had sent one hundred thousand yuan to the Yunnan quake relief effort, and one hundred thousand to flood relief the year before that. But this one felt different. Yang had to find the right balance: a donation large enough to calm the men, but not so large as to make it look like he had money to burn. The men complained endlessly about their wages and suspected that untold riches were piling up in vaults beneath the factory, money withheld from them expressly to scuttle their chances for advancement in the world. What if he fired them all on the spot, sold the factory to the highest bidder, and settled into a quiet life of mahjong and cold beer? And why was it his duty to compensate the men for their donations? It was the damned ingratitude that got him. How dare they hold his feet to the fire.

"Beijing Number Seven Peony Metal Fabrication, Limited, will match the donations of any and all employees," Yang said slowly, his eyes searching for any man willing to return his gaze, "and above that amount will donate three hundred thousand yuan to the relief effort."

That ought to shut them up, he thought. People think only of themselves, even when they believe they're helping others. It's every man for himself. Then he heard the applause. The men's faces, turned up to him like a band of starving children he'd fed from his own kitchen. Some were waving their hard hats. Amazing, he thought. But by tomorrow they'll have found a reason to turn against me. Three hundred thousand won't be enough. He turned abruptly and went into the office, the men's cheers still audible after he'd closed the door, like an ax chopping at him, breaking him up into pieces they'd throw on a fire to warm their rough hands. He fell into his leather chair and closed his eyes.

That was how Rabbit found him when he returned to the office after laying some more brotherly abuse on the men.

"Finally, you've died from stress," Rabbit said. "Now your daughter's treasures will be mine."

"Soon enough," Yang said without opening his eyes. "I'm down two pints to the relief effort."

"What a patriot. Hope you got a certificate."

Yang opened his eyes a touch, but Rabbit had concerned himself with a towering sheaf of invoices, his fingers playing up and down the jagged ridge of paper.

"What word from the proletariat?" Yang said. The factory was coming back to life, the floor beneath his feet beginning to thrum.

Rabbit didn't respond immediately. The office was arranged so that he sat with his back to Yang. It wasn't spacious, but was large enough for their two desks, both heavy wooden Qing Dynasty knockoffs, their chrome-and-mesh swivel chairs, several banks of file cabinets, and three boxy modular chairs for visitors. A small refrigerator stocked with kimchi and beer hummed against the wall.

Rabbit's fingers hovered at a corner of paper protruding from the stack before pincering an invoice, which he held close to his face, his upper lip retracted from his incisors as he peered over the top of his glasses. "It's fine," Rabbit said. "You know how the guys get. They say they're worried about their relatives, but mostly they're worried about their own skins, and they just want to get on with it."

Yang sighed and closed his eyes again. "Three hundred thousand," he said.

"It's enough. You're still a rich man no matter how much you give away," Rabbit said. He quickly added, "But no one thinks you're holding out."

"The men know I'm not a public speaker," Yang said.

"Don't worry about it. The rich always have trouble communicating with the poor," Rabbit said, dropping the page to his desk, satisfied with his inspection.

"I'm not the only rich one around here," Yang said.

"Noted," Rabbit said. "The difference is, I'm not the president of Beijing Number Seven Peony Metal Fabrication."

"So?" Yang said.

"You're not one of the boys anymore. You're tall, rich, and handsome."

"I'm supposed to apologize for being rich? I'm supposed to live in a shack and eat fried rice?" Yang said.

"No," Rabbit said. "But stop pretending you do. You're the big frog in this pond. You have to watch over the little frogs." Rabbit fixed his eyes on his friend. "You should have been here yesterday. You know what it sounded like? The cargo bay of a ship in a storm, creaking and groaning and everything sliding around. But the men, silent as a tomb. They were petrified, and where were you? They're your responsibility, for better or worse. That's how it is. You were absent in their time of need. You abandoned your children in their darkest hour."

Yang picked at the button of his shirt and didn't respond.

Rabbit searched Yang's face, but, finding only the same pair of sad black eyes he'd known for forty years, he nodded and went back to his paperwork.

For the rest of the week, Yang came to work and sat in his chair. The zone chief called five, six times a day, but Yang declined to answer. At first Rabbit managed to placate the zone chief, but eventually the chief refused to speak to him. It had gotten personal. Day after day, there Yang sat, placid as a frog in the mud. Maybe it was a calculated act of rebellion, but Rabbit couldn't understand for the life of him what his partner stood to gain by antagonizing the chief. The chief could make real trouble for them. Rabbit's own patience was wearing thin. He had enough problems trying to keep the men on the floor organized without having to play nursemaid to Yang.

During this time of silence, Yang came to understand the crisis in his own way: The workers would be satisfied by nothing less than strips of flesh from his back. The country would take nothing less than everything he had. Zone Chief Zhou was now leaving messages at all hours on his cell phone. He was cursing Yang in new and creative ways, threatening to shut the factory down. Yang smiled as he listened to a message from the chief degrading his mother.

Eventually, Rabbit lost it. "Did you have a stroke? Have you gone nuts?" he shouted at Yang.

Nothing.

"I'm calling a psychologist if you don't pull it together!" Rabbit yelled.

Yang smiled.

"I'm serious, you asshole!"

At home it wasn't much better. The first night Gong had paced around her husband, consoled him. The next night she screamed at him. Then she sat across from him, gnawing at her lip.

"You're under a lot of pressure," she said. "I understand. But that doesn't mean you have to act like a mental patient. You can't just hole up like this. Rabbit's told me what's going on. I don't want to wind up living on the street. I won't." She waited for a glimmer of recognition, a sign of concern. He gave her nothing. "You call back the zone chief and you do what he wants," she said. "You do exactly what he tells you to do. Why, on top of everything else, are you trying to bring the government down on our heads?"

She tilted her chin at him, waiting for an answer. When none came, she answered for him. "You are. You're trying to ruin us."

Yang got up and turned on the TV.

"You think this is a good example for Little Li?" she said. His smile cracked just a hair. Gong threw up her hands and left the room.

The news from near the epicenter of the earthquake in Beichuan County, deep in the Longmen Mountains, was horrific. Seven thousand dead in the town of Yingxiu, population nine thousand. In Dujiangyan, southeast of the epicenter, fifty children would be entombed in the rubble for weeks before workers could exhume them. Their parents encamped atop the concrete slabs, fighting with police to watch over the bodies of their children, singing them songs at dusk, telling stories to the rubble. Some had already been imprisoned for their defiance. Starving dogs and cats wandered over the wreckage, nosing into the rubble until rescue workers ran them off. Hundred-foot lengths of asphalt road had sheared off mountainsides and slid into valleys, sweeping away hamlets with no more pause than a drop of water rolling down a windowpane.

Yang considered the loneliness of dying beneath a slab of concrete, in the dark, mouth caked with dust and stone. He'd tried to be good, to do his duty, but what had he changed?

Newscasters sobbed as they reported on missing children reunited with their parents. Yet that was not what his countrymen concerned themselves with. The day after the quake, he saw in the *United Daily News* the total amount of donations by the ten richest people in China. In one day, 32.5 million yuan. And still, public outrage swelled. It was as though the benefactors had shat on the victims' graves. No donation was enough.

Chief Zhou had ordered a massive sign erected outside the zone gates listing, by order of size of donation, the twenty-seven companies located within. The names were in blocky script on a grid, framed on either side by cascading yellow and red bunting, the board rising to a height of two stories above the sidewalk. Included was each company's phone number and the exact amount, to the fen, donated to the earthquake victims. Passersby stood in front of the sign and dialed the listed companies, yelling indignantly at whoever picked up. If they couldn't get through, they pinned angry notes to a smaller comment board on the opposite side of the gate. The first-place company got as many calls as the last-place company, Yang's Beijing Number Seven Peony Metal Fabrication.

In the end it was the office secretary, a young cousin of Rabbit's, who ripped the phone cord from the wall and refused to answer any more calls until something was done. Rabbit went to Yang.

"I'm withholding your paycheck until you call the chief and sort this out," he said.

"So what?" Yang said.

"Just call the man," Rabbit said.

"I don't want to."

"Fine. I'll tell the men you're withholding our donation."

"So? They can read the sign," Yang said.

"They're under the impression the zone chief is putting the

squeeze on you for a kickback. You want me to tell them that you're keeping the money for yourself?"

"You'd kick your own mother in the balls," Yang said.

"My mother keeps her balls in a jar on the shelf, my friend, right next to yours."

Chief Zhou's office kept him on hold for five minutes while Yang listened to a tinny recording touting the zone's commitment to aiding the victims of the Wenchuan earthquake. The voice also reminded him that the zone was accepting applications for factory space, which could be modified to meet tenants' needs.

"Hello?" the chief said when he finally came on the line, as if he'd just run into the office and hadn't been sitting there fuming, fantasizing about various methods by which to disembowel Yang, the entire time.

"Chief Zhou, it's Bing Yang, Beijing Number Seven Peony Metal Fabrication."

"Bing Yang. Good to hear your voice. How have you been?" the chief said. His tone was calm and collegial, and if Yang hadn't known the man was exercising every muscle in his body to keep from reaching through the handset to crush his throat, he'd have thought they were on good terms.

"It's been busy, Chief. I'm sorry we haven't been able to speak sooner."

"Busy man, Yang."

"Busy."

"Yang, let's cut the bullshit."

"Bullshit cut, Chief," Yang said.

"I'm urging you to make a donation through the industrial zone. You've seen the board. It's a disgrace. You're one of only two companies who haven't helped the victims, and Beijing Heavy Transmission Eight is liquidating its holdings as we speak, so I might as well take them off the board entirely. Don't tell me you're broke, too."

"Oh, no sir, Chief. We've had better quarters, but we're okay."

"Good. So, how much will it be? They found a little girl alive in Beichuan, did you see that? Buried four and a half days."

"Amazing. It's a testament to the human spirit, Chief."

"I agree, Yang. So, how much?"

"Well, Chief, I've prepared a donation of three hundred thousand," Yang said. "We may end up bankrupt yet."

Chief Zhou didn't laugh. "That's fine, Yang. That might be enough to help me forget your behavior so far. When should I expect it?"

"Whenever you're ready to massage my scrotum," Yang said. Across the office, Rabbit gasped and made waving motions with his arms.

Yang waved back.

"What?" yelled Chief Zhou.

"Just cutting the bullshit, as requested."

"You son of a bitch!" Chief Zhou's voice shook. "All this time you keep me waiting? I've got cadres from the municipal government up my ass, and you're wasting my time with this? What have I ever done to you?"

Rabbit was pale, his breathing shallow.

"Let's avoid conflict, Chief," Yang said, holding the receiver away from his ear. "Why don't I just write a check to your personal account and we'll be done with it?"

Rabbit made a choking sound.

"You fucking hick," Chief Zhou sputtered. The line clicked and he was gone. Yang set his handset back in its cradle.

"Oh, oh, oh," was all Rabbit could say. He kept wiping his brow with a handkerchief.

"What's he going to do?" Yang said. "Add another zero to our tally on the big board? My conscience is clean. We'll give three hundred thousand directly to the Red Cross and we'll match the men's donations. I've given my own blood. Why is everyone so intent on draining my accounts?"

Rabbit stared at him. "You've lost your mind. Your wife calls me in tears. I'm maintaining your customers for you. Okay, my friend. That's one thing. But now you're messing with the Party. Chief Zhou is going to drop a bomb on us."

"He just wants his cut," Yang said.

"No shit. And he wants to keep his house and his Mercedes. If he doesn't get a donation from every company, in two weeks he'll be driving a dump truck in Xinjiang, spending Friday nights at the mosque."

"You're a Party member," Yang said. "Can't you have him reprimanded for trying to collect bribes? Doesn't that go against 'Love and respect honest labor and thrift'?"

"When did he ever solicit a bribe?"

"Come on!" Yang said.

"This is ridiculous. I can't go to the Party about Chief Zhou. I don't have the right connections," Rabbit said. "You're putting me in a terrible position. Let's make the donation together. We'll pull it from operating expenses, no cost to you or me. Deal? It's a business expense. It's an operational expense," Rabbit said.

"Not a fen. Not one single fen," Yang said.

Rabbit's face fell. "You're going to ruin us both," he said.

"Don't worry," Yang said. "I know you'll figure this out. I'm going home."

Yang opened the office door, the whine of the factory flooding in around him, and clanked down the stairs.

He passed his bus stop, intending to use the walk to the subway to clear his head, but when he got there he passed the entrance without giving it a second thought. His mood had begun to lift. It had been days since he'd exerted himself physically, and as he walked, effortlessly cutting through crowds, weaving around food vendors and CD pirates, he began to formulate plans for daily exercise routines that would get him back to peak condition. In his teenage years he'd been a distance runner, and from his distinction on the track he'd made connections that took him to Beijing. It had been the start of everything.

He worked himself into a state of exhilaration, awash in beneficence at the thought of tightening his laces at the edge of a track, joining the other early morning runners. He could turn everything around by donating more than any other company. He and Chief Zhou would have a good laugh about it afterward, and Rabbit would shake his head in admiration, as if to say, You sly old fox, I should have known you were up to something. He'd buy presents for Gong and Little Li in apology for his bad behavior.

By the time he turned in to his hutong, he'd laid out a plan for reconciliation that involved a banquet at the Kunlun Hotel and presents at everyone's setting. He would draw the people he loved into his orbit.

When he rounded the final corner, he saw Old Gao outside his gate, writing a ticket. Her back was to him, and Yang shuffled his feet and coughed to alert her to his presence. Her arm paused its scribbling motion, so he knew she'd heard him, but when he came up beside her, she flinched and said, "You startled me!"

"I'm sorry, Mrs. Gao," Yang said.

"Here," she said, holding out the ticket.

"I see." He studied her long, swooping strokes on the paper. She had quite beautiful script and he wondered if she'd been an intellectual in her former life. "'Improper disposal of garbage,'" he read aloud. "Thank you, Mrs. Gao."

"Don't be smart," she said. "Bing Yang, it's lucky I've found you. The neighborhood committee is receiving donations for the earthquake victims. Some of these foreign ghosts have given more than we Chinese," she said, waving her arm in the direction of his

German neighbor's compound. "It's a point of national pride, and I know we can count on you."

Yang's jaw began to ache. He felt his mood disintegrate like a stone wall crumbling to powder.

Then Old Gao said, "Mr. Bing. You're crying," as if to scold him for his breach of etiquette. When he didn't reply, she moved away from him, cane tapping rapidly, and called out over her shoulder, "You'll bring a donation when you can."

Yang pushed open his gate and went into the courtyard. Little Li had finally swept up the petals, but he felt no sense of pride in her obedience. He dabbed at his eyes with his sleeve and lowered himself onto a bench across from the denuded peach tree. It was late afternoon, pigeons and starlings circling above, their cries filling the courtyard as they looped over his house. Every once in a while a pigeon would flap down to attach itself to a limb, make some cooing noises, then fly back up to rejoin its kit. The light faded, and Yang stared at the tree for a long time, until its uppermost branches were only black outlines against the purple sky. He thought that if he had an ax, he would chop it down, but he didn't, so he sat, folding and unfolding the garbage ticket and trying to recall what it had been like to be poor.

THE CRYSTAL
SARCOPHAGUS

O n the morning of September 9, 1976, Comrade Zhou Yu-qing was awakened before dawn by the loudspeakers mounted on tarred poles outside his building. Chairman Mao was dead. Zhou rose in the dark and made for the bathroom, located at the other end of the building, across an open-air passageway. When he returned, his wife was up and getting dressed, and said she was leaving for the flower shop, which she knew would be open early and mobbed. Zhou tried to stop her. Lan Baiyu hadn't been well, and he didn't think she should exert herself. They lived on the fifth floor in an east-facing apartment that allowed them an unobstructed view of the rising sun over the rooftops of Beijing. The apartment, and its view, was a reward from the Party, but the building's only elevator was a rickety freight cage off-limits to residents. Zhou was afraid the climb back to the apartment would cause her to miss yet another day of research at the Academy of Sciences, where she was a mathematician. He demanded that she stay put. He would go for the flowers. She told him to mind his own business.

She was back with a bunch before he'd had a chance to get the tea water boiling, and she inserted one into the buttonhole of his chest pocket, pinning it there in an under-over-under piercing of the cloth that resembled a metal stitch and held the chrysanthemum neatly in place. She was breathing heavily from the climb, exhaling warmly on his neck as she worked at his pocket. He sat down at the table and looked into the dark reflection of the window. "The Great Helmsman has passed," he said.

Lan Baiyu said, "Very well, now, Director. You've marked the occasion. Put out the cups and get the leaves ready."

He arrived at the Glass Institute just as the dawn sky was waking the birds. The air was weeping with humidity, and his short-sleeve shirt was plastered to his back by the time he climbed to his third-floor office. He touched the flower to confirm that it was still secure, took his vacuum bottle from his desk, and went back downstairs to the communal kitchen on the first floor to fill it. Some researchers were gathered around a table, listening to a transistor radio, their faces buried in their hands. He recognized them from Institute political meetings, where they always occupied the front row. Their grief was real, he knew. They were Communist Youth League members, the raw red heart of the People's Republic. It had been a bad year for the people of China. Premier Zhou Enlai had died the previous January; then protests; then the disciplining hand of the government. Then, just over a month ago, the earthquake in Tangshan had killed hundreds of thousands of their comrades. And now this. If Zhou didn't feel exactly separate from their sorrow, he was insulated from it by his age and rank, and he felt an obligation to be a strong father for them. He opened the tap on the boiler to fill his bottle and tried to assemble some words, but he could only think to repeat the old adage that life is a dream, death a trip home. They wouldn't ken to that old philosophy. Bottle topped, he nodded gravely at the researchers and went back to his office.

All morning the speaker in the hall squawked the Chairman's poetry and passages from his essays. Zhou closed his door and worked until lunch, at noon walking downstairs to the cafeteria, where he sat rigidly during the vice director's speech, then delivered one himself entitled "Facing the Bright Red Sun in the East," which had been written by the Institute's political section.

As with everything from the political section, he found it over-wrought, hysterical in places, and he skipped entire sections. The four hundred assembled scientists, researchers, cadres, techni-cians, and students listened intently, many with eyes moist from crying. Stripped bare as a winter branch, the speech was neither beautiful nor moving, but it was politically correct, and as he drew to a close, the sobbing and wailing began in earnest. The Youth League members were sitting right in front of him, their faces upturned like hatchlings. One had grasped the sides of her head and was rocking back and forth as if possessed. Her cheeks glistened and her chest heaved as she struggled against her bench-mate, who had to embrace her to keep her from tumbling onto the floor. As Zhou sat down, the woman's mouth opened in an anguished rictus, the cords of her neck taut, her incisors bared. She howled like an injured animal. Zhou looked down at the ta-ble and studied the backs of his hands. She was right to display her sorrow, he just wished she wasn't so close to him. It was hor-rible to see anyone in such pain. Poor sad rabbit, he thought.

When the food lines wound down, Zhou took a tin bowl of rice and pickled vegetables and returned to his office. Everyone else stayed for a film of Chairman Mao's speeches, but Zhou wanted to get back to the reports he'd been reviewing that morn-ing, catalogues of glass injuries during the quake in Tangshan. The earthquake had come in the middle of the night and left the city looking like the target of an aerial bombing campaign intended to bring a war to a swift and decisive end. He'd been instructed to make recommendations for the installation of safety glass when rebuilding efforts commenced, and though, as with most direc-tives, this was nothing more than a cadre somewhere up the line covering his backside, Zhou would give the task his full attention. Of the hundreds of thousands dead, ten people might have died as a result of glass lacerations. But ten lives were ten lives.

Beijing was only 130 kilometers west of the epicenter, and

tremors still rolled through the city daily. When, that afternoon, the ceiling lights began to sway and the bookcases to creak, without looking up Zhou lifted his teacup from his desk so it would not spill, and went on with his work.

The welder Gu Yasheng was leaving the Beijing Railway Station, summoned back from his home village in Shandong Province by an urgent telegram. The messenger had come after midnight, and Gu had packed and left immediately. He'd walked the dirt road toward Red Flag Commune for a couple of hours before catching a ride on a farmer's horse cart, and he'd made it to Weifang just after dawn. Somehow news of Mao's death had already spread to the countryside. Every train going north was packed with keening peasants hell-bent on getting to the capital to mourn the Chairman. Only by showing the telegram to the political section head at the station had Gu been able to squeeze onto an express to Tianjin. He'd stood in the aisle for five hours, packed in with the farmers, those good folk, backbone of the People's Republic, many clutching small photos of Chairman Mao in their callused hands, wailing, sobbing. Eventually, he'd managed to work his way into a corner where he could hide his face in the crook of his arm and sleep.

At Tianjin he'd headed directly to the station political section secretary, who, upon seeing the telegram, personally escorted him to the next Beijing train. It rolled out a little after noon, and in the sun the carriage heated up like a steel furnace, reeking of garlic and loamy flatulence. The open windows did nothing but introduce gusts of hot air and bugs. The peasants' wailing and breast-beating intensified as they neared Beijing, and when the train pulled in and disgorged its passengers, they exited and stood dazed on the platform, as if awakened from a dream, unsure of what to do now that they'd reached their destination. Gu Yasheng pushed through them.

He hurried through the cavernous station, pausing just outside the exit, dazed by the harsh white light scouring the square, to put on his sunglasses, squinting even behind the green lenses. In the years immediately after liberation, proper welding goggles hadn't always been available, and in service to the revolution he'd contracted arc eye more times than he could remember. He was blind at night, and wasn't much better in the light of day. His sight was best in a welding shed.

The square was packed with travelers sprawled over their bags, casualties of the heat. Anywhere a structure threw a shadow, people had wedged themselves in like puzzle pieces. They sheltered under newspapers and in the skinny shade of light posts. A lucky few crowded under umbrellas. Waves of people pushed past Gu on their way to outbound trains. A fleet of long-distance buses idled to the west of the square, engines rumbling. Vendors hawking crabapple sticks and candies wrapped in bows had set up near the entrances. In Beijing, it was just another August day, the white sky sagging, the heat flavored with the charcoal smoke from a meat stand. Although a few passersby wore black armbands or chrysanthemums, there were no mourning masses at the station, and as the peasants from Gu Yasheng's train flowed out into the city, they were consumed, and vanished like a muddy river emptying into the ocean.

He walked across the roasting square, his bag on his shoulder, weaving around the supine bodies in a doddering fashion, like an egg rolling across a table. His legs were tight from standing, his calves hard, but despite the heat, his fingers felt bloodless and cold. He was nervous, moving as fast as his booted feet allowed, and he didn't feel the tremor that set the office lights swaying in Zhou Yuqing's office, but the synchronous up-leaping of everyone in the square made him stop. The tremor reached its inflection point, abated, the crowd tumbled back onto their bags, and Gu climbed onto a bus.

Many glassworkers had received the telegram. It told them when and where to report, offering no further information—but the signature, the name that had secured Gu's place on two trains where no tickets existed, the reason he felt a jumpiness in his chest, the propulsion urging him forward, forward, was the most powerful name in the country on that day, that of first vice chairman of the Chinese Communist Party Central Committee and premier of the State Council, Hua Guofeng.

Just before three o'clock, Gu arrived at the Glass Institute. To get to the door, he'd had to push through a crowd of researchers reading in unison from *Quotations from Chairman Mao Zedong*. He clutched the telegram tightly in his fist, his shield in case someone tried to force a Little Red Book into his hand. Inside the Institute, the chanting voices resounded through the open windows. He climbed toward the fourth floor, his feet squeaking slightly within the swampy confines of his steel-toed boots. He had not eaten since before dawn, and the detritus of the day's travel had settled in his lungs and hardened. He wheezed and bellowed, trying to crack that cement by whatever pneumatic force he could muster. At the third-floor landing he dropped his bag against the wall and slumped against the railing, elbows on knees, hacking.

The wet, clotted rasp echoed up and down the featureless stairwell. Gu had been gulping down hydrochloric acid vapor for years. It had wafted from the furnaces next to his workstation at the 505's special fused quartz workshop, and when he'd transferred to the 508 to train the welders there, their shed was in a perpetual fog of the stuff.

"Comrade," a voice said. Gu was still doubled over, and when the latest cycle of glottal torture ended, he spat on the floor, wiped his nose on his sleeve, and looked up.

"It's you!" Gu choked out.

Zhou Yuqing took the older man's hands. "Teacher Gu," he

said. He squeezed hard, then reached to embrace him, but Gu was seized by another coughing fit.

When it subsided, Zhou shouldered his old teacher's bag and the two slowly ascended the stairs. On the fourth floor, the clipped sound of the crowd floated in through the open window at the end of the hall and dueled with the speakers mounted on the wall, commingling to produce an almost pleasant drone, like the low buzz of insects in a forest. A portrait of Mao hanging at the hall's midpoint had been draped with black bunting.

In the conference room at the end of the hall their comrades waited. Zhou and Gu entered, and Lei Guangyu, former director of the Beijing 505 Glass Factory and an old oak of a man, caught them both in an embrace. More came forward, all the best glass-workers in the country. Tang Baorong, Fu Shuming, Zhang De-qui. There were about forty there that day, old hands who'd been reassigned to Task One from their posts at the 901, the 508, the Glass Institute, the Beijing Glass Instrument Factory, the Beijing First Light Industry Bureau, the Academy of Sciences. They beheld the faces of old friends, and their hearts rose up. Their spirits overflowed with joy.

Zhou Yuqing had worked with many of them at the 505 when it had been called the Beijing Second Spectacles Factory. They had supplied the revolution with lenses through which enemies were sighted and destroyed, stars charted—they had made the very glasses through which the Chairman gazed when he wrote his poetry. They were the technicians who'd cast the crystal lenses for *China-4*, the country's first spy satellite. Here was Tang Baorong, who had pioneered use of the rosebud on the oxyhydrogen torch. Tan Sitong, named after one of the six gentleman martyrs, but whom they called Sparrow, still bearing the long scar and chipped tooth from a supercooled bolus of fused quartz that had exploded during an experiment back when the silicon workshop was little more than a goat shed bolted to the side of the 505. Shang Min, the brilliant engineer who'd assembled the first modern oxyhydrogen furnace in China, pinching the cheeks of Old Teacher Gu between her stubby fingers.

At the front of the room stood Pan Caohang, the director of the 505, an elegant figure, tall, his ring of white hair cropped close to his scalp, geologic layers of skin drooping beneath his eyes. The creases on his forehead had only deepened since his colleagues had seen him last. He stooped a bit. The 505 had burned to the ground a year earlier and he'd overseen its reconstruction. Without fuss or undue hand-wringing he'd led his workers into battle and achieved victory.

Standing next to him was Beijing Vice Mayor Li Quan. The workers didn't know what to make of this politician. He appeared to be suffering mightily from the heat. Sweat cascaded from his face. He was stocky and his head appeared to have grown, unaided by a neck, directly from his shoulders. He looked as if, as a younger man, he might have been an explosive physical force. Now he wore his weight like a suit of chain mail. His heavy cheeks and thick lower lip glistened in the hard light shining through the windows.

Neither Pan Caohang nor Vice Mayor Li had slept in thirty-six hours.

Vice Mayor Li rapped on the metal desk at the front of the conference room. He held an official document labeled "Task One." He opened with a call to arms. "As a reward for your exemplary service to the People's Republic, you are instructed to build the crystal sarcophagus of the founder of the People's Republic, Chairman of the Central Committee of the Chinese Communist Party Mao Zedong!"

The workers clapped.

"Labor in harmony and with revolutionary spirit to achieve this goal within ten months!" Li read. They clapped again, but with diminished enthusiasm, and Director Pan had to step forward, clapping furiously, to rouse them.

As a political task, Task One took precedence over all other assignments. A special bureaucracy, Office Nine, had been created, with Li and Pan at the helm, to oversee construction of the coffin and the Memorial Hall. Everyone in the room was reassigned to the 505, effective immediately. Across the country, more workers were being rallied to the task. Even as he spoke, engineers and technicians were traveling to Beijing to complete the construction team.

Li went down a list of aesthetic requirements for the coffin, and made clear they would incorporate none of the crypto-mysticism that had crept into the design of Lenin's box. There would be no attempts to reanimate Chairman Mao, not now, not ever. This was not temporary storage. This design was to be eternal, elegant, pragmatic. It was to be an everlasting symbol of the People's Republic.

Technical guidelines followed: earthquake-resistant to magnitude 8.0, glare-proof, airtight, and, most important, the crystal was to be pure to 99.9999 percent—six nines to be confirmed by atomic spectography at the Beijing 401. And, Li Quan said again, waving his open palm forward to lead his troops to battle, it was to be ready in ten months.

Pan Caohang pulled a document from the folder in his hand and laid it on the table. The closest of the workers, Vitrics Professor Emeritus Hong Li, picked it up. He tentatively rotated the page, tipped his head and adjusted his glasses, turned it another ninety degrees. He tugged at his wrinkled earlobe. The document was a blurry facsimile from the embassy in Moscow, the image a rainstorm of ink surrounded by a fuzzy border.

"Director Pan," the old professor said, "my eyes aren't what they once were."

Vice Mayor Li lunged and snatched the facsimile from his

hands. He balled it up and flipped it into a corner. "It's Lenin's coffin! We don't need inferior Soviet technology polluting our design process!"

Soviet crystal coffin technology was, in fact, the most advanced in the world, which was why a delegation had already been dispatched to the Socialist Republic of Vietnam to study Ho Chi Minh's coffin. A gift from the Soviet Union, it was a back door to their superior fabrication techniques. But border skirmishes had soured relations between the People's Republic and Vietnam, and the delegation would spend a week sequestered in windowless rooms at the Red Star Hotel in Hanoi with nothing better to do than play cards. They would return to Beijing without so much as a weather report.

Vice Mayor Li and Director Pan had been dispatched on a mission as well, summoned in the dead of night to Premier Hua Guofeng's quarters and instructed to locate Dr. Sun Yat-sen's coffin. A furious storm had unleashed itself on the city as they left for the Temple of Azure Clouds.

It was well known that in 1925 the Russians had built a crystal coffin for Dr. Sun's remains, but that by the time it arrived on Chinese soil he had already been entombed. The coffin had gone into storage, and was believed to be somewhere in the basement of the temple, but there were many chambers, and the curator, to his great embarrassment, couldn't produce any documentation hinting at the coffin's location. A decade earlier Red Guards had ransacked the temple and there were no logbooks, no manifests for anything.

The storm had flooded the temple's basement, and after hours of wading through knee-deep water Li and Pan found it, buried beneath boxes of scrolls, covered by a moldy canvas sheet. One look and Director Pan knew the coffin would not do. The side panels were steel with nickel plating. Only the lid was crystal, an unacceptable solution, as mourners would be forced to look down on Chairman Mao. When Pan measured the coffin, it was too short for the Chairman.

Just before dawn they returned to Zhongnanhai with the news. Premier Hua, who appeared not to have moved from his desk, which was bare except for two telephones and an overflowing ashtray, accepted their report and dismissed them.

Later that morning, with the Central Committee and high-ranking cadres gathered to pay their respects at the Great Hall of the People, Premier Hua summoned Vice Mayor Li Quan to his side. Chairman Mao lay in state within a boxy acrylic coffin hastily fabricated by the First Plastics Factory. The premier leaned close to Li's ear, so close he could feel the older man's lips moving. "He looks like a catfish in a tank."

The premier withdrew, clasped his hands, and focused his attention on the honor guard. Li backed away. The premier's shame was obvious, and it was the fault of Li and Pan. There was no question: the final design must be eternal, cast in crystal, worthy of the father of modern China.

The vice mayor continued. Casting and fabrication teams would be housed at the 505. The Academy of the Arts would prepare an array of designs, and Office Nine would select the most suitable. "Ten months," he said again.

Zhou Yuqing, ever earnest, perhaps the only one by temperament unafraid of Li Quan, spoke up. "Comrade Vice Mayor, I mean no disrespect, but this task will be very difficult to complete in fewer than three years." There were some noises of assent in the room. What he'd meant by very difficult was impossible. They'd all done the math in their heads.

The annealing process could not be rushed. Crystal pulled too soon from the cooling furnace would have the tensile strength of rock salt. And for slabs of the size required by Task One, proper annealing would take at least three years.

Li Quan spoke over the tops of their heads, addressing the

back wall. "When completion of a task requires conditions that do not exist, create proper conditions!" He punctuated the words by slapping his palm onto the desk. Professor Emeritus Hong Li jumped in his chair.

"Comrade Vice Mayor," Zhou said, "we're just humble workers, and we can't defeat physical laws. There will be serious difficulties building the coffin if we don't have at least three years."

"You must be prepared to overcome all difficulties with an indomitable will and in a planned way!" Li Quan said. "No delays."

Zhou Yuqing resigned his challenge. Vice Mayor Li was powerful, and could have had him labeled a reactionary element and locked up. But more important, there was no sense in arguing with the Party. The Party outranked physical laws, scientific fact, logic. This knowledge was as essential to those in the room as the marrow in their bones. The Party was their water, their food, their thoughts.

Director Pan had a way of tucking his chin and speaking to his chest in a voice that made it difficult to hear, a mannerism that required the workers to lean forward and grant him their full attention. He was by reputation a clever leader. He said that he felt he should lend his support to Zhou Yuqing, who had shown the courage to speak his mind, even though he lacked a complete understanding of the political realities of the task.

"Comrade Zhou is correct to identify the problem," Pan said quietly. "There is no benefit to ignoring it. But in the end, the annealing protocols for this task present a problem like any other. We have been faced with insurmountable obstructions before, and we have defeated them. We are not afraid of a hard and bitter struggle. We will attack with revolutionary spirit and we will achieve victory."

Pan lifted his face. "For years we've been hunting mice. Now let us hunt tigers."

He fixed his eye on Zhou Yuqing.

"Director Zhou, will you serve as secretary of the casting and fabrication team? Will you lead your comrades into battle?"

Zhou instinctively put his hands up to wave away such an absurd suggestion. His cheeks darkened and he made careful study of a crack in the concrete at his feet.

"Lead this team into battle!" Pan called. "Destroy whatever obstacles stand in your way!"

Zhou stammered out a declaration of his unworthiness, but the workers shouted him down.

"Serve the People!" Vice Mayor Li shouted.

"Serve Chairman Mao," the workers called back.

"I am honored to serve," Zhou said, "but only if Comrade Gu Yasheng will serve as vice secretary."

The old welder nodded his assent.

In this manner Comrade Zhou Yuqing was made secretary of the team. His reluctance to accept the post was more than a standard show of deference. There was one thing of which he was certain: Task One was destined to fail. The impossibility of success was lost on no one, yet there was no doubt they would attack blindly, with full red hearts, like a cavalry riding directly into enemy cannons. Zhou would head the charge, and he would be the first to fall.

In two days, the 505's logistics battalion constructed a special workshop, approximately the size of a basketball court, in the northeast corner of the factory. Two brick walls lined with asbestos sheeting were erected to form the inner corner of the workshop and segregate their work from the rest of the factory. Casement windows on the outer walls were painted black. Wooden benches were installed along the walls for sleep. The team would work seven days a week, with meals delivered on rolling carts from the canteen.

The workspace was arranged around a central cluster of fifteen furnaces. Each apparatus consisted of a glass bulb affixed to a pair of reedy glass tubes, one attached to an oxyhydrogen torch, the other to a nozzle that sprayed silicon tetrachloride into the flame burning at two thousand degrees Celsius. Calibrating the mix was tricky, and the torches sputtered and belched blue-orange loops of flame down the tube unless properly tuned. When operating correctly, the furnaces hissed like a den of snakes.

From early days, Task One delivered a steady stream of furnace technicians to the infirmary. The tubing, after an hour of constant use, would begin to glow. Longer, and it became sensitive to minor temperature changes, vibrations, a vortex of air swirling off the arm of a passing worker, a cricket landing somewhere outside the workshop, culminating in an explosion, glass projectiles flying in every direction, those workers lucky enough to have their wits about them ducking as shards smashed against the wall. It was Technician Shou who, after a few weeks, noticed a pre-explosion creaking beneath the hiss, like that of river ice before it fissures, and became skilled at predicting when a tube was about to shatter. She'd throw her hand up and yell, "Cover!" and everyone in the immediate vicinity would drop to the floor.

Another array of furnaces, metal boxes the size of refrigerators, for casting quartz cylinders, was situated next to the glass furnaces. Grinding and polishing units occupied the southwest corner, and in the northwest corner, natural-gas-fueled annealing ovens resembling kettledrums had been lined up in two neat rows. Overlooking them, behind a thick window the size of a blackboard, was the clean room, which housed the mainframe that controlled the annealing temperatures. The mainframe was cooled by a compressor on the roof, and a branch line funneled air into the cramped lab where optical properties and silicon purity were tested. None of the cool air bled into the main workshop, where the ambient temperature was sweltering, rarely falling below thirty degrees Celsius.

By the middle of that first week, the last of the engineers had arrived from Shanghai and Chengdu. There were now sixty-four workers assigned to casting and fabrication, and Zhou divided them into two teams. Team One would experiment with quartz dust produced from silicon tetrachloride, a volatile liquid stored in drums labeled *Cooking Oil*, a security measure. The drums, about a hundred of them, were stacked in steel racks along a wall of the workshop.

Team Two, under the supervision of Gu Yasheng, would work from sacks of sorted crystal chunks delivered by a special train from the Donghai mines. Each 140-kilogram brown hemp bag had the characters for *Sandstone* stenciled in red on its side.

Four days after the first meeting at the Glass Institute, Team One turned on the silicon tetrachloride compressors and lit their furnaces. The compressor nozzles were opened, spraying mist into the tongues of flame, perfectly tuned and burning hotter than jet afterburners. Up and down the line, the blue needle of flame met the spray and small, glowing mounds of silica began to accumulate in the glass bulbs.

The process produced something else: hydrochloric acid vapor. Despite the ventilation fans, it accumulated at head-height and crept like fog across the workshop. The workers' eyes watered, and then they began to cough, almost politely at first but before long giving way to full-throated hacking. At first Zhou gagged and spat and struggled to maintain his composure, just like the rest. But, believing it was his duty as a leader to suffer without complaint, he forced himself to stand up, rigid as a soldier on review, arms at his side, eyes streaming, and suck the evil-smelling stuff through his locked teeth. Gu Yasheng coughed like the rest, but he detected hominess in the acrid atmosphere, almost as comforting as the childhood memory of his mother's cooking. He might have smiled just a bit when the acid hit his throat.

Across the workshop, Team Two dipped shovels into the sacks

of quartz crystals and loaded the pulverizer. The machine's engine screamed and bucked, crushing the crystals with percussive pops that gave way to a more sustained grinding. As the screw mashed them to dust, workers added more, the cacophony joining the furnaces' violent hissing to create a storm that buffeted their ears and turned all communication into pantomime. The pulverizer exhaled a thick white dust that mixed with the vapor over the furnaces and expanded to cover the entire shop in a white haze. A layer of fine snow collected on their lab coats and hair. It wasn't long before someone had dubbed the southeastern end of the shop the Yulong, after the mountain in Yunnan Province.

By the end of the week, Office Nine had selected a final design, trapezoidal, bearing a striking resemblance to the shape of naturally occurring quartz crystals, not unlike a military structure, perhaps a pillbox on a beach or the hardened airplane hangars some of the workers would have recognized from their time on bases in the south. Three long panels for the sides and top, and two smaller panels for the ends. These would be the largest single slabs of fused crystal ever cast in the People's Republic. Zhou tried not to betray his worry about the larger slabs, as big as doors, thick as medical texts, unfathomable dimensions. Unachievable. Impossible. He struggled to maintain correct morale. For ten years, his research had focused on lenses—discs of crystal the size of the bottom of a drinking glass. Now this. It was not a problem of science but of time. He'd been directed to transform a pile of flour into a baked loaf of bread, and he'd been given two minutes to do it.

Over the coming weeks the teams struggled, and they suffered. They sang revolutionary songs and chewed ginseng root to stay awake. They sucked in the dust and fumes, they sweated, and they failed.

They failed every day in September. The night of October 1,

they climbed to the roof of the factory to watch the National Day fireworks over Tiananmen. Did the lights in the sky, "The Internationale" pouring from the factory's loudspeakers, the clear fall air revive their flagging spirits? Perhaps some, but Zhou Yuqing hardly saw or heard any of it. His mind never left the workshop. When the show was over, he followed his comrades down the stairs and got back to work. Later, he confessed to Gu Yasheng that he feared they'd leapt from a plane without their parachutes.

"Perhaps the ground will be soft," Gu said.

October was a failure. By November, Team One had succeeded in producing only two patties of the required thickness. Their clarity was, at best, 90 percent. Trace amounts of calcium, sodium, magnesium, and iron fouled the mix, and short annealing times created bubbles. Every day brought a new disaster. The silicon tetrachloride furnaces shattered with alarming regularity, releasing clouds of toxic vapor into the workshop that doubled over even the toughest technicians.

There were flash fires—fabric, sheets of notepaper, anything combustible left near the furnaces ignited. Everyone sported burns, from fresh white furrows to late-stage menisci pulling tightly at the skin. Exhausted, they fell asleep at their stations. They all wore bruises and cuts. They smashed their fingers in furnace lids and walked into low-hanging ductwork.

Sleeplessness made them sloppy. Technician Du, changing out an empty hydrogen cylinder, failed to completely close the valve, allowing the remnants of the tank to bleed into the hot workshop air. The combustion cracked like a gunshot. Everyone, by then well conditioned, hit the floor. After a moment, they rose, dusted themselves off, and went back to work. Aftershocks from the Tangshan quake rattled the workshop every day, agitating the barrels of Cooking Oil, setting the furnaces clanging. They carried on.

Failure. Endless failure. If their task had, in fact, been to bake bread, nearly two months after starting they'd still have been try-ing to figure out how to sift the flour. Zhou paced the workshop at all hours, his hands behind his back, pausing to inspect the various workstations before resuming his loop. He slept no more than an hour at a time. He had the best equipment and the best vitrics squad in the country. They were working at maximum out-put. He insisted that the failures were a result of his leadership, and he met with the teams weekly to criticize himself. It was a lonesome sight and, for those who'd lost track of time, a dreaded signal that another full week had passed.

Zhou would call an assembly and demand that the workers struggle against him, as though they were back in those dark days of the revolution. They had nothing to say against him. He was working as hard as anyone, and he was always generous with his encouragement. He'd push on, his voice rising, insistent. Eventu-ally he'd call a name. The worker would say, "Secretary Zhou, we believe that you work too hard and could benefit from more sleep," or, "We notice that you sometimes forget to drink. You must maintain your intake of warm fluids or you'll get sick."

Their weak criticisms failed to satisfy him, and in frustration he'd turn on himself, sometimes with great violence. "I fail to lead according to the principles of Mao Zedong thought, choos-ing instead to rely on my own selfish ideas. I lack courage and strength, and my weakness has led to the continued failure of Task One. For the rest of my life I will rise in the morning and think first of my weaknesses and failings as they pertain to my poor leadership of the fabrication and construction teams of Task One. My failures this week are as follows: I failed to adequately explain safety protocols to Comrade Hu Shutou, who was subse-quently injured," and so on. Comrade Hu, in all likelihood, had gone to sleep on his feet and fallen into a furnace. No safety pro-tocol could have helped him, but Zhou would go on like this, enumerating his failures, until he'd listed every mishap from the previous week and taken personal responsibility for them. It felt indecent to watch, but the workers had no choice.

After self-criticism, Comrade Zhou left for his meeting at Office Nine. He could have filed his weekly reports to Office Nine via messenger, but he preferred to appear in person, pedaling his Flying Pigeon an hour across town to Huangchenggen South Street, to a square sand-colored building crowded into the background by the neighboring broad-shouldered ministry buildings. Its relative anonymity, the lack of flags or insignia of any sort outside the front doors, was a sign of the secret work that went on within. From the moment he swung into the courtyard, Zhou felt the eyes of the door guards on him, and even as he ascended to the meeting room, alone in the stairwell, he knew he was being watched.

Once he was in the conference room, Vice Mayor Li Quan set upon him: "Your teams are working at full capacity?"

"Yes," Zhou said. "They only leave the workshop to attend to injury or matters of personal hygiene."

"And you have full control of your test teams?"

"I do, comrade. The failure is entirely my fault."

"I see," Li said, pouting with that fat lower lip of his. "And the testing continues?"

"Yes, comrade. Testing continues."

Testing continues. Those words could have been struck in steel and hung over the workshop's door. Heat, fumes, explosions. Time. The intractable nature of time, the casting of quartz slabs, slower than the formation of fossils. The daily tremors that shook the barrels of Cooking Oil, setting the steel shelf frames creaking. The dreamless sleep, waking to nostrils packed with silicon dust. Through it all, testing continued. The workers of Task One would, Zhou assured the cadres of Office Nine, achieve the first goal: a perfect block of crystal eighty centimeters square, eight centimeters thick—the size of a board game as thick as a dictionary.

"You're receiving adequate supplies?" Li Quan asked.

"Yes, Comrade Vice Mayor. The supply lines are operating without interruption."

"The test block will be available to view by the end of the month?"

"We will increase our efforts and improve our methods," Zhou said.

While Zhou catalogued various experimental methodologies his teams had adopted, Vice Mayor Li Quan saw the end of his political career looming in the distance. A failure of this magnitude would guarantee him a post on a provincial revolutionary committee somewhere in Tibet. He had already secretly instructed the Beijing 901 Factory to begin work on a prototype coffin made of K9 optical glass. He had told no one at Office Nine of his plan.

Zhou ended his report as he always did, with his resignation.

As always, Li ignored him. If he could have found someone to replace Zhou, he would have, but who would have taken the job?

"Your report has been received, comrade," he said.

"Serve the People!" Zhou said.

In October, Zhou's wife had come down with a case of the flu. After she'd been confined to bed for a week, her neighbors tried to convince her to go to the infirmary at the Academy of Sciences, but she insisted she'd be fine until Zhou could visit again. Lan Baiyu had grown up in Shanghai. Her parents were dead, and her few living relatives were too old to travel. She relied on the kindness of an older neighbor, the mother-in-law of a fellow researcher at the academy, who brought her soups and emptied the bucket. The sickness pinned her to the bed like a vise. Fever induced wild dreams. She told herself it was not possible to feel her organs aching, but within was a deep pain she'd never before experienced. She hated most the inability to think—she could only lie in the bed, sweat, and try not to provoke the pain. When she tried to compose a thought about her research she found she could barely muster the correct terms. They would float in her imagination, then fade if she tried to add more. Equations were impossible. Eventually all her efforts went into arranging her body in the least painful position. It was as though she were made of broken glass. Movement was agony, but when the urge became too insistent to ignore, she reached down, pulled the bucket across the concrete floor, positioned her buttocks, and released.

It was that urge, a deep pressure in her bowel, that compelled her from her bed in the middle of the night. Although she had eaten little and hadn't risen in more than a week, in a fever state she rose to make the trip outside their apartment, down the open passageway to the toilets on the other side of the building. Like the high floor, their apartment's location far from the reek of the bathroom had been a reward for scientific and technical service to the people. She wrapped herself in a long PLA winter coat and stepped outside onto the landing. The concrete was cold beneath her bare feet, the toilets a day's journey. She'd made it halfway, gripping the chipped metal guardrail for support, when her right leg gave out with an electric jolt that cut through the fever and brought her at once to full consciousness. Her bladder and bowels released. Then she was down, her face on the sooty concrete, her heart slamming, breath shallow and fast. She could smell her mess, and she knew she was hurt badly. Out of shame she tried to drag herself back inside instead of calling for help. She didn't make it far, and a neighbor found her the next morning, her fibula and tibia snapped, shivering, in shock from pain and exposure.

Beijing University Hospital was not far from Office Nine, but Zhou would leave the meeting as though he were pedaling back to the 505. He'd go two blocks south, a block east, before turning right and ducking into the hutongs that led to the neighborhood where his wife was receiving radiation treatments. It was November. Zhou had told no one at the workshop, not even Gu Yasheng, that she had bone cancer and that it was unlikely she'd survive.

Did anyone ask after her? No. The work was ever-present. Who would have thought such bad luck would befall those good servants of the people?

Testing continued. In December a powerful tremor caused a shelving bracket to snap, sending a row of Cooking Oil barrels cascading onto the workshop floor. Several sprang leaks when they hit, and those brave workers who leapt in to right the vessels suffered chemical burns on their hands and arms. They were both back the next day, thick with bandages, their eyes bloodshot, puffy, as though they'd been dipped in fire.

Then, incrementally, there was some progress. Advancing, receding, like the shift of season, a surge of spirit-raising warmth would give way to days of slate skies and cold, but then the sun would return. In this manner Team One developed a method of casting a clear crystal cylinder, which could then be ground down to a book-size square. They'd cool the brick of crystal in the annealing furnace for two weeks, and then Gu and his welders would attack the still-searing crystal with the needle flames of their oxyhydrogen torches to release any bubbles before final grinding and polishing. It was an inelegant method, but the resulting cube was 94 percent pure, with only a few bubbles, a few wavy striations. Zhou put Team One into high production, and by the end of December they had an acceptable test blank to present to Office Nine.

On a gray January morning, Zhou set out for his meeting at Office Nine, joined by Gu Yasheng. Comrade Gu couldn't understand why, but Zhou had insisted on traveling by bicycle, and both wore woolen long johns, an assortment of scarves, padded army-issue long coats, and fur-lined hats with doggish earflaps. Gu had a nice pair of sheepskin gloves lined with lamb's wool, designed for J-8 pilots, a gift from a cadre at the Ministry of Aerospace. Zhou's hands, in synthetic leather gloves, had already stiffened into claws by the time they rode through the factory gates.

The test slab was traveling in the back of a PLA troop transport, crated in a straw-filled box. The soldiers riding with it smelled the straw smoldering. Just beyond the gates, the truck rumbled past the cyclists, pumping black smoke from its diesel stacks. Gu waved farewell. It hadn't passed his notice that they were among the only cyclists on the road. Packed buses trundled by, windows fogged, exhaust pipes smoking.

"Why are you punishing an old man?" Gu said.

"The air clears the mind," Zhou said through his bundle of scarves.

Another bus passed them and Gu looked wistfully after it. The power lines over the street were whipping around, singing in the wind.

"Perhaps next week you could come up with another mind-clearing torture," Gu said. "Starve me, then make me watch dogs eat pies. Imagine the clarity I could achieve."

Zhou's usual route took him around the perimeter of Tiananmen Square, but Gu suggested they cut through. The southern end of the square was clogged with construction equipment and workers laying up the first level of Chairman Mao's Memorial Hall. As they pedaled past, Zhou couldn't help thinking that the hall would be completed on time, but his own failure to build a simple glass coffin would bring shame to the Task One project.

At the building on Huangchenggen South they wedged their bicycles in among the rest. Gu unstrapped his document satchel from his basket.

"That wasn't so bad, I guess," he said. Somehow the exercise and the cold had relieved his coughing, and he felt loose-limbed, perhaps even a bit younger. It was the first time Gu had left the workshop in four weeks.

Zhou was frozen to the bone, moving stiffly. "Didn't I tell you?" he said, patting Gu on the arm. "You're solid as brick." The older man did look healthy, indeed. He'd pulled away his scarves to expose his nose and mouth, which were steaming like a bull's. Zhou saw he'd drawn strength from the struggle.

Inside, they shed their coats and hats and were shown to a conference room by a buttoned-down young woman.

"Comrade," Gu said to her, "is there a bottle for tea nearby?" He flashed his straight white teeth.

"Right away, comrade," she said. She looked back as she went out the door.

Zhou shook his head. "You're spoiled. Who's ever said no to you?"

Gu thumped his chest and laughed. "Only my enemies."

Zhou believed it, and he was glad to have Gu on his side. Yet he was ill at ease. Always wary, always watchful. The unwatchful didn't survive audiences with Central Committee members.

The slab had been uncrated in a corner of the room, and Zhou walked over to it and inspected it from several angles. It radiated heat, enough to warm his hands as he held them a few centimeters off the surface. Blackened curls of straw lay on the floor. It didn't look like much. A piece of glass. It did not achieve six nines. He bent down and counted bubbles, and knew that even as he did, more were forming.

"It's not cracked, is it?" Gu said.

"Of course not, comrade. It's clear as water, rated to six nines, and earthquake-resistant to magnitude eight! It's perfect." He'd tallied twenty-seven bubbles so far, silver pinheads suspended in the crystal.

"Don't be nervous, little duck," Gu said. "Vice Mayor Li once told me himself that you possess rare qualities."

"Don't fill my head with shit. I'm just a humble worker."

The heads of Office Nine filed in, Vice Premier Gu Mu at the fore. It was his first appearance at a meeting, and after Zhou got through the technical details of the report, the vice premier commended him in warm, miasmic tones, phrases worn from overuse, applicable to any situation. "The Central Committee praises your team's effort and charges you to carry on the fight." When he finished, his mouth set into a tight line that stretched across his face like a guy wire. He rose and approached the slab. He touched it, and drew back his hand quickly, sticking his fingers between his lips.

"It meets the specifications?" he said.

"It is a test slab, Comrade Vice Premier," Zhou said.

The vice premier nodded. He pointed at a cluster of bubbles. "These little frog eggs. The final product will meet specifications, correct?"

"Correct, Comrade Vice Premier," Zhou said.

The vice premier bent down and examined the slab one last time, then sighed. "Engage in successful practices," he said, and walked out of the room.

Zhou knew that Office Nine had lost faith in him. After the meeting concluded, Gu Yasheng was called into a room to speak with Vice Mayor Li privately. Zhou was left waiting in the hall like a schoolboy, and when Gu emerged, he told Zhou that other factories around the country had been instructed to attack the problem and achieve victory where the 505 had failed. Having already completed the task a month earlier under the vice mayor's secret order, the director of the 901 announced to Office Nine that his teams had completed the K9 optical glass prototype in record time.

Factories in Shanghai, Harbin, and Kunming were working furiously to produce test crystal blanks. Zhou asked Gu not to speak a word of it to their comrades back at the workshop. Like a good father, he meant to protect them from harmful knowledge.

Zhou despaired for his workers, and for his failure to lead them to victory. He stalked the workshop, standing sentry at the oxyhydrogen furnaces like a condemned man, sweat rolling down his face, his lab coat a palette of stains and burns. He stared into the blue-white flame, yet nothing came to him. He'd stripped his mind bare.

Like everyone, he looked like hell. His eyes had sunk deep into his face, which had the texture of a rotten apple, the skin slack, waxen. To be heard over the noise, the workers shouted, the effort igniting epic coughing fits. They were going deaf, anyway, and had come to communicate largely by resigned shakes of the head, mournful twists of the mouth. Zhou's exit through the workshop door to make his weekly report at Office Nine had become a ritual of hopelessness, the workers watching him go, cursing themselves for their failure to invent the groundbreaking methods that would save Zhou's skin.

Toward the end of February, the winds came hurtling down from the north, bashing Zhou as he made his way across town. By the time he arrived at the Office Nine building, his body would be numb, and he'd huddle by the boiler for ten minutes while his coughing subsided. When he entered the room to deliver his report, Vice Mayor Li Quan would sit motionless, his hands flat on the table, and, when the report was done, offer him nothing more than a perfunctory farewell. Zhou expected to be removed from his post any day, the workshop disbanded and everyone sent back to their home factories.

Lan Baiyu's health was declining, and Zhou's visits to her hospital room had become rituals of their own. These were final days. They were tender with each other, speaking only of their past together, the odd patchwork of their marriage. When she asked about Task One, he dropped his eyes and listed the latest failures. Though she knew it was embarrassing for him, she never failed to ask, and she listened with great attention, her head ticked to the side of the pillow, recording every failed test, every miscarried theoretical approach. Every once in a while she'd ask a question—something like, Were the bubbles silver or white? Zhou would think, answer, then go back to the catalogue, still fresh in his mind from his report to Office Nine. She'd urge him on, reminding him of his great successes in the past, the reasons the motherland had entrusted Task One to his leadership. After he left, she closed her eyes and moaned into the sweat-soaked pillow. Radiation treatments had fried her skin. Her thirst was unquenchable, yet she vomited out anything she drank. Her bones ached as if some horrible device were bending every one just shy of breaking. Her tongue was a salted slug, her eyelids sand. She clutched at the sheet. She knew she would die. That would be the way out of her predicament. But she couldn't imagine how Zhou Yuqing would find a way out of his.

Through the end of winter, Comrade Zhou continued to deliver his weekly reports to Office Nine: minimal progress. Did the workers notice a change in him then? No, of course not. They were ghosts all, haunting the workshop and rattling the furnaces. Morale was a dry husk. Zhou lost his wife without a word of complaint to his comrades at the workshop. Only a week later did he tell Gu Yasheng.

The annual sandstorms came in late March, spitting against the workshop windows and clogging the mainframe's cooling unit. It was in April that Office Nine dispatched Comrades Zhou and Gu to the Shanghai 133 to exchange methods and information. The 133 had been testing a special induction furnace, and reports had been positive.

Their orders came through in the morning, and Zhou and Gu had just enough time to collect their personal effects before catching the train to Shanghai. As it rolled south, the air became warmer, thicker, and at every stop along the way the food handed up by vendors got spicier. Zhou was quiet. He rarely turned his face away from the window. Gu had fallen asleep instantly, and his head rested on Zhou's shoulder. The heartbeat rhythm of the telegraph wire rising and falling, the plowed fields whipping by, walls, slogans, low adobe houses, pigs and chickens. The train creaked and swayed farther southward, revolutionary songs crackling through the speakers over the doors.

Zhou felt as if long-dead nerve endings were reanimating, coming alive to his grief. His seatmates, provincial cadres returning to Hangzhou, south of Shanghai, gossiped about enemies in their danwei. They were speaking standard Chinese, but their Shanghainese would break through from time to time, the sounds indecipherable, an echo of Lan Baiyu's childhood language. She'd learned perfect Beijing Chinese at university, but when she was tired she'd swap a sound here and there, a hint of who she'd been decades before, a skinny girl pulling her father's fishing net out of the greasy Hangzhou Bay.

The cadres paid Zhou no attention, which suited him fine. On his lap he held a cedar box with ornate brass hinges. He'd made it himself years ago, planing the wood from a gnarled hunk he'd found on a visit to Anhui. In the light from the window, the lacquer deepened and the wood glowed. It was a simple box that bore no inscription.

He watched the landscape in Shandong Province with unusual attention. Lan Baiyu had been sent to May 7 Cadre School there, and he took care to recall her descriptions, aligning them with what he saw now: endless fields converging in the distance, the impossible expanse of flatness. Flatness after flatness, perspective lines converging in mist. The land of a good people, she'd said. She'd been away then for eight months, and every week a letter had come bearing stamps depicting Iron Man Wang Jinxi, vanguard fighter of the Chinese working class. She'd never been shy with him, and the stamp was a private joke, after she'd one night in bed called Zhou an iron man. Political monitors read everything, so they filled their letters with revolutionary prose glorifying the workers and praising the wisdom of the peasants. Some of her letters were nothing more than long excerpts of the Chairman's poetry or admonitions to wage revolution with all his vigor. Neither Comrade Zhou Yuqing nor Lan Baiyu existed in those letters. The stamps carried all their passion and longing, more than they'd have been able to confess to each other had they been face-to-face.

When Comrade Zhou one day received a letter bearing the image of a giant panda, his heart plunged. He tore open the envelope, but was unable to focus on its contents. He held it crumpled in his hand and fell against the wooden table in his spare living quarters. He looked again. "Comrade Zhou," the letter read, "aren't these lovely Giant Panda stamps the postal service has issued? I do miss the proud face of revolutionary hero Wang Jinxi, but do not fear: the Iron Man's red heat will burn inside me forever." Like a man breaking through the surface of the water, Zhou gasped, his body rejoicing in the sunlight and the air searing his lungs. He became aroused, almost painfully so, and he loosed his pants and brought himself off in a hitching convulsion.

Eventually she returned home to Beijing, but within a month he was sent away to May 7 Cadre School in Guangdong. He never questioned why they hadn't been sent away at the same time, but Lan Baiyu wasn't content to sit quietly by, and she lodged complaint upon complaint with the Commune Committee until they gave way to the Revolutionary Committee, which wanted no trouble, and kicked her right up to the section secretary.

For Lan Baiyu's troubles, the section secretary had her assigned to teach at the newly established Nanjing Technical University, a thousand kilometers away. By the time Comrade Zhou's reeducation in the countryside was complete and he'd returned to Beijing, she'd been in Nanjing for three months. They wrote yet more letters, though the Iron Man was by then out of print. She came back to Beijing for National Day, the Spring Festival, and he went to Nanjing for New Year's. In total, they saw each other thirteen days that year. Seven the next. Eight the next. When he was made director of the Glass Institute, Zhou began lobbying to have her transferred back to Beijing. It took another two years, but finally in 1975 she was assigned a post at the Academy of Sciences.

By then they'd given up hope of having a child. They shared meals, spoke kindly to each other, tended to the household, and at night they lay down to bed.

They'd had two years together before Zhou was assigned to Task One. Since Lan Baiyu had been admitted to the hospital he'd missed only one Monday, and on the last morning, after he'd left, she mustered her strength and shuffled to the window, where she put her hands on the cold sill to steady herself. She looked down five stories, a satellite view of her husband walking his bicycle out to the street. He pushed off, threw his leg over the seat, and rode away. She would have recognized him in a crowd of thousands. He had an unusually formal posture on the bicycle, as though astride a stallion in a parade, his legs working up and down in a controlled, martial rhythm. She laughed. Ridiculous man, out in the freezing weather on a bicycle when, given the importance of his task, he could have had a private car ferry him to his meeting, the hospital, anywhere. But that was her husband. He adhered to his routines. He'd ridden his Flying Pigeon to the first meeting at Office Nine. Therefore, he'd ride it to every meeting. As he turned onto the street, she craned her neck to see him through the veiny tree branches, and then lost him as he rode south, beyond the window frame. She wished she'd been able to come up with a solution to his problem, but by then it was difficult for her to remember her own name.

When Zhou and Gu's train arrived in Shanghai, they were met by representatives of the 133 factory. Zhou was eager to see the induction furnace, but the 133 director was evasive. He insisted they tour the facility before there be any discussion of progress on Task One.

It was, Zhou thought, an impressive facility, full of cutting-edge technology. A vascular system of pipes clogged the rafters and delivered silicon tetrachloride, hydrogen, and oxygen to every part of the factory. Almost the entire working floor had been given over to Task One. The walls were plastered with "Learn from Daqing" posters depicting square-jawed peasants with glaring white teeth and broad shoulders, model oil-field workers. Zhou complimented the director on his factory's political orientation, and received a shrug in reply. "We serve the people," the director said.

"They've still got the revolutionary spirit down here," Zhou whispered to Gu.

"They haven't been failing as long as we have," Gu said.

After a look at the ventilation system, the director clapped his hands and said, "That's it. We have a banquet prepared in your honor."

"Where's the induction furnace?" Zhou said.

"Perhaps we can speak about that after the banquet," the director said.

"Better to confront obstacles ceaselessly," Zhou said.

The director tugged on the hem of his coat, straightening the fabric. He stood tall, as if delivering a message to Mao himself. "We have retired the induction furnace."

Zhou nodded. Whatever schadenfreude Zhou might have felt was eclipsed by the knowledge that if the 133, clearly a more advanced facility, hadn't been able to improve on the work done at the 505, there was little hope for Task One.

"If the experiments were conducted according to protocols and didn't achieve the expected outcome, that was no fault of yours. This is a task unlike any we've ever confronted," Zhou said.

"Yes, comrade. Our tests produced substandard synthetic crystal. I had hoped to give you better news."

"Testing continues," Zhou said.

"Tomorrow we'll visit the brickworks," the director said. "Our comrades there have attacked the problem with great force, but their success has been limited."

"Who?" Zhou said.

"The Shaseng Brickworks," the director said. "They were experimenting with a modified furnace and managed to make some nice little pieces of glass before the whole thing blew up."

"The brickworks?"

"The furnace. We'll have a full tour tomorrow. Many members of the municipal government are eager to meet you tonight, comrades."

"They produced good crystal at the brickworks?" Zhou asked.

"Small samples."

"Comrades," said Gu, "perhaps our food could be allowed to go cold in the name of Task One?"

The director winced and looked at his watch. "Fine, fine. Let's go. I envy your revolutionary spirit, comrade."

The director of the 133 called for his car to come around and meet them. It was a short ride to the brickworks, a sprawling gray building overlooking a stagnant canal overgrown with algae. Pylons of brick were stacked around the perimeter, and clusters of chimneys chugged out white smoke. The director led Zhou and Gu through the arched front doors and across the floor to a corner of the factory where some workers were tinkering with a tangle of pipes, canisters, and blackened, shredded metal.

"Comrades," the director said. "This is the modified casting furnace I mentioned."

Only one of the workers looked up to acknowledge them.

"Comrade," the director said in Shanghainese, "here are Comrade Zhou Yuqing and Gu Yasheng from the Beijing 505. They're interested in your experiment."

The worker wiped his brow with his forearm, leaving behind a greasy brown streak. "They interested in explosions?"

"They're interested in the product of your experiments," the director said.

"Then they must be from a bomb-making unit," the worker said. He was smiling crookedly at them. He didn't have many teeth, though he looked to be only about twenty-five years old.

"Comrade, they have traveled from Beijing in service of the motherland," said the director.

The worker's smile dried up. He looked at Zhou and Gu, then reached over to a table stacked with tools and shards of red and yellow brick, plunged his hand into a sack, and pulled out a clear lump of unpolished crystal, which he handed to Zhou. It was substantial, slightly bigger than his fist.

"Have you tested this for purity?" Zhou asked the director, who relayed his question in Shanghainese.

"Didn't need to," the worker said. "The special filter was cooking silicon dust pure to six nines."

"It's pure to six nines," the director said to Zhou.

"Why didn't anyone report this to Office Nine?" Zhou said.

"It's not even big enough to qualify as a test blank," the director said. "You've made blanks twice this size. Why would we bother Beijing with something so insignificant? You might also note that the furnace blew up."

"You know why it exploded?" Zhou asked.

"A weak valve," said the director. "They built the furnace from spare parts."

"We've never once achieved six nines," Comrade Zhou said. "Not even at this size. We can't defeat the annealing problems."

Gu had drifted over to a slab of glass, about knee height, leaning against a wall.

"Comrade," Gu called out. "Who produced this?"

"That thing's a disaster," the director said. "Don't bother with that."

Gu waved Zhou over. "Look at what these clever brickworkers have done."

The two men crouched down to examine the slab. It was made up of about twenty smaller cubes of quartz, each welded to the other by a seam of molten quartz, a glass quilt. The welding was a mess, and it was still radiating enough heat to cook a pig.

"If the cubes are cast small enough, they won't need much time in the annealing furnace," Zhou said. "You can make the welds clean?"

Gu grunted. "Am I not a proud worker of the 505 special crystal workshop?"

"When did you make this?" Zhou said.

The director turned to the worker and spoke to him quietly. "Last week," the director said. "But no one could stay at it for very long. It was just too hot. Plus, it's impossible to lay down clean welds. They had their best welders going at it but, without intending any disrespect to them, look at it. A terrible disaster."

Gu was inspecting the slab, his nose so close he could smell the heat. He rose slowly, bracing himself on Zhou's shoulder, and walked back to the worktable, where he picked up the lump of raw crystal. He spat on it, rubbed it against his pant leg, and held it up to a dangling lightbulb. Perfect clarity.

"How did you do this?" Gu said.

"Wei Lun there designed the filter," the director said, pointing at a pair of legs sticking out from beneath the blackened hulk of the furnace.

"Can he build another one?" Zhou said.

"If he has materials."

"Can he build twenty?"

The director of the Shanghai 133 looked at the exploded furnace. "Yes, comrade," he said.

"You'll need to rebuild that thing, as well," Zhou said.

———

Before leaving Shanghai, Zhou found a fishing boat willing to take him out to Big Gold Mountain Island, a journey of about an hour. Gu went along without asking what Zhou had in his satchel, just as he hadn't asked what was in the box Zhou had kept on his lap the entire train ride from Beijing.

When they reached the island, the fisherman barely registered surprise when his passengers declined his offer to slide up on the beach so they could walk around. There was no point in trying to understand what went on inside the heads of northerners, and he silently swung the bow around and headed back to Shanghai. The mast creaked as the sail filled with wind, and the hull slapped at the waves. As the island receded, Zhou pulled the wooden box from his satchel and opened it. Gu spoke softly to the fisherman, and they both trained their eyes on the shore, affording Zhou a moment's peace. Lan Baiyu's ashes swirled out and lay down on the choppy water where as a girl she'd dived from the gunwales of her father's fishing boat.

When they returned to Beijing, Comrade Zhou immediately reported the breakthrough to Office Nine.

"The problem has been solved?" Vice Mayor Li said, his eyes wide.

"We are near to a solution, comrade," Zhou said.

"Near?"

"Variables remain," Zhou said.

"How did brickworkers achieve victory where our country's best glassworkers failed?" Li said.

"I do not know, Comrade Vice Mayor."

"Brickworkers."

"Yes, comrade."

"Coffin construction will be completed on time, then?" Li asked.

"We are dedicated to the task," Zhou answered.

Vice Mayor Li ordered Zhou to begin producing crystal cubes as soon as the new filters were fitted to the furnaces. He sent word to the Shanghai 133 and the Shaseng Brickworks to begin production of crystal cubes as soon as their furnaces were ready. A special airlift operation would transport the completed cubes to Beijing. Once enough cubes were available, Gu Yasheng's welding team would begin welding together the five slabs needed to construct the coffin.

"Comrade Zhou," the vice mayor said.

"Yes?"

"We are out of time."

"Correct, Vice Mayor."

"Complete Task One and cease all failure."

"Understood, Vice Mayor."

Zhou ordered the workshop sealed tight. Windows were caulked shut and special clean passages were built outside the doors to trap dust. The floors were to be kept wet at all times to cut down on silicon dust. Workers from the Shaseng Brickworks arrived the next day to construct special filters and install them on the casting furnaces.

The workers of the 505 attacked with renewed fervor to produce perfect cubes of crystal. Only because "The Internationale" blared through the loudspeakers did they know another day had ended. When "The East Is Red" played, they knew the sun had risen again. They ate when food was placed in front of them. They slept when Comrade Zhou told them to. Comrade Gu's welding team was made ready.

The first quartz blanks came out of the furnace in cylinders thick as a thigh, and the workers sliced them like sausages, then ground the segments into twenty-centimeter squares. Immediately they could see a noticeable difference, an increased clarity, a smoothness deep within the glass. The filters had worked.

After achieving grade-one polishing, the grinding technicians inserted the squares into welding brackets. The welders shot white-orange spears of flame at any surface imperfections, melting out craters, releasing trapped gas, and patching the hole with melted quartz from a slender rod the size of a straw. Even in protective gear, no one could work on the cubes for more than a couple of minutes at a time, so hot was the quartz.

On June 6, Gu's team finished cleaning the first batch of cubes. They arranged them in clamps that held them within tenths of millimeters of each other. The squares were still baking at a thousand degrees Celsius, as hot as napalm. The flame of Gu's torch, about twenty-two hundred degrees.

Everyone gathered to watch as he climbed into his proximity suit, acquired from the Ministry of Aerospace, designed to protect firefighters at launch pad explosions. Layered in asbestos and coated in aluminum, the silver suit made a sharp, crackling sound, like the cellulose on a package of cigarettes. Its hood was the shape of a barrel. The visor was impregnated with gold, but couldn't protect against arc eye, so Gu wore welding goggles underneath. He'd been practicing in the top half of the bulky suit, welding crickets from scrap metal, and even in the unwieldy gloves he moved gracefully, clicking the striker only once to light his torch, adjusting the flow nozzle with ease.

With a fist of welding technicians gathered behind him, he set to stitching the cubes together, torch in his right hand, his left applying the thin rod of quartz to the seam. It was a familiar pose, his feet planted firmly shoulder-width apart, a slight bend at the knees. Many of the workers had learned calligraphy this way, taught by an old master at the blackboard with his horse-hair brush and cup of water, the strokes applied with energy and spirit from the heart, the characters appearing, then glistening, vanishing from the slate as the students hurried to copy them in black ink.

Each seam had to be flawless. He worked from the top to the bottom, right to left, as if composing a poem. It was a laborious process, and upon completing a seam, he snapped his wrist, making the supply hose jump and recoil itself by his silver moon boot, leaving behind a ghost loop on the wet concrete.

Gu had reached the age of constant discomfort, and while at the slab he fought mightily to keep his mind focused. His comrades had seen that upon waking, whether on a bench in the workshop or the dormitory bed he sometimes retired to, he tested his knees as he unfolded them, as he might the hinges of an old chest. They were serviceable but delicate. His hands were petrifying with arthritis, his shoulders ramped, scapulae sharp and protrusive. He had sand in his hips and thorns stabbing the balls of his feet. The first steps of the day were always experiments. When nothing shattered, he tried to go about his business as though he weren't a broken-down machine headed for the scrap pile. Of course, he coughed endlessly.

It was on the second seam that Gu's gloves began to smolder. He'd felt the heat on the first, but that wasn't unusual, and there was nothing to be done about it. He carried on. He didn't notice the smoke from his gloves until Xi Xifeng, one of the welding technicians, shouted at him. "Fire!" he yelled, jabbing his finger urgently.

Inside the hood, behind the goggles, Gu's eyes went to Xi, then back to his work. It was hard to hear, and he was having a bad enough time trying to concentrate with all the heat. There was no problem with sweat condensing on the inside of his visor, as they'd feared, because at fifty degrees Celsius, any moisture that touched the inside of the visor sizzled away.

"Fire, Teacher Gu! Fire!" Xi was yelling. Gu then noticed the smoking knuckles of the gloves. He killed the torch feed and set it and the quartz rod down atop the mixing cabinet. Xi had marshaled a hose and as soon as his teacher turned toward him, he opened up the nozzle. Gu held out the gloves, steam pouring off his suit. In no hurry, he turned his hands in the water, as if rinsing them after a wash. He'd been on fire plenty of times.

Rooster Yan approached with a pair of medium-weight tongs and held them up to Gu's visor, opening and closing the paddles to indicate his intentions. Gu held still while Rooster tugged at the gloves, first the right, then the left. Once they were off, he held his hands up, palms out, in front of the visor. The little hairs between his knuckles had melted into balls of keratin. He felt the heat from the hood on his bare skin.

"More water," he said, pointing at the hose, and Xi obliged, soaking him down, more steam billowing. With some assistance, Gu removed the hood and jacket, shaking out of them in a staggering dance, careful to protect his hands. The pants were held up by a pair of wide suspenders. On the floor, the hood sizzled in a puddle of water. He nudged it with one square toe.

"That worked well," he said before sitting down heavily on the concrete, then tipping over, felled by heat exhaustion.

"Oh, my," said Xi, dropping the hose and running to Gu's aid. Being a stout fellow, the son of farmers, he easily hoisted Old Gu onto his shoulder and carried him to the infirmary. Saline was administered and Gu was back in the workshop a few hours later.

It had been a full moon the night Gu received the telegram calling him back to Beijing from his home in Shandong Province. He'd told the story many times. Blind as he was, he'd set out walking, glad for what little light there was, especially when the road passed by forests known to be inhabited by wolves. Twice he heard their cries, and his grip on his walking stick tightened. He could have turned back to wait for daylight, but he'd forged ahead. He was acquainted with a wolf from those woods, one his neighbor had trapped, a long gray male with pale blue eyes. He seemed to have quickly become domesticated, but Gu recognized the intelligence in this animal, and he knew the wolf was only waiting for his opportunity. He lay in his cage with his head on his paws, his eyes tracking every moving thing. Gu Yasheng thought about that wolf when the cries stopped, knowing that they could be tracking him, waiting for the right moment to attack, but he made it to Red Flag Commune without incident. It's best, he told his comrades, to act with courage. Most times you won't need it.

The workers were all thinking of the story and Comrade Gu's quiet bravery when Comrade Zhou ordered a galvanized metal tub to be positioned at Gu's welding station. He would stand in the tub while technicians would rotate past, dumping buckets of water over him. The tub would catch the runoff. Every seven minutes, Gu was to step back from the slab and into a second tub for three minutes, where technicians would continue to douse him with water.

In reality, Gu remained at the slab for up to an hour at a time before stepping away. The tub overflowed. His gloves smoldered. In the first week, he burned through a set of gloves a day, the skin beneath undergoing a slow crisping process. The pain became unbearable, an agony that threatened to drive him insane. When the technicians removed his hood to pour cold water down his back, he babbled at them about fishing for carp on Xihai Lake, and his eyes settled on those around him but he didn't see them. His work didn't suffer, though, and after a ten-minute break they'd re-hood him and lead him back to the slab. After the tenth day, the affected nerves died, and the pain went away. He became himself again. He completed the final seam on July 16, forty days after he'd begun.

While Gu had been at work, the Beijing First Tool Works had modified a giant German milling machine and installed it in the 505. When Gu finished a panel, the grinding team would wheel it away and immediately begin smoothing the surfaces and edges. The slabs were still hot when they were laid on the polishing stands, which caused the polishing paste to decompose at an increased rate, but they were ready with vats of abrasive powder and tubs for mixing new batches of slurry. They stood watch over the slabs as the bobs spun across the surface, and at any sign of thinning viscosity stripped out the paste and applied a fresh coat.

Four technicians were standing watch over the first slab, intended to serve as the lid of the sarcophagus, when a powerful tremor rolled through the workshop. It was, according to the Municipal Seismological Bureau, the 197th registered aftershock from the Tangshan quake, and it was sharp, a muscular flinch like a horse twitching its flank. Everyone in the factory felt it. The polishing technicians shut down the polishing wheels and crouched by the slab, waiting. The lights above them swayed. A fluorescent tube shattered and rained down on them just as a duct cover rattled loose and crashed to the floor. Without thinking, two of the technicians, Zhu Meiling and Song Jianfeng, threw themselves onto the slab to protect it from any more falling debris. They howled in pain until the tremor subsided eight seconds later and their comrades pulled them off. Both were wailing, their clothes seared away, third-degree burns along the length of their bodies. Polishing continued.

After polishing was completed, the coffin was laid up and shipped to the Glass Institute, where it was vacuum-coated in a nonreflective film.

On August 18, the coffin was crated and loaded into a covered troop transport. There was no color guard, no celebration at the 505. The workers were not yet finished. The transport driver, chosen from the ranks of the Central Guard regiment that protected members of the Standing Committee, had practiced the route for two weeks and departed the 505 at exactly eleven forty-five in the morning. Two white-clad People's Armed Police on Chang Jiang

750s roared out in front, followed by a jeep, then the transport, and two more CJ750s bringing up the rear. The caravan did not exceed forty kph. The route had been laid out not for expedience, but for the quality of asphalt. Thousands of people straddling bicycles blinked from behind roadblocks. The truck was unmarked, but its funereal pace and police escort led many to believe they were viewing the procession of Chairman Mao's body. He would come the next night in a specially equipped, refrigerated Red Flag hearse.

The caravan rolled across the cobbles of Tiananmen Square, approaching the Memorial Hall from the south. A Jiefang construction crane was ready at the entrance to the hall, and the truck pulled into a corral beneath the crane's hook. Soldiers removed the canvas awning and bamboo support ribs from the bed and ratcheted tight the straps threaded underneath the crate and up its sides, cinching them together at the top like a bow on a present. The coffin in its crate weighed as much as an adult Holstein. The crane's hook came down and a soldier threaded the loops, gave the cable a tug, and up went the crate. It swiveled overhead, where workers from the 505 had assembled on the stairs, the crate swinging gently as it reached its target area; four construction workers in hard hats reached up with gaffs and guided it onto a wooden dolly. Once it was down and secured to the dolly, the 505 workers began to push. The rubber wheels squeaked against the marble peristyle.

Inside, their Task One comrades waited, along with hundreds of other model workers selected from factories in Beijing. At the door, the dolly was handed off and rolled through the main hall by a rotating succession of workers, until it had reached the entrance of the tomb itself. The crate was opened. The coffin would make the rest of the journey on a platform designed especially to navigate the space. The sixty-four workers from the special shop at the 505 would take the coffin to its final seat, a titanium gutter on which an engineer from the Sichuan Chemical Research Institute laid a neat bead of silicone sealant. Once inside the inner room, the coffin was tethered to a small hand-cranked crane, the chains slowly ratcheting up until they had clearance and the arm was swung over the rectangular cavity in the black marble base that would allow Chairman Mao to descend every night into the bowels of the Memorial Hall, where his corpse would lie until morning in a darkened cold storage unit.

There was no shouting, no barking of orders by cadres competing to exert control over operations. The crane operators, selected from workers at the 621 steelworks, communicated by hand signals with their riggers and spotters. Technicians from the Jinzhou 155 Glass Plant helped guide the base onto the bead of sealant. A single photographer, An Youzhong, recorded the event. His cameras were arranged on high tripods in two corners of the room, with lights rising above them. He stood off to the side with air bulbs in his hands, and the clicking of his shutters was the only sound other than the hiccupping ratchet of the crane's chains lowering, ever so slowly, the coffin onto the base.

A Leica hung from a strap on An's neck. He lifted it slowly, like a sniper shouldering a rifle, to catch the face of Zhou Yuqing, whose cheeks were sunken and shoulders slumped at the unmistakable angle of exhaustion. He wore a white cotton shirt damp at the armpits, and blue cotton trousers. He stifled a cough from time to time. This photo would have to be destroyed, An thought, even as he shot. All his film belonged to the people. His eye belonged to the people, as did the finger that pressed the shutter release. Zhou Yuqing belonged to the people, too.

The coffin was seated, checked, and Zhou, with a small team, stepped over the low glass parapet surrounding the base and approached the coffin. They wrenched loose the bracing clamps on the coffin, working in unison to avoid asymmetrical pressure on the coffin's seams. Once they'd unscrewed the metal arms, Comrade

Zhou counted down in a firm voice. Three. Two. One. They pulled the vises away.

Their work finished, they averted their eyes from the immortal home of the Chairman. To stare any longer into his empty tomb, to see the pit from which the body would rise—that was not their role in Task One. They filed out carrying the braces. A washer pinged against a bolt, and Comrade Zhou stopped them, hand-tightened it, and they resumed their march through the hall and out into the humid day. The sky was heavy with storm clouds, and later there would be thunder but no rain, and then the clouds would clear.

They return the next day for the official dedication, the workers receiving two buttons each commemorating their efforts, one depicting the Memorial Hall, one depicting the departed Chairman, which they pin to their cotton jackets. Collars buttoned tight, they stand at attention in four ranks, sixteen abreast, the victorious workers of the Beijing 505 Glass Factory special fused quartz construction team of Task One. The most powerful men in the country, members of the Central Politburo Standing Committee, file by, their shoes clapping on the stone, each one carrying a bouquet, which he lays at the base of the white marble statue of Mao Zedong, who is seated, one leg swung casually over the other, a grandfather beckoning to his grandchildren. In muted blues and grays, Deng Xiaoping, Hua Guofeng, Ye Jianying bend to set down their flowers as tripod-mounted flashbulbs pop. Each rises slowly and rejoins the others.

The leaders enter the inner sanctum, where Mao's body lies, leaving the sixty-four alone in the outer hall. Gu Yasheng's grating cough echoes off the marble walls. His complexion is that of a high-altitude climber, his cheeks mottled brown and pink where the black skin has peeled. Some dark crusts levitate, speared by the shafts of his gray stubble. His nose has been roasted, his eyebrows and lashes burned away.

He purses his lips, spits into his handkerchief, and painstakingly corrals the globule of phlegm, no easy procedure, as his hands are balls of gauze. He folds the handkerchief with an attention usually reserved for a flag or wrappings for the dead. His bandages are stained with muddy brown spots, seepage. Only the tips of his fingers protrude, like charred tree stumps on a mountainside, enough for him to manipulate the handkerchief, but the task requires determination and a little ingenuity when it comes to keeping the joggling mass from sluicing out of the fabric after he makes the first fold. His thumbnails have melted away. The rest of his fingers are cracked, black. He's not distracted by the pain. He has a method: he brings the handkerchief close to his face so that he might focus all his concentration on it, and makes a little basket so that the expectoration can soak in before he joins the four corners, then a quick perpendicular fold, and he's done. There is speculation among his comrades that Task One has taken a mental toll. The heat was immense, and Gu seems to have become more childlike in the wake of his work on the slab.

Witnessing this is like watching a songbird with a broken wing flapping in the dust. Yet his comrades keep their fingertips on their pants seams and do not reach to help him. He is a fire immortal, an old master, more than capable of handling his own snot rag. Most hold handkerchiefs concealed in their hands. No one would dare spit on the floor of Chairman Mao Memorial Hall.

More coughing down the first rank. Zhou Yuqing. Shang Min. Zhu Meiling and Song Jianfeng, the technicians who threw themselves on the searing slab to save it from damage, their coats tight, lumpy from the bandages beneath. Gu brings his big mitts back up to his mouth, coughs, spits, encloses, folds. They are a chorus of bronchitics. Outside in the world it is late August, but inside the Memorial Hall it is fall, the atmosphere cool as the recesses of a cave, and it is arid, gentle on their ravaged lungs. The sixty-four stand at the end of their battle, burned and blasted, weak with exhaustion, suffering from exposure to hydrochloric acid vapor.

Soon the hall will open for public viewing of the departed Chairman. The line will snake through Tiananmen Square, doubling back endlessly before spilling onto The East Is Red Avenue. *People's Daily* will report that the carpet surrounding the sarcophagus itself becomes sodden with mourners' tears, requiring daily extraction and replacement. Many lower-class peasants, the most exalted of the Five Reds, will, upon viewing their Chairman, find themselves felled by heartrending grief and will have to be carried from the inner chamber on stretchers by memorial guards. Many will sink into despair. They will refuse food. There are many who still follow as the child follows the parent, without questioning, with incorruptible love.

While the sixty-four have worked so diligently to complete the sarcophagus, so have the people of China labored to construct this Memorial Hall. Farmers have run snap lines for cornerstones laid by a troupe of actors from the Political Department at Beijing University. Rebar has been cut and installed by bus drivers, submerged in concrete mixed by printing press operators. Electrical panels have been wired by schoolteachers. The Memorial Hall is a shambles. Chairman Mao will lie in state for one week, and then the hall will close for another year of repairs.

But the coffin is flawless. It is unbreakable. It gives off no reflection. It is otherworldly, a miracle, a triumph of the revolution. The workers of the 505 have defeated the laws of physics.

Look upon the coffin, the sixty-four say, each of its eight seams milled to a tolerance of two-tenths of a millimeter, the thickness of a sheet of paper, joined with astronautical-grade silicone sealant, earthquake-resistant to a magnitude of 8.0. If Beijing were to be struck by an earthquake as powerful as the one that leveled Tangshan, this Memorial Hall would collapse around the intact sarcophagus. Several months from now, the pillow of silicone gel between the quartz slabs and the titanium base will be stripped and reinjected by technicians. The gel will be examined for fatigue and chemically reconfigured, if necessary. But the coffin itself will need no improvements. It is, and will remain, as glorious and eternal as the Forbidden City.

After a time, they are called in, all sixty-four, a single corpus. The room is not designed to accommodate so many, and quarters are tight.

The tan carpet muffles their footsteps. The walls are faced in light fir, and small potted pines from Yan'an line the walls, infusing the room with the antiseptic smell of an evergreen forest. The crystal coffin is set atop a base of Taishan black marble, into the sides of which have been laid the hammer and sickle; the emblems of the state and the army; and the dates of Mao's birth and death. Three borders of Kaffir lilies surround the base, in turn enclosed by a low glass parapet. The effect is that of a parade float parked in an opulent bedroom.

Within hours of his death Chairman Mao's doctors had shot his corpse so full of formaldehyde that it oozed from his pores and caused his ears to rise out from the sides of his head like an elephant's. His fingers and toes had swelled like sausages, as had his scrotum and penis. Since that early triage, the process has undergone refinements, and the Great Helmsman's face is pink, hale, a countenance of peace and slumber, the result of careful embalming and tuned xenon lighting in fiber-optic tubes hidden along the inside of the coffin's seams. He is at rest, the Party flag as tight across his chest as a soldier's bedsheet.

The sixty-four are close enough to the Standing Committee to see the hairs in their nostrils as they collectively gaze on Chairman Mao's corpse. Deng Xiaoping dips his chin and a tear rolls down his cheek. For what? The folly of political life, the fear that he would yet again find himself thrown in prison, the Chairman's ghost for a cellmate? Chairman Mao's is a heavy death, like that of a massive tanker sinking, pulling down with it anything unfortunate enough to stray into its watery vortex.

A camera shutter clicks. Hua Guofeng makes a wrinkle of his mouth, as if he's chewing on a bitter root. His reign as premier will be brief, and he knows it. He makes no effort to weep over the dead body in the glass case. Even the humble workers from the 505 can see he is a marked man.

The march into the inner sanctum aired some of the cobwebs from their lungs, but the glue's settling again on those ruined alveoli, and the chorus starts up anew. They struggle to maintain proper attitudes of respectfulness, but their bodies rebel. Stifled, controlled expectorations only lead to more retching, gagging. The room fills with gasping, pained hacking. The PLA special guards' eyes wheel left and right at the noise. Hua Guofeng has had enough and begins to shuffle out of the inner sanctum, but is stopped by a guard, who points at the photographer on the other side of the crystal coffin. One more. The camera clicks and the Central Committee files out. The coughing explodes now, filling the room. They are drowning. All decorum is lost. Bent double, faces flushed red, purple, their cheeks balloon and webs of sputum fly out. The guards hiss at them to be quiet and wave their white gloved hands, but what can the workers do? Finally, unwilling to lend witness to this catastrophe of mourning, the guards usher the workers out, herding them through the narrow door like cattle.

AN EVENT AT
HORIZON TRADING
COMPANY

No one had seen Boss Zhou for weeks. After the markets tanked he disappeared. Rumor was he'd hit the road, looking to unload the firm on some unsuspecting Russians. Only the top earners would survive a sale, so everyone was scrambling to stake out his little patch of scorched earth. Other firms were jettisoning their traders by catapult. Things were bad. Above the waterline, we were in flames. Beneath, the structural integrity of lace. Then word got around that Boss Zhou had been spotted at a Hanfu ceremony, and suddenly Brother Kang was the most popular guy in the office.

Brother Kang was head of the institutional sales desk, and since discovering the glory of the Hanfu lifestyle movement, he'd tried to convert anyone who'd listen. Before festival weekends, he'd show up for work in his flowing robes and putou hat and pass out instructional pamphlets on leading an ethical life and returning the motherland to her once-exalted status. He was solicitous, bordering on shy, in his recruitment efforts, but if he managed to catch your eye, he'd add on a pocket copy of the *Analects*, and you could be sure he'd be back to ask if you'd read it. According to his brochures, from Xinjiang to Shanghai, the movement was gaining momentum. So far at Horizon Trading Company, only the most desperate cases had walked the Hanfu path—guys who missed their monthly bogeys or wanted a promotion or transfer out of institutional sales, or were otherwise in hock to Brother

Kang. That's how he'd gotten me. My accounts bombed when the markets turned, and he'd made me a little company loan until everything recovered, on the condition that I join him at an archery ceremony, which was how I wound up spending a long Sunday sweating into a set of secondhand robes. My Hanfu reeked of mold and the hat's strap gave me a rash on my jaw. Except for the ones I shot into the ground, all my arrows sailed over the target, and Brother Kang took care to explain that my bad aim was the result of my spiritual shortcomings—not because I hadn't held a bow and arrow since my elementary school days. The ceremony was a test of virtue, and I had been found lacking. When it was all over I didn't ask to sign up for another ceremony—no one ever did—but now there was a stampede to get in on the action.

Across the trading floor, Kang's office looked like a rush-hour subway car, guys spilling out the door, jostling for position.

"It's moments like these that make me proud to be Chinese," Slick Lips said.

The glass wall shuddered as more guys wedged themselves in. I could see Kang waving his arms above his head.

"Look. He's drowning in happiness," I said.

"Oh, boy," Slick Lips said. "He's got the album out." Indeed, he was holding it over his head so everyone could see. As a primer for my outing, he'd shown me photographs of all his previous historical reenactments. He could get so worked up about someone's glue-on beard or sash fabric. All the serious lifestylers made their own Hanfu, sewing the belts and undershirts, some even going in for embroidery classes. It was tricky business getting the geometry of the robes correct, according to Brother Kang. I envied him a little. I personally didn't have many outside interests. Girls, maybe. I pretty much lived at the office. Kang had blacked out the faces of some reenactors whose historical accuracy failed to meet the standard.

"There is honor in the Hanfu," he'd told me. "It's not just an old style of dress. It's not just about a family tree proving you're Han Chinese. This is a system of beliefs. Rule one: live as a gentleman. Two, filial piety. Three, behave honorably and reciprocate acts of honor. These are the principles we've lost. The rituals of our ancestors provide a solution, a new path."

"Technically, the new path is the old path, right?" I'd said.

Brother Kang had stared back at me like I'd kicked over his sand castle.

What did I know about Brother Kang? He lived alone. His face had an adolescent sheen, and whenever I saw his thick fingers fumbling through a stack of research reports, I couldn't help thinking of him in his apartment, his face blued by the computer screen, those stubby digits attacking his little JJ with the same disorderly haste. God help any woman he got his hands on. His tongue had a way of curling out of the corner of his mouth when he was concentrating. His favorite saying was, "I'm not here to make friends," and by any measure he'd succeeded wildly. He spoke to his subordinates as if addressing dementia patients. When in the presence of a superior, he was the first to throw blame onto an absent colleague. Naturally, he was a rabid nationalist.

Across the floor we could see him slowly turning the pages of the album, tapping specific photos with his index finger. About this time, Ai Ai sidled up. He crossed his arms.

"Well, this makes me puke," he said.

"What doesn't?" Slick Lips said.

"This especially," Ai Ai said. "I went with him on Saturday. Worst experience of my life. Two hours on a bus so I could stand in a field all day and observe the proper attitude for ethical rejuvenation. I said, 'What the hell ancient ceremony is this?' and he says, 'No ceremony today. We're doing spiritual maintenance so that we'll be prepared to fully engage in next weekend's ceremony.' Can you believe it? I didn't even get to go to a real guan li! Did I mention this took place in a field? The grass is ankle-high, and all day long harvest mites are having a buffet on my legs. Then it starts to rain. Finally the thing shuts down and we leave, and by the time I come home, Mei Lin's gone. She got bored and went out with her friends. All night I'm calling her. My legs are driving me crazy and I'm developing a sinus issue from the rain. She never picks up. Turns out she's met this guy, some longhair Australian—"

"I've heard this part," Slick Lips said. His feet were up on the desk and he was flipping through an auto magazine. His shoes were some kind of lizard skin with silver buckles. Definitely Italian.

"Same here," I said. If we hadn't exactly heard it before, we knew where it was going. This was Ai Ai, after all.

Ai Ai looked at us with wounded eyes. "Well, I couldn't remember what I'd told you. But you see why this makes me puke extra."

"Easy come, easy go. You'll get a new girlfriend," Slick Lips said.

"The worst part of it is," Ai Ai said, "Kang gave the Indo accounts to Liu Weifang this morning, so it was all for nothing."

"The injustice! Brother Kang must pay," Slick Lips said without looking up from his magazine.

"Don't make light," I said. "Poor Ai Ai, abandoned again. What kind of person are you, beating a wounded dog?"

"Who's making light?" Slick Lips said. "Fuckers like Brother Kang only react to strong countermeasures. Revenge is the only solution." He flipped the car magazine into the trash and pulled a soccer magazine from the top of the stack he refreshed every Monday. He never seemed to do any work, but consistently led our desk in profits. "If you don't have the balls to do what needs to be done, don't flop around on the deck like a fish, moaning about how you lost your girlfriend and Brother Kang's ruining your career."

"You're an asshole," Ai Ai said.

"You better believe it," Slick Lips said. "But I've never had to play dress-up with Brother Kang, either. Here's my advice. Swear off women for a while. Maybe you'll have better luck with men."

I laughed into my collar.

Ai Ai looked at the ceiling. "I'll tell you what, you bastard. Grow a dick and you can be first in line," he said.

Slick Lips looked up. "Oh, Little Ai, so forceful."

Ai Ai stared pensively in the direction of Brother Kang's office. "I hate that guy."

"Vengeance," Slick Lips said.

By the end of the day, everyone in the office knew the best places to buy Hanfu. Electronic versions of the *Analects*, formatted for handhelds, had arrived in our in-boxes, courtesy of Brother Kang.

It was well known that Boss Zhou was fiercely nationalistic, so it didn't sound unreasonable that he'd have taken up the Hanfu lifestyle. I'd heard that he owned the jawbone of one of the Japanese commanders responsible for Nanjing. At Horizon Trading, everyone in management was Han, but there were some Huis here and there. In some regions, it's just smart business practice to have a native son approach investors. There were a couple of Mongols, a guy who was half Xibe, a Uyghur, a couple of Yaos, some Koreans. For a while, we even had an American, but he was lazy and got fired. Out of two hundred on our floor, about forty were from minority groups.

The next day, every one of them showed up decked out in Hanfu. It was as though a plague had swept across our war-torn land, infecting first the weak, the wounded and starving. They were spread out all over the floor but impossible to miss, the patient zeroes of the coming pandemic. For once in his life, Slick Lips was struck dumb. Not Brother Kang. He got on the squawk box and let everyone know what a great idea he thought it was. "Honored fellows! This is the first step toward a new China!" and so on. I kept my head down and pushed securities, but I was a little sad inside.

Brother Kang went around personally congratulating everyone wearing a Hanfu, and then he bought them all lunch. It wasn't only the minority guys who'd heeded the call—I'd say 40 percent of the floor was wearing Hanfu. The trading desks were a mélange of business suits and bright silk robes. Even some of the girls had gone in for it. One was wearing a diyi and a phoenix crown. She finally took it off because her phone was getting tangled in the pearls every time she tried to place an order.

"This really, really makes me puke," said Ai Ai. He was wearing a gray suit, a white shirt, and a purple tie, double Windsor. The suit had roped shoulders and was cut perfectly, probably one of the Gieves & Hawkes he'd picked up on his last trip to London.

"Everything makes you puke," Slick Lips and I said in unison.

"Boss Zhou's not even here to see this," Ai Ai said. "Isn't he in Moscow all week? These people would walk around naked with grenades in their mouths if someone told them they'd get a promotion."

"Are we sure this isn't a joke?" I said.

"I was in a meeting with the desk heads this morning, and all they could talk about was the tailoring on their Hanfu," Ai Ai said.

"Cowards," Slick Lips said.

"Annoying is more like it," Ai Ai said. "I'm sitting between a couple of guys over there who spent half an hour arguing about whether or not default swaps contribute to societal harmony."

"Maybe they'll quit their lives of crime to study for the imperial examinations," Slick Lips said. "You look terrible. You drinking for breakfast again?"

"Up all night fighting with Mei Lin. She can't decide between me and the Australian."

"What the hell is wrong with you?" Slick Lips said. "Were you abused as a child? Kick her out!"

"If I'd just stayed home Saturday, none of this would have happened," Ai Ai said.

"I think I'd better buy a Hanfu," I said.

"What?" Ai Ai shouted.

"No, you're not," Slick Lips said.

"I think I'd better, just to play it safe," I said.

"Heart of a kitten," Slick Lips said.

That night after work I went to Wangfujing and bought a blue cloak with a nice double-luck design embroidered in gold, a pair of white pantaloons, a sash, the whole lot. The salesman assured me it was top-of-the-line. I had trouble sleeping, and the next morning I decided to wear a suit, one of the buffalo-horn-button custom jobs from Hong Kong, and keep the Hanfu in my bag in case I needed it.

When I got to work, there were even more in robes than the day before. I'd estimate the office was about 75 to 80 percent Hanfu. At the division meeting, I was the lone suit in the room. The entire derivatives desk had placed orders through their regular tailor in Kowloon, and he'd flown in that morning with two racks of robes. They'd disappeared into their conference room wearing suits and emerged wearing red Hanfu.

"Idiots. They look like waiters," Slick Lips said. He was wearing a suit, his tie loosely draped around his collar, as usual.

"Strength in numbers," I said.

"At least you reconsidered," Slick Lips said.

"Ah . . ." I said.

"Ah, what?" Slick Lips said.

I pointed at my bag.

"You are the lowest form of human life."

You do what you have to do. I didn't get into this line of business because of my acute sense of ethics. I was here to make money, and to survive, not always in that order. I'd been on this track for as long as I could remember. Slick Lips had every reason to hate it here. He had a PhD in organic chemistry from Tsinghua, and had been studying nanotubes or something, advancing our great nation's store of scientific knowledge. His parents were Party members and money had never meant anything to him. Then his father died.

"You realize you've distinguished yourself as both a sheep and a coward?" Slick Lips said. "At least put the fucking thing on."

"I'm keeping my options open."

Slick Lips picked up his phone and punched the keypad, mumbled into the headset. Across the floor Ai Ai stood up, receiver to his ear. He was wearing a suit and tie. He flipped me off. I shrugged. What was I supposed to do? I just wanted to keep my options open. I didn't get much action from Slick Lips or Ai Ai the rest of the day. I was there until late, and they both left before me. Usually we'd wait for each other and grab dinner at Shintori or hit some dives in Sanlitun. I wasn't hurt. I went to Shintori by myself.

Fine if they wanted to make me pay for my transgression. I deserved it. It's why I liked them. The employees of Horizon Trading had about as much personality as traffic lights. Grinders. Optimists. Willing to do anything to get ahead. Good soldiers. Not Slick Lips and Ai Ai. They were bad attitudes and they expected the same of me.

On Thursday a BTV news crew showed up. They'd set up lights by Brother Kang's office, and were doing live feeds to *Happy Morning Beijing*. All the flat-screens on the walls, usually tuned to the financial channels, showed Kang's shiny face as he pontificated about the great Hanfu movement. The first time the camera swung across the trading floor to show the Hanfu army, I ducked. I don't know why. It's not like I knew anyone who would see the show and laugh at me. Everyone I knew worked at Horizon Trading. The next time the camera panned, I looked right at it.

That's how I wound up being interviewed. When the lights went down, the reporter walked over.

"So you're a holdout," she said. She was thin and pretty and wasn't wearing much makeup. I'd always thought TV reporters were caked in the stuff. Probably an idea I picked up from a movie when I was a kid.

"I don't think I'm the only one," I said.

"Do you see anyone else in a suit? Let's talk on camera," she said.

I hadn't seen Slick Lips yet that morning. His chair was empty, and the reporter lowered herself into it, swiveled, leaned in, and held the microphone to her mouth. The cameraman hit the floodlight and I went momentarily blind.

"Rolling," he said.

"What's your name?" the reporter said, then pushed the microphone at my chin.

"Uh, Zhang Wei," I said.

"Mr. Zhang, among a sea of Hanfu supporters, you're one of the few who've opted not to take part. Could you explain your reasons?"

"Ah," I said. "No reason, really. Ah. I just feel more comfortable like this, I guess."

"Is it possible that you're staging a quiet protest against the Hanfu movement in your office?" the reporter said.

"No, no. I'm just wearing my suit."

"Do you consider yourself a bold supporter of our great nation?"

"Of course I do," I said.

"But you've chosen to stand outside and observe your colleagues' national pride without taking part yourself. You must feel that the Hanfu is overly nationalistic."

"Ah, absolutely not. I'm a strong nationalist. A strong supporter," I said.

"And yet you've chosen not to wear the Hanfu?"

"Ah," I said. I was sweating, naturally. I couldn't think. I reached down for my bag and opened it.

"What's this?" she said.

I pulled out my Hanfu. "I was just waiting for an opportunity to put it on."

The reporter looked up at the camera and made a cutting motion with her finger. The light went off.

"Thanks for your time," she said, and extended her hand.

I took it. "Okay," I said.

"We'll follow up after you've changed," she said.

"Ah. Oh, okay. I have a lot to do today," I said.

"It'll only take a second."

"Right," I said.

They moved off, the reporter calling, Sir! Sir! after one of the derivatives guys who'd made a hat of a paper cup with a chopstick jammed through it.

"Nicely done," said a voice from behind me. I turned around. It was Ai Ai. Slick Lips was with him. They had on raincoats.

"Oh, there you are," I said. "What's up with those?" They were wearing old-style red star liberation caps. They took off their raincoats to reveal identical olive-green Zhongshan suits with brown belts, like it was 1967 and they were off to a struggle session. They had the red patches on the collars, and Slick Lips's red armband read "Smash Running Dog Capitalists!" Copies of the Little Red Book peeked out of their chest pockets.

"You are fucking kidding me," I said.

"Promote Mao Zedong thought!" Slick Lips screamed. I'm not exaggerating when I say every head on the trading floor turned his way. The cameraman's spotlight swung around, too, illuminating the two revolutionaries, casting long shadows behind them.

Ai Ai pulled out his copy of Mao's *Quotations* and, holding it aloft in a perfect revolutionary pose, screamed, "Let one hundred flowers bloom! Drive out the old and bring forth the new!" The veins in his neck bulged. His eyes were wild.

I thought the reporter was going to kill herself trying to get back across the office. Brother Kang tried to insinuate himself between her and the end of our row, but she dropped her shoulder and plowed through him. "Hey!" he said. His beard had come loose and was dangling from one ear. "You can't film that!"

It was too late. She was in Slick Lips's face with the microphone.

"Sir, are you an employee of Horizon Trading?"

"A proud worker, comrade," he shouted. *Comrade*, being slang for gay, got the Hanfu guys around me snickering.

"Why aren't you wearing robes like everyone else?" the reporter asked.

"The Hanfu lifestylers are puppets of the Japanese government!" Slick Lips said.

The reporter leaned in closer. "You say the Hanfu lifestyle is a plot by the Japanese government?"

The guys next to me stopped snickering. One of them said, "Hey, now, that's unnecessary."

Slick Lips answered the reporter. "My comrade and I are following Chairman Mao's instructions to seek truth from facts. True patriotism is rooted in liberation, not the imperial lifestyle! The Hanfu lifestyle is inauthentic. The Japanese wear the same robes, they just call them kimono! We've heard that the Japanese fully approve of the Hanfu lifestyle!" He looked around the trading floor. "Anyone who supports the imperial way of life is an imperialist!"

"Shut up," someone yelled weakly from the direction of corporate bonds.

The reporter was beginning to piece it together. I could see it in her posture. "Ah. You're some of the famous angry youth?"

Ai Ai took this one. "We don't adhere to any platform except Chairman Mao's. We reject the imperialist jingoism of Hanfu. We follow the teachings of the Great Helmsman."

"What do you hope to accomplish with your mode of dress?" she asked.

"We intend to stage a thought revolution!" Slick Lips screamed. "Who's with us?" He was waving his Little Red Book again. "Who will reject outmoded thought?" he shouted. It seemed louder this time, probably because it was directed at me.

I was still holding the rumpled Hanfu on my lap. I looked down at it, mostly to avoid my friend's eyes. The reporter took care of that.

"Mr. Zhang, you remain undecided. Who will you join?" she said. The microphone was under my mouth. I made a laughing sound.

"I don't think anyone really cares which side I join," I said.

"Your colleague cares," she said.

"Well, I don't know," I said. "I'd have to hear both sides' arguments," I mumbled into my chest.

"Would you consider a debate?" the reporter said, holding the microphone to Slick Lips's face.

"Ready and waiting," Slick Lips said, saluting.

"Who will debate the Hanfu side, then?" the reporter said, looking around dramatically. She really knew what she was doing. "Mister Kang, what about you? You're the leader of the Hanfu movement at Horizon Trading."

The camera was on Brother Kang. "We're not going to have a debate about this," he yelled, throwing his hands up at the absurdity of such an idea. The reporter and the cameraman scrambled over to him. "I won't address it. These employees are just trying to stir up trouble. Horizon Trading does not sanction dressing up like Red Guards."

"Horizon Trading only sanctions the Hanfu style of dress?" the reporter said.

"Horizon Trading doesn't sanction anything!" Brother Kang said. "We've chosen to show our national pride by wearing the Hanfu, and that's it."

"So it's your personal choice to wear the Hanfu? It's not company policy?"

"That's right. Personal choice," Brother Kang said, shaking his head and waving away any doubts.

"Are these employees," the reporter said, pointing at Ai Ai and Slick Lips, "allowed to make personal choices about their wardrobe?"

The Hanfu guy sitting next to me leaned back and, without taking his eyes off Brother Kang, whispered, "She's very clever. No wonder you looked like such an ass on camera."

"I see what you're doing," Brother Kang said to her. "No more questions. No more questions."

"Just a few more questions. We're almost finished," the reporter said.

"No, no, no." Brother Kang was swiping at the camera, and the cameraman was dodging and weaving like a cobra to avoid his grasp. "Turn it off. Interview's over," Kang said, waving his hand in front of the lens, the sleeve of his blue robe flying about. His beard had fallen off completely.

"Fine. We've got enough," the reporter said. "Let's go." As the light went out, Brother Kang made a last lunge for the camera, and this time got the square lens hood in his hand. There followed a struggle over possession of the camera, and Kang appeared to be winning, but at the last moment he seemed to feel he'd proved his point, and he shoved the thing away and started ordering people around.

"Back to work! Phones, people!" he said. "Someone have security escort this woman from the premises."

Behind me, Ai Ai said, "I hate him a little more every day."

I turned around and made a plaintive, agreeable face. He ignored me.

"You two! In my office!" Kang shouted at him and Slick Lips. They made a show of moving as slowly as possible across the trading floor, and Slick Lips leaned against the office's glass wall once they were inside. Kang slammed the door and started yelling. He went on for about ten minutes, and then it got quiet. When the perpetrators were released, Ai Ai looked like he needed a transfusion. Slick Lips, naturally, looked like he'd been napping on the beach. Ai Ai went to his desk and collapsed into his chair. His head disappeared behind his terminals. Slick Lips came over to his own desk, put his cotton-shoed feet up on the keyboard, and yawned.

"Nice move. Been a pleasure working with you," the Hanfu guy between us said. He'd taken over the chair to observe the debate and didn't appear to be going anywhere.

"I'll be your boss by the time this is all over, dummy," Slick Lips said.

"He didn't fire you?" I said.

"Who are you, again?" Slick Lips said.

"Come on. What was I supposed to do?" I said.

"Maybe we'll give you a second chance if you swear an oath to the Chairman," Slick Lips said.

"How are you still here?" the Hanfu guy said, shaking his head like he'd just seen a bear riding a bicycle.

"I threatened to sue," Slick Lips said. "Brother Kang can't dictate my lifestyle choices. Article Thirty-five. Freedom of speech."

"Article Thirty-five of what?" the Hanfu guy said.

"The Constitution." Slick Lips gave me a look like, Can you believe this guy? "I'm persuasive. Plus, I told him that if he tried to get rid of us, I'd go straight to Boss Zhou and tell him Kang was trying to suppress our nationalistic expressions."

"So you're going to keep wearing that getup?" the Hanfu guy said.

"Look at it this way. If there's going to be a battle over who's got more Chinese pride, I want to be on the side that destroyed feudalism and liberated the peasants, not the side that oppressed the masses. I'm just saying, if it weren't for the Red Guards, we wouldn't be here today," Slick Lips said.

"Yeah. Maybe so," the guy said, nodding and doing his best to look thoughtful.

"Maybe so?" Slick Lips said. "You think you'd be wearing gel in your hair and silk boxers? You'd be dragging a plow while some landlord beat you with a cane. Forget about this stuff." He tugged at the guy's silk robes.

By the next morning, Slick Lips had lobbied every employee on the floor. His pitch came down to a simple notion: What would best impress Boss Zhou? Pretty much anyone could wear a Hanfu. It took real balls to put on the Red Guard uniform. Between the malcontents, those who held grudges against Brother Kang, and the spineless bastards like myself who would always do whatever necessary to cover their own backsides, he'd convinced a band of about fifty to switch allegiances. I, being a unique species of spineless bastard, arrived at work with a Hanfu in my bag and a Red Guard uniform wrapped in brown paper under my arm. This wasn't valiant behavior, but I wanted to survive, and that meant playing the odds. I'd called my doorman the day before and had him run out to the market at Fuchengmen to buy one. He gouged the hell out of me, but I deserved it.

By the time I showed up, arguments had already broken out

between the Hanfu and the Red Guards, little gangs throwing around high-minded language and political slogans, people who worked long hours in close quarters finally given a forum in which to settle old scores, air petty betrayals and hurt feelings. Alliances formed over many beers were put asunder. It appeared that the derivatives desk had split right down the middle, and they were shouting unintelligibly at each other, shoving, behaving in a generally Paleolithic manner. It was impossible to hear anything but yelling. I slid into my chair and tried to look like I was working too hard to get involved.

Then Slick Lips climbed up on a desk in a corner of the trading floor and rallied the Red Guard faction. They formed up and started chanting slogans against the class enemies at Horizon Trading Company, stamping their feet and clapping their hands. "The counterrevolution cannot smash us! Smash the counter-revolution!"

Brother Kang, not to be outdone by this pack of screw-ups, took to the squawk box and announced that the Hanfu lifestylers were to gather outside his office.

I peeked over the top of my terminal. Empty seats. I looked behind me. More empty seats. My row was vacant. There wasn't anyone left. Everyone had chosen a side.

I saw Ai Ai jogging over, a Little Red Book in his hand.

"What's in here?" he said, nudging the brown package with his toe.

"Laundry," I said.

"Liar," he said. "You've got a uniform in there. Show me what's inside."

"It's nothing. It's a blanket."

Ai Ai made a play for the package but I kicked it deeper under the desk. If he wanted it, he'd have to go spelunking.

"Come on! Join the costume party. I know you've got that Hanfu stashed somewhere around here, too," he said, rifling through my file drawers, slamming them closed when he saw they were empty except for napkins and orphaned chopsticks.

"I think I'm better off staying neutral," I said. "This has gotten out of control. Carry on without me. I have calls to make."

"Oh, no. I had to decide which way to go, and you do, too. You can't pass. In or out." Ai Ai took my arm and pulled. "There's no neutral."

Brother Kang came striding over, his robes flapping.

"Wei," he said, "why are you sitting out here like a rock in the sea?"

"He's about to join us," Ai Ai said, tugging on my arm again, this time with meaning, like a kid trying to pull a root out of the ground. "He was just about to unwrap his uniform."

"You're joining them?" Brother Kang said. He sounded hurt.

"I'd prefer to stay neutral," I said, yanking my arm back.

"How can you take them seriously?" Brother Kang said. He calmed himself. "I think I understand. You don't want to abandon your friends. It's an honorable position. It's exactly the sort of honorable position a follower of the Hanfu path would take. But don't make a mistake. You've always been careful. That's what I like about you. Weigh potential outcomes and do the right thing."

What a salesman. Brother Kang had never spoken to me with such decency. Even at the archery ceremony, he'd been officious and distant. I'd bought lunch and snacks and he'd never offered to reimburse me.

Some of the Hanfu faction had drifted over to see what was going on. Behind them, a few of the derivatives traders were angling for a better look. The Red Guards had stopped chanting.

I tapped my screens. "Wouldn't it be easier if I stayed on the desk here? Someone ought to be getting some work done."

"Collective decisions are the essence of high morale," Brother Kang said. "We're nurturing the life of the firm."

"What life of the firm?" Ai Ai said. "We're done for. This place is a grease stain on your fat ass!"

"You're a rotten egg!" Brother Kang said.

No one talked that way anymore, but it was just the sort of thing Brother Kang would say. Some of the Hanfu crew started laughing.

"Shut up!" Brother Kang shouted.

"There he is," Ai Ai said, slapping his legs. "There's the Brother Kang we know. You fucking bully. You fat pig flopping around in the mud."

"Have you lost your mind?" Brother Kang said. It was a reasonable question. Slick Lips could get away with that sort of talk, but Ai Ai?

Ai Ai lifted his chin just a hair. "Fat little emperor in a dress," he said.

"Stop it before you say something you regret. Apologize," Brother Kang said.

"Impotent."

"Last chance," Brother Kang said.

"Oink," Ai Ai said.

"You're fired." Brother Kang did not raise his voice. He'd whispered the words, in fact, and the Red Guards, who'd been milling about, casually eavesdropping, suddenly didn't look so casual.

Slick Lips charged over. "On whose authority?" he said. His face was close enough to Brother Kang's to plant a kiss on him, but Kang barely flinched. He merely assessed the set of eyes across from his. He didn't push Slick Lips away or back up. It was fairly terrifying.

"You're causing more than your usual share of trouble this week," Brother Kang said.

"You're crazy, and you're sick. You fired one of the firm's best guys just because he called you a name?"

"What are you talking about, one of our best guys?" Brother

Kang said, laughing. "He hasn't hit a bogey in months. Look at him. He's a mess." He was right. Ai Ai looked terrible. But he hadn't said anything to me or Slick Lips about his profits falling off.

"Hire him back and we'll forget about the Red Guard stuff," Slick Lips said.

"This isn't a joke," Brother Kang said. "I've acted ethically and in the best interests of Horizon Trading Company. My decision stands."

"Fire me, too, then," Slick Lips said. "Fire your top earner if you're so sure of your position."

Slick Lips had barely had time to cross his arms and look around the room smugly when Brother Kang said, "All right. Now you're both fired." It was hard to tell whether he'd been pushed into it or had seized on the chance to finally rid himself of an employee he'd never approved of, no matter how much money he brought in.

No one moved except Ai Ai, who dropped into a chair with a moan.

"Stupid, fat, moronic pig," Slick Lips said. "Boss Zhou's going to throw you off the roof when he hears about this."

"Sure," Brother Kang said, Slick Lips nothing more than a bad memory, before directing himself to me. I could see this was a new Brother Kang, not someone I wanted to cross. "And you. Still want to join this Red Guard movement?"

I shook my head.

"Good. I'm happy to welcome you to the Hanfu lifestyle." Brother Kang addressed the Red Guards. "Come over, friends. All is forgiven."

To get to the Hanfu side of the trading floor, the Red Guards had to squeeze between my chair and the row of desks behind me. They queued up like ducks.

"Unlawful termination. Coercion," Slick Lips said. "You don't have the authority to fire anyone!"

"Lower your voice, and get out before I call security," Brother Kang said.

"What about Article Thirty-five, comrade?" came a voice from the Hanfu crowd, followed by a dim sort of laugh.

"Where's that Hanfu you've been too neutral to wear, Wei?" Brother Kang said.

"Wei," Slick Lips said sharply, as if to wake me up with a warning that there was bad weather ahead, that we'd better get moving.

I didn't respond, and I didn't look at him. I gave him and Ai Ai time to get to the elevators, and only after I was sure they were gone did I unzip my bag and pull out the robes. That was my tribute to our friendship. Even though I'd been carrying them around for days, the robes were heavier than I remembered. Not in a portentous way. The robes felt heavy because the fabric was high-quality, and when given a choice I'll usually go with the more expensive option. I was glad I'd sprung for the best. They lay nicely across my lap, draping like a waterfall down my legs. No one could say they weren't nice robes, and I didn't want to be sitting around in a cheap Hanfu, not when Boss Zhou could return at any moment.

SWITCHBACK, 1994

A Public Security Bureau officer banged on the bus doors and pulled himself inside. He looked down the aisle, past the sacks of vegetables, at the stack of bricks. The driver knew the PSB had him. The bus was grossly overweight. Through the windscreen, the passengers in the front rows saw three trucks, a minivan, and another bus parked in the crook of the next switchback. They'd been creeping through the mountains since midday and it was getting dark. Even if their driver had his papers in order, and enough for a bribe, it wasn't likely he'd be able to get the battered green school bus moving again. They'd barely been moving as it was. The engine had cooked itself miles ago. It gave off raw grinding yowls when forced into a lower gear. It yowled when they climbed. It yowled on the short level stretches. Its shocks had been cut from granite.

Only on the downhills did they make any speed, and then the driver didn't so much steer as ride the thing like a brakeless train, flying around corners, the doors flapping open, blasts of icy wind washing through the cabin, tires making that horrible ripping sound on the pavement that it seems can only be followed by the dead silence of their complete detachment from the road. In the mountains, everyone drove like this, all over the road, drunk on the freedom of locomotion, but there was an element of pragmatism to their fear of low speeds. In a head-on collision, speed gave you a survival advantage, your momentum propelling you, like a plow parting sod, through a slower, ascending party. The hulks of buses driven by the slow and unlucky lay in nests of shredded trees down in the valley.

Their only hope of getting through the mountains was to maintain momentum. Now they were stopped cold on an incline. In the middle of the bus, a chest-high stack of mud bricks blocked the aisle, the handiwork of a peasant who had, one armload at a time, carried aboard five hundred pounds' worth while her husband dutifully stacked them. It had taken forever because, as it turned out, half the passengers were experts on brick-stacking, and the husband had to stop every five seconds to defend his methods. At first he'd just muttered and waved off their commentary, but after ten minutes he was openly engaged in shouting matches with at least three different farmers; another faction was shouting at the first to leave him alone so he could finish, and yet another was shouting at everyone else to shut up. The job eventually got done, and it was then that the driver, in a blue parka and green track pants, rose from his seat where, feet up on the dash, he'd been smoking dreamily for the duration of the episode. He sidled back to the brick stacker and said, "You can't put these here. They'll throw off the vehicle's center of gravity. Move them back there." He waved his cigarette at a spot five feet aft.

Half the passengers were Tibetan pilgrims, and he was counting on them to mind their own business, but in the face of this despotic behavior they united with the peasants and really let the driver have it. He gave as good as he got, threatening to eject everyone from the bus if they didn't shut up and move the pile back. He picked up a brick and held it by his head like a religious totem, using it to punctuate his points more than to directly threaten the passengers, but it was lost on no one that, should the confrontation escalate, there were plenty of bricks to go around.

Eventually, in a stirring show of brotherhood, the pilgrims and peasants defeated the megalomaniacal overlord, rising up against the driver and shouting him back to his seat. His protest was a bravura performance. He threatened to charge everyone a transportation tax for the bricks. He told the bricklayers he'd make them ride on the roof. In a final show of anger he dashed his brick on the steel floor. He called them bandits and accused them of conspiracy, but with an exasperated sigh, he relented. It was high time to get the old bucket moving again.

The PSB looked down the aisle at the bricks and examined the faces of the passengers. This time the Tibetans were silent. They weren't going to go out of their way to antagonize a PSB, but a few of the Han Chinese on board made some noise about the unscheduled stop. They shut up when the PSB swiveled his boxy head in their direction. Everyone figured this for just another instance of government-sanctioned highway robbery: a toll or road improvement tax cooked up on the spot by an enterprising officer. The driver would pay the bribe and they'd get moving. But after a quick conversation with the PSB, he cut the idling engine and followed the officer off the bus. The passengers groaned weakly, and everyone, the Tibetans, the Hans, a pack of old Muslim ladies whose faces were studies in erosion, clambered over the bricks, squeezed past the bundles of vegetables farther up, and disembarked.

The late afternoon sky was passing from light blue to purple. Down the slope, terraced rice fields tripped toward the river like the contour lines of a topographic map. In the valley, the roofs of a village overlapped one another like the scales of a tremendous snake. A cold sliver of sunlight cut into the shank of the mountain high above them. The bus's hood tinged as it cooled, smelling of ozone and burnt oil, hot metal.

The passengers followed at a safe distance from the PSB, past the three flatbeds loaded with sacks of cement and scrap metal, past the minivan, past the other bus, and around the switchback. As they rounded the corner, they saw farther up the road a

Russian-built cargo truck, probably a troop transport in a former life. There was a familiar gracelessness about it, a uniformity of design that hinted at the existence of a factory that manufactured gray Communist boxes of various sizes. A size-five box would become a car. A size-five box bolted to a size-twenty box, a troop transport. A thousand size-twenty boxes, a ministry building in Beijing.

The truck's tires were as high as a grown man. Tiny birds picked at insects spattered against the steel bars of the truck's grille.

There was a crowd, and there was a man in the road. The snarled bicycle lay beneath the front of the cargo truck, and a pack of cotton-jacketed farmers stood off to the side, their rakes and hoes rising above their heads like aerials. The truck's driver, a slouchy-looking man with a cigarette dangling from the corner of his mouth, was playing back the accident for some very skeptical PSB. The more he waved his arms, the tighter the grim set of the PSB mouths became. He was in big trouble. He'd killed a man.

At the center of all the commotion lay the victim, his blood pooling on the road. There was his foot, the black slipper, the thin white sock embroidered with a line of four brown diamonds, a single blue thread bisecting the diamonds and disappearing beneath the cuff of his long underwear. Black creased pants. His face was turned away from the crowd. He was not mangled, but he was in a position no living man could withstand, his limbs at jagged angles. There was gray dust in his black hair. Blood trickled from his ear and dripped steaming to the pavement. The pool of blood had grown a custardy skin in the cold, so that as the wind blew, it strained and jiggled. Birds hopped from the truck's grille to probe its edge. The Tibetan pilgrims began to pray, beads clicking in their hands.

The farmers know the man on the pavement. His name is Tong Fushan, and he lives with his family only a short distance up the road. He'd almost made it home. Fushan was a college graduate, thirty years old, a teacher in the village of Longliebu down at the base of the mountain. He also ran a bookkeeping service for the farmers, which brought him a stipend from the government. A farmer had set off on foot to inform Fushan's parents.

They were a bad luck family. The Tongs' daughter had been struck by a seizure while planting rice, and though the water had been shallow, she'd been alone and had drowned. Afterward, Fushan had returned home from Nanjing to help his parents, but, despite being an educated man with a good salary, had not been able to find a wife, and now the family name would die out. These acts of fate were inexplicable. The Tongs were honest people who worked hard. They shared with their neighbors in lean times and had always repaid favors. In any person's life it was possible to find tragedy, but in some equal measure, also happiness. The Tongs were out of balance. There, looking at the corpse, an old farmer named Lung Bonu, whose family had lived in the mountains for five generations, theorized that a Tong ancestor had acted in bad faith during his life and his family was still paying off his accounts.

The whacking sound of the Tongs' two-stroke farm vehicle echoed off the mountainside. It resembled a mantis, and came creeping slowly down the road above the switchback, navigating the PSB vehicles arranged to block passage, the rime at the edge of the roadside crunching beneath its tractor tires. Tong Po was in the plow seat, driving by manipulating two long rods fitted with levers. His wife, Lu Meifang, was sitting in the cargo flat behind him with the farmer who'd brought them the news. Her back was to her husband, facing away from the place of her son's death, her right hand holding the rough wooden railing, her left hand on her thigh. Her padded cotton pants and jacket made her appear much rounder than she was. The farmer, seated on the wheel well opposite her, balanced two quilted blankets on his lap. His brown, creased hands lay atop them. His nails were cracked, knuckles fat with arthritis.

A PSB jogged toward the vehicle, at first waving his arms, then planting his feet and insisting that they stop. The vehicle bore down on him, but at a comically slow velocity, like a slug approaching a rock. Just before the front tires met the officer's black boots, Tong Po released the gear lever and applied the brake. Po could see the crowd, made up of strangers, but he could not see his son or his friends, the farmers, who were standing beyond the body.

"There's been an accident here," the PSB said over the popping engine. "You'll have to dismount until the road has been cleared."

In his seat, Po was taller than the PSB. He looked at the crowd, back at the officer.

"He is my son," Po said.

The officer stepped forward, grimacing, tapping his ear. "Turn off the motor."

"My son," Po said, louder this time.

The PSB digested this, said, "Wait here," and walked back into the crowd. The bus passengers knew without being told that the man on the farm machine was the father, the woman in the back the mother. If he'd been a farmer trying to get somewhere, he'd be arguing and fighting his way through the crowd. But this was his final destination. There was no urgency in the man. He sat atop the machine, saturnine, unblinking, his mouth hanging slightly open, a portrait of ruin.

The PSB pushed back through the crowd, followed by two more officers, who had hung back when the first had approached Po.

"Shut it down, follow me," said the PSB.

Po reached down by his foot and killed the motor. He climbed off the seat and went around back. "Come on," he said to Meifang. She followed him, shuffling numbly, the bundle of blankets beneath her chin. She was a glacier about to calve, her eyes looking nowhere, seeing nothing. The crowd parted to let them through. No one spoke. The wind shushed through the leaves of the trees, and the passengers' heavy coats flapped in the gusts.

The sight of her son's body crippled Meifang. She went down in a crumple, all her will extinguished. The crowd closed around her, arms under her arms, arms around her back to lift her up. Po saw his son and tried to recognize him. He studied the face carefully, then the jacket, pants, socks, shoes, the hands. His son's face was dusty, his eyelashes covered in gray flecks, lips dry. There was nothing familiar about him. The pool of blood like pig's blood on the slaughterhouse floor.

Po crossed toward the truck, where most of the PSB were standing, passing by his dead son as if he were a tree fallen in the road. The senior officer stepped out to meet him.

"I should take my son home," Po said.

"Honored one," the PSB said, "we are conducting an investigation. This is a crime scene."

Po looked back at his son's body, the truck, the bicycle. He saw the driver standing in the shadow of one enormous tire, his eyes wild with fear, scarcely breathing, a cornered rabbit who might well die before the dog's teeth sink in. He saw his friends, their hoes and rakes.

"There's no need for that," Po said.

"Old uncle, it's not for you to decide. The state must finish collecting forensic evidence."

Po looked up at the sky. "It's going to be dark. The wolves are going to come down."

"We're properly trained, old uncle. Nothing will happen to your son."

Meifang's sobbing rose.

"How long will you make me wait?" Po said.

"We're nearly finished," the PSB said. "We had to call down for a camera, but it's just arrived."

"You'll make photographs and then we can take our son?"

The PSB sighed. "Yes, old uncle. We won't waste time."

This satisfied Po, and he went back to Meifang, who was squatting on the asphalt, face in her hands, body heaving.

"They'll let us take him soon," Po said, squatting down beside her.

"He needs to lie in his bed," she wailed.

The sun had dropped behind the range across the valley, and suddenly it had become night. Passengers were softly asking their driver when they'd be able to get going. He didn't know.

A flash illuminated the roadbed. Another one. The PSB moved to get a different angle. The flash went off three times in quick succession. The body lit up, threw shadows, disappeared. The PSB turned on their sedan headlights to help. More flashes.

The process took time, and the PSB wanted to document everything properly because of recent investigations into police practices that had resulted in officers losing their jobs. A provincial-level deputy political commissar had even been thrown in jail. But this wasn't a complicated case. The old farmer hadn't even asked to speak to the truck driver who'd killed his son, and the officer in charge took that as a sign that he wouldn't have to deal with this patch of road again, at least not until someone else died here.

He sent one of his juniors over to collect information from the victim's family. When his man returned and handed over the notebook, he told the junior officer to let the family know they could remove the body.

Po and Meifang rose and walked over to where their son lay. She knelt down in the headlights and took his head in her hands. It was so heavy. In the harsh light the pool of blood was just a black mark on the road. Po went about straightening his limbs, first the left arm, then the right, then straightening the left leg, then the right. Po looked up, toward his friends, and they all moved forward, laying down their tools and surrounding the two parents and their child. Meifang cradled his head in her lap, brushing the dust out of his hair, then gently lowered it to the concrete without a word and reached for a blanket.

"Underneath," she said. Their friends took his body and lifted it while Meifang spread the blanket on the cold road beneath him. They laid him down on it, and she brought up the sides of the blanket to cover his arms. Po draped the second blanket over his son's body.

The farmers lifted him up and carried him slowly toward the crowd, which again parted to let them through. The bus driver who'd stopped first had cranked up his engine and turned on the lights so they could see where to go. They processed toward the Tongs' vehicle and laid the body in the back. Meifang climbed in beside him and sat down on a wheel well, her hand on his chest. Po climbed up into the seat and started the engine. They had one motorcycle-style light attached to the front, but it was enough. Po knew the road with his eyes closed, and he released the brake and executed a tight loop in the switchback, then pointed up the road toward their house. The banging of the two-stroke echoed over the valley.

A PSB climbed up into the Russian troop transport's cab and another couple of officers wrestled the bicycle out from beneath its front axle. They tossed the mangled frame into the scrub on the side of the road and climbed in on the other side. Gears grinding, it headed down the mountain to the station, followed by the PSB sedan.

The crowd dispersed to their buses and trucks. The first bus, already warmed up, roared off, followed by the scrap metal and the concrete trucks. The third truck and the minivan pulled away as the last passenger boarded the second bus, where the track-suited driver was priming the engine, praying the thing would start. When he turned the key and pressed the starter, the engine chugged, caught, then chugged some more. He could hear the belts rasping, the fan blades cutting the cold air around the block. The lights dimmed and flickered with each revolution of the crankshaft. He took his finger off the starter. The bus was quiet except for the creaking of the passengers' seats as they settled in the cold. It was dark outside, dark inside. The only lights were far down in the valley, pinpricks in a black sheet. He tried again. The engine chugged, then caught, and roared as he gave it the gas. He let it run for a while, warming its bones, revving the engine every so often, before depressing the clutch and pushing the gearshift. It knocked back, shuddering in his hand, but he waited for a gap and pushed it forward again. The bus fell into gear and he released the clutch, gassing it up, giving it what it wanted, letting it strain against the brake before lifting his foot, the bus then groaning forward, toward the bend in the road, its tires breaking loose the frost that had settled in their treads. He cranked the wheel around the switchback's arc, over the dark stain on the pavement, meaning to look down to make sure he didn't guide the tires directly through it, spreading the poor man's blood all over the road, but he looked too late and couldn't be sure that he hadn't. He checked his watch, raising the luminous dial right up to his nose. Behind schedule, and three more stops before he'd be able to sleep. He could make it up on the backside of the mountain. Once they'd crested the pass, he could really open it up and let it run.

ACKNOWLEDGMENTS

Thank you to Sean McDonald for his gentle ministrations; to Courtney Hodell for spotting this book when it was only a speck on the horizon and for guiding it into port; to Anna Stein; to Antoine Wilson, Brigid Hughes, Ben Howe, and Lysley Tenorio; to Hawlin Wu; and to my family: Jennie, Eleanor, and Anna.

He just wanted a decent book to read ...

Not too much to ask, is it? It was in 1935 when Allen Lane, Managing Director of Bodley Head Publishers, stood on a platform at Exeter railway station looking for something good to read on his journey back to London. His choice was limited to popular magazines and poor-quality paperbacks – the same choice faced every day by the vast majority of readers, few of whom could afford hardbacks. Lane's disappointment and subsequent anger at the range of books generally available led him to found a company – and change the world.

'We believed in the existence in this country of a vast reading public for intelligent books at a low price, and staked everything on it'
Sir Allen Lane, 1902–1970, founder of Penguin Books

The quality paperback had arrived – and not just in bookshops. Lane was adamant that his Penguins should appear in chain stores and tobacconists, and should cost no more than a packet of cigarettes.

Reading habits (and cigarette prices) have changed since 1935, but Penguin still believes in publishing the best books for everybody to enjoy. We still believe that good design costs no more than bad design, and we still believe that quality books published passionately and responsibly make the world a better place.

So wherever you see the little bird – whether it's on a piece of prize-winning literary fiction or a celebrity autobiography, political tour de force or historical masterpiece, a serial-killer thriller, reference book, world classic or a piece of pure escapism – you can bet that it represents the very best that the genre has to offer.

Whatever you like to read – trust Penguin.

read more
www.penguin.co.uk